BEYOND THE

DARKNESS

A DARKNESS NOVEL

Katie Reus

Cover art: Jaycee of Sweet 'N Spicy Designs
JRT Editing
Author website: http://www.katiereus.com

Beyond the Darkness/Katie Reus. -- 1st ed.
KR Press, LLC

ISBN-13: 9781942447023
ISBN-10: 1942447027

eISBN: 9781942447016

*For my family, thank you for putting up with my
insane schedule and your constant support.*

Praise for the novels of Katie Reus

"…a wild hot ride for readers. The story grabs you and doesn't let go."
—*New York Times* bestselling author, Cynthia Eden

"Has all the right ingredients: a hot couple, evil villains, and a killer action-filled plot. . . . [The] Moon Shifter series is what I call Grade-A entertainment!" —Joyfully Reviewed

"I could not put this book down. . . . Let me be clear that I am not saying that this was a good book *for* a paranormal genre; it was an excellent romance read, *period.*" —All About Romance

"Reus strikes just the right balance of steamy sexual tension and nail-biting action….This romantic thriller reliably hits every note that fans of the genre will expect." —*Publishers Weekly*

"Prepare yourself for the start of a great new series! . . . I'm excited about reading more about this great group of characters."
—Fresh Fiction

"Wow! This powerful, passionate hero sizzles with sheer deliciousness. I loved every sexy twist of this fun & exhilarating tale. Katie Reus delivers!" —Carolyn Crane, RITA award winning author

Continued…

CHAPTER ONE

Keelin strode across Bo Broussard's establishment, holding an armful of all types of bagged blood as she headed for one of the open bars. She wasn't sure exactly where the half-demon owner got the blood for his supernatural-only club, but she knew it wasn't stolen. The male probably had another side business.

"Thank you!" Cynara, the other bartender working this part of the club with Keelin exclaimed, grabbing half the small bags from her as she stepped behind the sleek, wood bar.

Soft music pumped through the speakers and mostly vamps were on the dance floor tonight—or in some of the back rooms behind the red door. A door Keelin had no desire to ever open. She wasn't into BDSM thank you very much. Or, she didn't think she was. Although she might make an exception for one annoyingly sexy dragon shifter she hadn't been able to get off her mind for the past month straight. Ugh, why couldn't she stop thinking about him?

"Hey, sweet cheeks. Can I get a fucking drink?" A surly looking vampire with spiky blond hair at one end of the bar growled, his eyes flashing amber. He watched her with annoyance. Gritting her teeth, Keelin let her beast flare in her eyes, a warning to the male who quick-ly straightened and cleared his throat. "My apologies. When you get a chance, I'd like a drink."

She nearly snorted at his abrupt change of manners, but nodded politely. He wouldn't know what type of shifter she was but vamps tended to have a healthy re-spect for shifters in general, especially one as young as this male appeared to be. He couldn't have been turned for more than a few years by her guess. At almost fifteen hundred years old, she was good at estimating age. "What type of blood?"

After he told her, she quickly poured his drink and then six others for patrons who were patiently waiting. It was Friday so it was typically busy, but with Bo doing a vamp-special night there were more of the species here than usual. Not that she minded. Bo's bar was neu-tral ground, even in the deadly wolf shifter, Alpha Finn Stavros's, territory. Finn let the demon operate here as long as he remained neutral—and the half-demon tended to pass along any intel he received to the Alpha that might be useful. At least that's what Keelin had heard. She'd only been living with the Stavros pack for the last month. She wasn't a wolf but the pack had given her shelter since their healer was now mated to Keelin's brother and living up in Montana.

Three hours later, it was almost eleven and time for Keelin's shift to be over. It wasn't as if she needed the money, but she liked working here. It was the first time in . . . ever, that she'd had such independence. Still, she

couldn't wait to get off work because she had plans tonight. Another bonus to her new freedom. She could go
out with whoever she wanted, *whenever* she wanted.

"Hey, why don't you get out of here a few minutes
early," Cynara said, pushing a few locks of her shocking-
ly purple hair behind her shoulder—hair Keelin was certain wasn't dyed.

"You sure?" she asked, stacking clean martini glasses
in a pyramid on one of the shelves. Their bar was mostly
cleared now, with patrons either dancing, in one of the
private booths or in one of the private rooms. They'd
get another rush in the next half hour when the new
shift came in. Cynara was working a double though so
she'd be staying.

"Yeah, I know you've got plans with your girls. Just
keep Nyx out of trouble," she murmured. "Bo will freak
if anything happens to her."

Keelin glanced over her shoulder, automatically
looking for Nyx. They'd started working at the club at
the same time and she wasn't exactly sure what type of
supernatural being the other female was. She was sweet
to be sure, incredibly graceful looking—and a huge klutz.
Keelin started to respond when a sharp awareness filled
her chest, the warmth spreading out in a burst of sensa-
tions, slamming into her nerve endings without warning.

She sucked in a breath as understanding of what was
happening set in. Blood rushed in her ears and her hands
started to tremble. It took Cynara's hand on her forearm

to bring her back to reality. Blinking, Keelin looked at her friend and tried to get her erratic breathing under control.

"You okay?" Cynara frowned, her purple eyes bright with concern.

Swallowing hard, Keelin nodded. "Yeah. I'm good." But she wasn't good. Not at all. Her parents, two of the most powerful dragons on the planet, had just come out of their Protective Hibernation. All members of a dragon clan were connected to an extent and when one was born or came out of a Hibernation, they all felt it.

She loved her parents, but they'd guilted her into Hibernating with them hundreds of years ago—because of their fear of losing her—and she'd foolishly given in. She'd lost hundreds of years of her life only to emerge a year ago into a new, modern world she loved. She refused to go back to that sheltered existence living on her clan's land up in Montana. Something akin to fear slid through her veins at their awakening, even though she knew it was stupid. She controlled her life now, not them.

When she realized Cynara was still watching her curiously she pasted on a smile. "I'm going to go talk to Bo then head out with Nyx." Their other friend Ophelia should be there soon too. She was meeting them before they headed to the underground supernatural fights. Which weren't actually underground at all, but it was what everyone called them.

As she stepped out from the bar, she watched as Nyx collided with another server weaving her way through the black high-top tables, sending empty glasses flying in all directions. They crashed to the ground, glass shattering everywhere. Keelin cringed and immediately went to help them clean up when Bo appeared as if out of nowhere.

Damn that male was stealthy. Tonight his eyes were gold and his hair an amber-ish color. He was always changing his hair and eye color, with magic she guessed. And pretty much anything he chose looked great against his café au lait skin. The man looked like a work of art he was so beautiful. With a wave of his hand, the glass pieces molded back together. Some vamps around them gasped at the display but Keelin had seen him do it before. Nyx smiled gratefully as she helped the other server put the glasses back on her tray. It was too crowded to hear much but Keelin was pretty sure the other female mumbled a thank you to him. Her cheeks flamed crimson as she looked away.

Bo just watched the female as if he wanted to devour her.

Keelin was so getting Nyx to talk about him tonight because those two needed to hook up. When Bo started to head to the front door, probably to talk to one of his security guys, she waved him down. "Hey, you got a sec?"

He nodded toward a white door on the other side of the club. "My office?"

"Sure."

Once the door closed behind them the noise from outside dimmed dramatically. The walk down the hallway to his office was quick and quiet. In his office, she couldn't hear anything from the club. Considering her supernatural hearing, that was saying something about his insulation. Or maybe he had some sort of spell in place.

"What's up?" he asked, heading to his desk and rifling through a set of papers, a frown on his face.

She hovered near one of the chairs in front of it, deciding not to sit. "Nothing much. I..." She wasn't really sure how to say what she was feeling and suddenly felt stupid for asking to talk to him. It wasn't as if her parents could swoop in here and demand Bo fire her or something. But that fear had spiked inside her moments ago, that with this sudden reemergence they'd try to rip her away from her new life. She didn't even know if they'd woken up yet or if this was just the beginning stages. Sometimes it could take weeks or even longer for a dragon shifter to wake up fully.

When she didn't continue, he looked up, still standing behind his desk. "Everything okay? Anyone give you a problem tonight?" His eyes flashed angrily.

She loved that he took his employees safety so seriously. "Oh, no. Nothing like that. I just, I wanted to say I really like this job, that's all."

His expression softened and he sat, motioning for her to do the same. "You don't make small talk, so what's going on?"

Sighing, she collapsed onto one of the seats. "It's nothing, really. I could be wrong, but I'm fairly certain my parents have woken from their Hibernation." Unlike the majority of supernatural beings she came in contact with, Bo actually knew what she was—he'd seen her brother burn a hole into his ceiling and through the front of his club not too long ago. Kinda hard to hide what she was after that awesome display.

Bo's eyebrows raised a fraction. "Okay."

"They will not be pleased that I've left our land or that I'm working in a demon-owned bar."

"Half-demon," he murmured, almost absently, before continuing. "So what are you worried about?"

"Nothing. I think I just had a panic attack, thinking they'd storm down here and, I don't know, try to force me to quit or something." She felt weak and pathetic even saying the words aloud. For too long she'd let her mother's fear suffocate her, living only a half-life.

Bo seemed to understand though. "I know who you are and that you don't need to work. As long as you want a job, you have one here. No one has ever told me how to run my business or who to hire or fire. I doubt your parents would try to use any persuasion on me, but if they do, don't worry." There was a bite to his words, reminding her that he was a powerful being.

"Thank you." His words soothed her but she still felt a tiny bit pathetic. She needed to get over this crap with her parents. Standing, she headed to the door. With her hand on the doorknob, she half-turned. "Nyx is going with Ophelia and me to the fights tonight."

Bo went preternaturally still at her words in that way that only supernatural beings could. "Nyx is going?" Each word came out clipped, as if it pained him to speak.

Keelin nodded. "Yep. Thought you'd want to know." Without another word, she left, making her way to the end of the hallway. Apparently Bo had once used the rooms behind the red door frequently but ever since Nyx started working for him, he hadn't slept with or looked at another female in a sexual way. Keelin had no idea if the former was true, but she knew the latter was. He had eyes only for Nyx.

Stepping out into the club, Keelin was immediately inundated with all the sensory details; flashing lights, music, the scent of sweat, sex and perfumes. She loved it. Being in this new world was fascinating. She moved around the outer edge of the dance floor, making her way to the front. Ophelia and Nyx were already waiting, both females practically jumping up and down with excitement.

Good, because she was too. She'd been in Biloxi a month and this was her first time going to the fights. Well, technically she'd been once before, but that was when she and Conall had been looking for their brother Drake. That hadn't been for pleasure.

She planned to make this a night she'd remember. Because she was tired of thinking and reacting like her former self. New Keelin had taken charge of her life and she wasn't going back to her prior, boring existence.

* * *

"Thanks for having someone pick me up from the airport," Bran Devlin said as he shook Finn Stavros's hand. The other Alpha nodded once and turned back to the punching bag that must have had some extra reinforcement for the way he was slamming his fists into it.

Bran had been picked up at the private airport he'd flown into—he'd decided to use normal transportation instead of flying in his dragon form—and escorted directly to the Stavros pack's mansion in historic Biloxi. Then he'd been led down to a lower level floor and to a state-of-the-art gym.

Finn was the only one in the room, the tension and aggression rolling off the other male and filling the room with a bitter scent. Bran didn't think it was because of his presence, but he needed to be certain. Having two Alphas under the same roof wasn't a long-term option, even when they were different species. Not that Bran planned to stay long. "If you'd prefer I stay elsewhere it won't be an issue."

At that, Finn stopped and faced him. The Alpha's jaw clenched tight, his breathing and heart rate slightly increased as he watched Bran. "No, I'm honored to house another Alpha, especially from your clan. I want to discuss an alliance with you—that I hope will eventually extend to multiple dragon clans. We've already formed one with the Petronilla clan, as I'm sure you know."

For centuries dragons had lived in secret, even among other supernatural beings. By necessity more than anything. Dragons had been hunted for millennia for a multitude of reasons. They still didn't flourish the way other shifters did, but that had a lot to do with the way they mated—when one mate died, so did the other. As far as he knew, they were the only shifters on the planet like that. He figured it was Mother Nature's way of controlling their population as they were inherently powerful. "That's something I'd like to discuss with you also." Even if it wasn't the reason he was here.

"So, why are you in my territory?" The question was blunt, but with no rudeness.

Bran had been vague and unfortunately he couldn't be completely truthful. Not yet. Not until he'd done some recon. "Two reasons, one being a female." Something he never thought he'd say, but his fucking dragon hadn't left him alone for a month straight. It'd been clawing and raging under the surface, determined to get to Biloxi, just to *see* the female who filled his fantasies. He'd been edgy and surly to everyone in his clan. They were glad to be rid of him for a while, he was sure.

Finn raised a dark eyebrow, but something about his expression told him he wasn't exactly surprised. "What's the other?"

"I'm investigating something."

"Something?"

"It's paranormal in nature. Other than that, I cannot discuss any more details—yet. I ask for your patience while I see if it's worth even discussing with you." Truthfully, what he was doing in Biloxi was classified. Not that he wouldn't bend the rules for another Alpha, but until he knew more about his off-the-books 'assignment' from his former boss in black ops, he didn't want to say anything. He'd been headed to Biloxi when his old boss had called, the timing likely not coincidental. His former handler had probably known he was headed here and decided to ask him for a favor.

Finn was silent for a while, contemplative, his ice blue eyes assessing. "Is this related to your clan or your job before a year ago?"

Bran stilled. "What do you know of my previous job?"

A corner of the Alpha's mouth lifted a fraction. "Nothing, which is why I'm asking. I know you didn't become Alpha of your clan until your parents passed a year ago so I looked into you. And I found absolutely *nothing*. Your reaction tells me enough—for now. Drake and Victoria trust you, and so does Rhea so I'm extending that trust."

But it was on a short leash, something the male didn't have to say. Relief slid through him as he nodded. "Thank you. If anything in my investigation will affect your territory, I'll inform you immediately."

Finn nodded and started to respond when a new scent filled the air. Female, like winter and moonlight. He turned toward the entrance to see a tall, lean teenage girl who was clearly Finn's daughter strolling in. Just like that, the tension in the room eased, disappearing as if it had never been. So that had been the source of the Alpha's distress.

"You're back," Finn said, his voice soft.

"Well, you did give me a curfew, even though I just turned *seventeen*." She snorted, flipping her inky black hair over her shoulder. The girl might be young, but there was an aura of power surging around her that surprised Bran.

"You're lucky I let you go out with that human at all," the male growled.

"I almost wish you hadn't," she muttered. "It was awful."

And that was Bran's cue to leave. He cleared his throat and nodded toward the exit. "I'm going to head out but I'll be back later. Thank you again for the hospitality."

Finn nodded. "She's at the fights."

He blinked. "Who, and what?"

"Keelin. She just got off work about half an hour ago and is on her way to the underground supernatural fights."

Bran's dragon rippled beneath the surface, his talons scraping against his insides. He knew about the fights. Keelin's brother, Drake, had been visiting Bran's clan the last couple weeks and had told him about them. How brutal they were. He didn't care that Keelin was a dragon and could naturally take care of herself.

She shouldn't be at a place like that. A month ago she'd almost died, had been shot and nearly killed in a savage sacrifice by an insane dragon trying to open a Hell Gate. The female was too damn naïve about this modern world.

Not trusting his voice, he just nodded and strode from the room, everything else funneling around him as he pulled his cell phone from his jeans pocket. He could have asked Finn where the fights were but he was going to go right to Drake and get the location, to find out if this place was as bad as the male had said.

The other dragon's roar of anger when he told Drake where his younger sister was, was all the answer Bran needed.

Bran's dragon clawed even harder, desperate to take over and get to the female. His reaction was not normal.

Somehow he managed to rein his dragon in from shifting and grabbed a ride to the fights with one of Finn's packmates. For how he felt now, he didn't trust his dragon completely, wasn't sure he could control himself in animal form. The fact that his animal was already so close to the surface, begging for freedom, told him everything he needed to know.

That had never happened, not even when he'd been a child. But something about the petite, blonde female made him savagely protective. And possessive, something he didn't like at all.

CHAPTER TWO

One month ago

Keelin slipped her thick robe on and fought the shiver that rolled through her. It was no use. Normally she could regulate her body temperature so that she was comfortable in any setting. Not this morning. Not after . . . she shuddered, still not able to believe everything that had happened in the last twenty-four hours.

She'd healed from her gunshot wounds, but whatever her cousin had poisoned her with had left her weak and exhausted. All she knew was, she was going right back to bed. She'd thought she was ready for a shower but even that had exerted too much effort.

When she opened the door from the en suite she sensed Bran Devlin before she'd even stepped into her bedroom. What was he doing here? His scent, which reminded her of a dark winter night, all woodsy and masculine, tickled her nose. It vaguely registered that she found it more than just a little appealing, but she was too exhausted to care. The fact that she hadn't heard or scented him earlier said a lot to her state of healing.

"Bran." All she could manage was his name. They'd only had a few conversations. He was Alpha of another dragon clan and seemed decent enough. Fia, one of her oldest friends, was mated to the male's brother and said Bran was a stubborn ass, but Fia thought anyone who didn't cater to her every whim was an ass. And Keelin knew intrinsically that this male would cater to absolutely no one. It was a good quality in a true leader.

He stood next to her roll-top desk, dwarfing the delicate piece of furniture. Like most dragons, he was big in human form too. Big and far too sexy for his own good. Something she didn't want to be noticing. A female like her wouldn't have a chance with a male like him. She might be considered royalty, but she wasn't strong or even physically built like the majority of her species. Not that she even wanted to be with this male anyway. The attack she'd just been through had been a wakeup call. It was time to start living her life on her terms. To get out from under the watchful eye of her clan.

He took a step forward, his sapphire-green eyes flashing. Well, one did. The other was slightly cloudy. She wondered at that for a moment until he spoke. "Do you need help?" His deep voice rolled over her like a seductive balm.

She shook her head and fiddled with the tie on her long robe. "What are you doing here?" She was surprised her brother Conall had even let him in her house. Her other brother, Drake, was likely with his mate right now, as he should be, after everything they'd been through.

"Your Aunt Alma sent me up with tea." He motioned to the silver tray he'd set on her desktop.

"Oh." So her aunt had bullied him into this. That made more sense. Apparently even Alpha shifters had trouble standing up to that woman. "Well, thank you. I'm tired so don't feel like you have to stay or anything."

He frowned at her, but didn't respond as she slowly made her way to her bed. She appreciated him bringing the tea but she couldn't be bothered with it. She just needed more sleep. And she wanted him to leave. It wasn't normal for her to have males outside her own clan in her home and definitely not in her bedroom when she was just wearing a robe.

Keeping her robe on—she'd undress only when she was alone—she slid under the covers with a sigh. As she pulled her thick gold and cream-colored duvet up over her, he picked up one of the small ceramic cups and brought it to her. Steam tendrils curled up from it, the cup instantly warming her hands as she took it.

"Thank you," she murmured, expecting him to leave after that, surprised by his thoughtfulness. As an Alpha he had better things to do than play nursemaid, especially to a near stranger like her.

Instead, he grabbed one of the tufted high-back chairs from near one of her windows and pulled it over so that he was sitting next to her. He leaned forward, placing his hands on his knees, everything about him coiled tight. "Do you need food? Something else? Your aunt said you hadn't eaten anything since...you've been home."

"I'm okay, but thank you." When he just sat there watching her, she plucked at her comforter, unsure what to say. Even though manners had been drilled into her since she was a child, she simply didn't have the energy for small talk. And if she was honest, his presence was making her uncomfortable. She wasn't sure why, he was just being kind, but having him in her room was strange.

He reached up and scrubbed a hand over his black, closely cut hair. The muscles in his arms flexed, as if on display just for her. Feeling stupid for noticing, she fought the heat flooding her cheeks and glanced down at her tea again.

"I just wanted to make sure you were okay," he finally murmured. "If my presence bothers you I'll wait in the hall."

Surprised by his words, she looked up. He hadn't said he'd leave, just that he'd wait in the hall. That was...odd. But maybe her aunt, or even her brother, had asked him to watch out for her. After one of their own clan members had nearly killed Keelin and Victoria, Conall could be in over-protective mode. "You don't have to wait at all. The threat is gone."

"I know I don't have to. I want to." He watched her carefully, as if searching for something.

When he looked at her with those green eyes, she found herself getting flustered and wasn't sure why. "I'm probably just going to sleep," she mumbled, feeling self-conscious and more than a little out of sorts.

"Okay. You're sure you don't need anything now?" he asked, standing, his body language still tense, all those fine muscles pulled taut.

"I'm sure."

He nodded once, that frown still in place. "I'll be in the hall if you need me. Just say my name."

Before she could formulate a single word, he was gone, the heavy door shutting behind him with the barest whisper of sound. The sweetest, spiciest scent lingered in the air after he'd gone, something that smelled a lot like desire. But that couldn't be right.

* * *

Present day

"Three sexy males coming our way, ladies. At your ten o'clock Keelin, so look alive," Ophelia murmured, the petite female with dark curly hair grinning as she took a sip from her black and pink leopard-pattern flask. At five feet flat, the woman was an inch shorter than Keelin. Tonight she seemed even smaller because she was wearing a pair of pink and white Converse sneakers. The shoes didn't have any height. A short denim skirt about the size of a bandaid and a black, skintight sweater with pink skulls on it completed her ensemble.

She might be over two-hundred years old but she looked like a college-aged student.

Next to her, Nyx's cheeks flushed pink. It didn't take much to get her flustered, Keelin had noticed. It was one of the reasons she liked the female so much. Nyx seemed just as fascinated by the world as Keelin did and didn't always get idioms—which told her that Nyx had likely been sheltered too. Wearing dark jeans, black kitten-heel boots, a black turtle neck and a cardigan, she was definitely more buttoned up than most of the women here. Not that it stopped any of the males from checking her out. Her long black hair hung down her back in an inky waterfall and there was an inherent grace about her. Well, until she started moving. Then she normally tripped on something or knocked something—or some-one—over. "You do all the talking, Ophelia," she whispered, her statement not surprising either of them.

Keelin glanced away from the fighting ring in front of them, which was currently empty, and over to the three males heading their way. A twenty minute break had been called after the last battle between two vampires. She'd never seen vamps fight before and it had been interesting—and incredibly brutal.

All around them people were talking, laughing, and gossiping about anything under the sun. It was all supernatural beings too, no humans allowed. Humans would likely freak anyway if they ever stumbled upon this place. Not that it was likely to happen.

Since it was standing room only, with no seating around the octagonal-shaped ring, she wasn't surprised when someone jostled her from behind. It was a miracle they'd gotten a spot right up front. Or maybe not considering Ophelia had shoved her way up here, using her status as the head healer to the Stavros pack to her full advantage. Everyone was a little terrified of her apparently, not that Keelin could understand why, she was so sweet. But they'd recently lost Victoria since she'd moved up to Montana now that she'd mated with Drake so maybe they were worried about pissing off their only healer.

"Hello ladies," one of the males said as he and his two friends, all with dark hair, stopped in front of her and her friends. They almost looked like brothers with the same sharp facial structure, dark eyes and olive-colored skin.

Keelin forced a smile, something she normally didn't have to do. Something about their scent was off but she couldn't place it. She didn't like not knowing what species a supernatural being was. A quick glance at Ophelia and Nyx revealed they didn't seem to notice anything so she internally shrugged. As she focused on them, she realized how incredibly good looking they were. Too bad they did nothing for her libido. *Damn that Bran Devlin.*

"I'm Marshall," the one who'd first said hello spoke again. "And this is Martin and Milo." When Ophelia's eyebrows raised he laughed. "Our mother liked the letter M."

"So you're brothers?" Ophelia asked.

He nodded and Keelin realized one of the other males, the one named Martin, was staring at her intently. She half-smiled but he didn't return it.

"Who are you guys here to see fight?" Marshall—if that was really even his name—asked.

As Ophelia answered, everything swam before Keelin's eyes for a moment. Like reality shifted, the edges of her vision turning fuzzy as the male's face warped into something…dark. She swallowed hard, trying to tear her gaze away from him. The way he made her feel was as if…she needed to take a long shower to wash an oily residue off her skin. It was revolting.

His face blurred in front of her, to be replaced with something else, as if she was watching a movie play out. The male was straddling a naked female, his face was covered in blood, his eyes black pits of nothingness, a dark abyss she felt as if she was drowning in. He threw his head back and laughed, his eyes glittering under streams of moonlight filtering in from bars covering a window. They were in a cell of sorts. He grabbed the female's wrist and bit down—

Everything fizzled, the vision in front of her dissipating like smoke.

Blinking, she shook her head and realized Ophelia was watching her. "You okay?" her friend asked in concern.

Maybe she'd just been standing there staring off into space like an idiot. Whatever, she didn't care, she just wanted away from these males. "I promised some of the pack we'd meet them. We need to go. Now." Keelin didn't bother looking at any of the males, not caring how rude she sounded. Whatever had just happened was real, she was certain. She might not know what she'd just seen but she didn't want to be around any of these males for a second longer.

Just like that Ophelia said goodbye to the males and linked her arms through Keelin and Nyx's and dragged them through the throng of people. Once they'd reached the outer edge of the growing crowd, closer to the exit in this warehouse-type building, Ophelia pulled to a stop.

"Okay, what was that about?" the healer asked.

Keelin glanced around, the back of her neck tingling, but she didn't see the males anywhere. Still, she wasn't going to tell her friends what had happened in a public place. She was going to wait until they were alone and see if they had any idea what freaky thing had just happened. "Nothing, that guy just creeped me out," she said, turning to face them.

"Me too," Nyx murmured, wrapping her arms around herself.

"They were kinda weird, huh." Ophelia nodded, but she was still watching Keelin speculatively. As if she knew Keelin was holding something back.

"Yeah, and listen, don't talk to them anymore, okay? There was something off about them. I...sensed it. Just don't be alone with any of them."

The other two females nodded, but before they could respond, two of Ophelia's packmates strolled up; Solon and Jason.

Solon wrapped an arm around Ophelia's shoulders and kissed her on top of the head. "Hey, half-pint. What are you guys up to?" he asked, looking at all of them.

"Just watching the fights," Keelin said, knowing Nyx likely wouldn't say much. She served drinks well enough at Bo's place, but she didn't flirt—not that it hurt her tips any—or make much small talk.

"Your boy find you?" he asked Keelin as Jason started talking quietly to Nyx.

Keelin's eyebrows pulled together. "Boy? I do not have a boyfriend." Nor did she want one, thank you very much. But perhaps Solon meant something else. She was still getting used to so much of the modern slang.

Solon snorted. "No, I mean Bran Devlin. Heard he was here and looking for you. Oh, there he is..." The male trailed off, staring at Keelin in confusion as she ducked down lightning fast. "What the hell are you doing?"

"Where is he?" she demanded, ignoring his question as she crouched down like a complete lunatic.

"In the crowd, coming this way. And I hate to break it to you, but you're not going to be able to hide very long."

Still hunkering down, she swiveled only to see a mass of bodies blocking her from having a visual of the fighting ring and thankfully, Bran. Wherever he was. God, she'd masturbated to thoughts of him yesterday. She hadn't seen him in a month, but it hadn't dulled her attraction to him. He'd been all protective and surprisingly possessive of her before she'd left Montana. It made no sense, they had no real ties. But she hadn't been able to stop thinking about him. She didn't want to see him right now. And she didn't care how insane she was acting in front of her new friends.

"I'll see you guys later," she said, ducking around Solon and Ophelia—who was laughing at her—then made her way to one of the exits. As she hurried, she used people to block her so she wouldn't be seen. Luckily she was short and most shifters tended to be tall. It made her getaway easier. Yes she knew she was acting like a crazy person.

She just didn't care.

What the hell was Bran doing here in Biloxi? She'd made it perfectly clear a month ago that she wasn't interested in anything romantic. Had he followed her here? Freaking Alpha shifters.

As she stepped through one of the side exit doors, she passed by Vega Stavros. The seventeen year old's eyes widened when she saw Keelin, probably because she wasn't supposed to be here. She was supposed to go straight home after her date earlier.

"Isn't it past your curfew?

"I went directly home after my date. Just like I was supposed to," Vega said, almost sulkily.

"Then what, young lady, did you sneak out right after you checked in with your parents?" Keelin demanded, not caring about Bran at this point.

Vega straightened, her violet eyes filled with amusement. "Young lady?"

"Yes, that's right." Oh my God, she was so her mother. She glanced over her shoulder and saw Bran moving through the crowd. He hadn't seen her yet. Her heart started beating triple time. "Never mind," she said, turning back to the girl. "Make sure you stay out of trouble. Solon and Ophelia are here, go find them or I'm calling your dad right now." Without waiting for a response, she ducked out of the place and into the cool air. If Keelin didn't think everyone in the pack would be looking out for Vega she would have stayed but there had been two dozen Stavros pack members at the fights tonight. And the truth was, seventeen or not, Vega could take care of herself. Keelin could sense the girl's power and it was staggering for someone so young.

Sucking in a deep breath, she hurried across the parking lot, her three-inch heels crunching over the gravel. It was almost spring but there was still a surprising bite of cold in the air. Not that it bothered Keelin.

As she moved in and out of the vehicles, she glanced around. The parking lot was full, but the warehouse was far from the main road, hidden back enough that no one would accidentally stumble on it. There weren't any people out here, not with all the action inside. Which was good for her, she'd have privacy to strip and shift so she could fly back to the mansion.

A burning scent accosted her about two seconds before the three males from inside appeared as if from nowhere, stepping out from behind a black SUV with dark tinted windows. Her alarm bells went off, but she didn't panic.

Inhaling deeply, she only scented the three of them. Okay so it was unlikely someone was trying to attack her from behind. Still, she wasn't letting her guard down.

"You smell delicious, little dragon," the one named Marshall said. Apparently the leader of the trio.

And he knew what she was. Just great. "Get the hell out of my way," she demanded. Shifters or any supernatural beings only respected strength. She was pretty sure these three were out here to ambush her but she knew well enough to always stand her ground, no matter how afraid she was.

"Not after what you saw back there," the other one—maybe, Martin—said.

Somehow she kept her expression blank. "Saw?"

"You're special, aren't you little dragon? Not everyone is powerful enough to see or contain the power." Marshall spoke again while the third one stepped to the left, as if he was thinking about moving around one of the vehicles to cut off her escape.

She was about tired of the 'little dragon' comments. And she had no idea what he meant by 'contain the power'. She pinned him with a stare, her dragon's fire tickling the back of her throat. Tonight was definitely going to end badly. Probably with her clothes shredded and these losers burned to a crisp. She knew her animal was in her eyes already, was barely containing the urge to shift.

But she'd be weakest when she underwent the change, just for a few moments. She needed to put some distance between them before she let her dragon take over. "Special?" she asked, wanting to keep them talking as she took a couple steps backward.

They followed, one having to fall behind the others in the tighter space between the vehicles.

"Very special," the creepy one she'd seen biting that female said in a sing-song voice. The sound of it felt like ice trailing down her spine. His eyes darkened and she scented that fire again. Demons. They had to be. "And now you have to die."

Fire erupted in one of the male's hands and she didn't think, just let her instinct take over.

Not bothering to shift, she unleashed the fire that had been tickling her throat, a scorching stream releasing at the two closest males. She nailed one of them in the arm and face.

He screamed and the other male went for a weapon. A gun. He yanked it free from the back of his pants. Before he could lift his arm she whipped her fire at him, ready to fry him when a blast of bright orange flames fell from the sky, lighting up everything around them.

She jumped back, lifting an arm to shield herself from the brightness. Her fire died in her throat as the flames from above ate up the three males, incinerating them and four vehicles around them in seconds, as if the fire itself was hungry enough to devour everything in its path. She could feel the heat but just barely. As a dragon she could shield herself—to an extent—from other dragons' fire, but whoever was breathing it was specifically guarding her against its destructive power. She sensed it bone-deep.

She stared at the sky but whoever it was had shielded themselves—until a shimmering bluish-green dragon with scales the color of the Mediterranean suddenly appeared, landing in the ashes of the demons and destroyed vehicles with a thump. He spread his wings, a beautiful pale blue that gave off the illusion of flowing water and stared at her with sapphire-green eyes.

Eyes she would know anywhere.

Before she could move or even think, the male shifted to his human form. Bran stood there, all six feet four inches of sexy, pissed off male. His expression was one of pure rage as he stepped toward her. Not that it stopped her from checking out every single naked inch of him. And the man was *built*. All those hard lines and striations looked as if he'd been carved from marble.

She knew she should be more worried about what the hell had just happened but as he stalked toward her, it was hard to remember her name.

"Keelin," he growled out and it registered that he was angry—*at her*. "What the hell were you—"

She stomped her heel against the gravel, not caring if she looked childish. "Don't you fucking lecture me!" She couldn't take it from him of all people. Not now, not ever.

He let out another growl, this one filled with something else. Not anger.

He fisted her hips, tugging her to him faster than she could blink. She'd barely let out a gasp of surprise before his mouth crushed over hers, hard and demanding.

CHAPTER THREE

Bran's tongue teased against Keelin's, the simple taste of her setting him on edge. Of course there was nothing simple about her or this situation at all. When he'd seen those three males follow Keelin outside—as she unsuccessfully tried to hide from him—his dragon had clawed at the surface, ready to destroy her attackers.

But he'd remained in control, had followed them like the hunter he was. He'd remained in the shadows, cloaked and looking out for her. Until that fucker had said Keelin was going to die. He'd never lost control of his animal side like that, as if he was barely hanging on to his humanity by a thread. Everything he'd just done was a fiery haze.

Everything except the way Keelin was grinding up against him, her petite form arching into him. He'd been going crazy for a month wanting her. It was hard to believe she wasn't pushing him away. Growling low in his throat, he nipped her bottom lip between his teeth and tugged.

She moaned and dug her fingers into his shoulders. It wouldn't take much to get her undressed. He backed her up against the side of a truck—as far away as he could manage from the charred remains of demon and metal.

He skimmed his hands up her hips and over her waist, wishing he was touching more than just her skin-tight black dress. When he'd first seen her inside the warehouse, his entire body had gone on red alert. Much like the first time he'd met her. He lost the ability to think, much less talk.

The dress hugged all her curves, accentuating that perfect ass. He'd seen other males looking at her, wanting her, and he'd had the irrational urge to incinerate every single one of them. And even though the hem was an inch below her knees, the heels she wore helped accentuate those toned calves. Calves he'd fantasized about having wrapped around his shoulders because every inch of her body was a subject of obsession for him. Against his will too. He hadn't thought he wanted a mate, but his fucking dragon had other ideas.

When she slid her hands down his chest, her greedy fingers trying to touch every inch of him, he rolled his hips against her, his cock thick and hard and desperate to get inside her.

She moaned again and all reason fled his mind. Grabbing her hips again, he hoisted her up the side of the vehicle—then realized they had a problem.

Her damn dress was too fitted for her to move much. And he wanted those fine legs latched around him, her high heels digging into his ass.

Reaching for the hem, he shoved it up her legs until it bunched against her waist. She immediately wrapped her legs around him, rolling her hips against his. Oh God, just a thin scrap of material separated them now.

He shouldn't do this. She deserved better than rough and frantic up against a vehicle mere feet from where he'd just killed three demons, and where anyone could stumble on them. When he met Keelin's gaze again, her gray eyes were heavy-lidded and sparking with lust. They'd gone almost pure silver.

That was when he realized she was glowing. A gold light emanated from her, illuminating their position perfectly. Cursing, he glanced around and as he did, the spell of intimacy between them was broken.

"Oh my God! *No.* No, no, no!" she chanted, frantically shoving at him, realizing what the glow meant as fast as he did. He didn't want to let her go but he did. Before her heels hit the ground she was already tugging her dress down. She took an unsteady step away from him, face flushed. The second she did, the glow dimmed, but he knew what he'd seen.

When dragons started the mating process it manifested in different ways. Since his brother was mated to a Petronilla dragon he knew exactly what that glow was—it was a Petronilla trait for when their animal side wanted to start the mating process. Her dragon was clearly on board with him. Unfortunately, as Keelin glared accusing daggers at him, it was clear her human side didn't like the thought of mating with him at all.

She might as well have punched him in the nuts. He knew he wasn't a fucking prize, but...*fuck.*

Her long blonde hair was rumpled, her full lips swollen as she glanced around, finally taking in their surroundings. When her gaze landed on the burning embers of what had been the demons and vehicles she shook her head. "What the heck was I thinking?" she muttered. Then her gaze snapped back to his. "What were those things?"

Yeah, he could go for a subject change. Better than focusing on the fact that she didn't want him. Or didn't *want* to want him anyway. He still wanted her though, no doubt about it. "Demons I think. And they followed you out of the club." His jaw clenched. For centuries dragons had lived in anonymity, even among other supernatural beings.

But months ago that had started to change when Keelin's brother escaped from Hell.

Literally.

His escape had caused an earthquake in New Orleans and he'd subsequently been given shelter by a wolf shifter pack before his clan found him. And now said pack—and the Alpha's vampire mate—wanted to enter into alliance talks with his dragon clan. They were already basically allies with the Petronilla clan. And Finn's mating with a vampire meant those alliances would eventually extend to vamp covens as well. Which could be a positive thing.

The downside to the situation was that others seemed to know more about dragons now. Not that he'd ever fooled himself into thinking they'd been completely anonymous but if those demons had tracked Keelin because of what she was he'd...well, he couldn't do much more because they were already fucking dead.

She wrapped her arms around herself and shivered. Instinctively he wanted to pull her close again, but resisted, knowing she'd reject him. "I talked to them inside. One of them..." She trailed off at the sound of footsteps crunching over gravel.

He'd heard one of the doors of the warehouse open about twenty seconds ago but clearly Keelin hadn't been paying attention.

Her two female friends and the two Stavros pack males approached. Solon, who had a similar skull trim to Bran, stepped forward and surveyed the damage. "A vampire came inside talking about a light show out here so we came to check it out . . . What the hell happened here?"

"Three demons attacked me so I killed them," Keelin said before Bran could even think about answering.

Damn it. He couldn't call her out. The smoldering scent of flesh and metal covered up the scent of her lie. He knew why she'd taken the credit for the kills. He was an Alpha in another Alpha's territory. Maybe she was worried about him. Which was kinda sweet if a bit misplaced. The kills had been more than justified.

Solon flicked a glance at Bran and his lips pulled into a thin line. So maybe the guy didn't believe her either but damn, Bran couldn't contradict her in front of everyone. Not when they were on unsteady ground enough as it was. It would just piss her off and alienate her. And probably embarrass her in front of her friends.

"And you decided to just take out some vehicles while you were at it," Jason, the other one muttered. "That was *my* truck, Keelin." His voice was more resigned than annoyed as he pointed at one of the piles of ash.

Ophelia rolled her eyes. "Big deal, the pack will get you a new one. It's not like the thing wasn't insured."

"For a dragon attack? There's not even a frame left for the insurance adjuster. And my iPod was in there."

"I'll take care of it," Bran said, stepping up next to Keelin and ignoring her huff of annoyance. "That's not the issue anyway. Those demons were tracking Keelin."

Solon frowned. "You're sure?"

He nodded. "Yeah."

Solon's frown deepened and he ran a hand over his skull trim. "Wait...demons or half-demons?"

"I...don't know." Damn it. He probably should have let one of them live so he could have questioned them. But he hadn't been thinking tactically before. All he'd cared about was eliminating the immediate threat to Keelin.

"You think they were after her specifically or just any single female?" Solon asked.

"Okay, 'her' is right here," Keelin snapped. "And they knew what I was. They called me 'little dragon' and said I smelled delicious. They also called me special more than once, though I'm not sure what that was about.

And..." She cleared her throat, as if choosing her words, before continuing. "Then they said I needed to die."

Bran only realized he was growling when everyone turned to look at him. He also decided to cover his junk as best he could. He didn't mind nudity and it was clear the other shifters didn't either but the female with black hair, Nyx he thought her name was, was looking anywhere but at him, as if uncomfortable.

"So then you just killed them," Solon said.

"They attacked me first. And I got a little carried away with my fire." Her voice was dry as she said the last part.

Bran snorted softly. If she expected him to apologize later that was never going to happen. He'd level a city block to save her. Period. As an Alpha he was more strongly in touch with his animal side than most of his kind and he wasn't going to fight the instinctive need he felt to protect her.

"Damn it. All right..." Solon looked around. The lot was empty of other people and Bran had a feeling it would stay that way for a while. There had been a full lineup of fights for the next couple hours. Apparently they often fought until day break. "Jason and I are going to take care of this. The rest of you, head to Bo's club. I'm calling Finn. He'll meet you there."

"Shouldn't we go back to the mansion?" Keelin asked.

But Bran understood the other male's reasoning. If someone had targeted her or others were watching them—though he didn't sense it and his natural ability to detect when he was being watched or hunted was in-born and sharp—they wouldn't want to lead them direct-ly back there and put the other packmates at risk.

As Bran expected, Solon shook his head.

"Okay, well, you know Vega's in the warehouse right? Maybe we should—"

"Lyra's watching her," Ophelia said. "Apparently she checked in with her dad at her curfew, then turned around and headed here. Sneaky little thing." There was a note of amusement in the woman's voice.

Keelin instantly relaxed. Bran couldn't tear his gaze away from her. She'd just almost been attacked and was worried about someone else. Yeah, his dragon had picked the right female.

When she realized he was watching her, she glanced up at him and frowned. Then turned away and com-pletely ignored him. When she practically marched away from him, he couldn't help but watch the sway of her ass. Damn the woman got him riled up.

"We need to leave now," the one named Nyx said quietly, something in her tone making the group go still.

"What do you sense?" Bran asked, stepping closer to the group of females, wanting to be as close to Keelin as possible.

Nyx met his gaze, her blue eyes grim but there was a trace of confusion. "I'm not sure, but someone is watch-ing us."

Bran inhaled deeply, pushing his hunter's senses outward, but all he felt were the people in the warehouse. Too many scents filtered through the air, made worse by the scent of ashes, that he couldn't get a lock on anything else. But he believed the female.

Ignoring her gasp of annoyance, Bran clasped Keelin's elbow. It was time to leave. "We should go then."

* * *

"Is she the one?" Shar asked, his hands shoved into the pockets of his jeans.

Naram nodded without glancing at him, watching the petite blonde getting into a vehicle called an SUV with some wolf shifters and another dragon. After being woken from a millennia long coma—one he'd been put in by the female's grandmother—he was once again free thanks to a natural disaster. "She looks just like her grandmother and she's wearing the bracelet." Soon he would bathe in her blood—if he could destroy her. Then he would take back what was rightfully his. That bitch was wearing his talisman.

His.

"Perhaps she's not as powerful. The male killed our scouts, not her."

Naram shrugged, liking the feel of being in a human body again. When he'd been imprisoned, his spirit had been trapped in a sacrificial urn. The sensation of the wind blowing over his skin now was welcome. "That means nothing. Male dragons are protective of their mates. They are not rational when it comes to females."

Something he knew well. And the truth was, if she wasn't inherently powerful she wouldn't have been able to even wear the bracelet. Only a certain line of female dragons was able to possess it without dying. There was simply too much power contained inside it.

"They are mated?"

"I don't know." And he didn't like that. His kind and dragon shifters had been enemies since the beginning of time and for all he knew of them, there were still many secrets they kept. At least they had when he'd lived on the earth. He assumed it was still the same.

"Is it odd that they are aligning with wolf shifters?" Shar asked. The young demon hadn't been out of Hell long and didn't know much of the human world.

Unfortunately Naram was still adjusting to this world too. Eight months out of his imprisonment and he still wasn't at full power—and he wouldn't ever be until he eliminated his problem and retrieved his bracelet. He'd only recently released Shar to assist him. "Years ago it would have been unheard of, but now I think things have changed."

They'd located the female a week ago and had found her working at a bar owned by a half-demon and living with wolf shifters. She must have only recently put the bracelet on or he never would have found her. But it had allowed him to track her to an extent.

Her living arrangements didn't make sense and while he wanted to outright kill her because of her blasted bloodline, now he realized he'd have to be more subtle, to get her alone before that happened. Especially if she was mated. Mated dragons were more powerful and could prove a death sentence to one such as him. Because if he moved in too soon she might take off the bracelet, then go into hiding and then he'd never get the chance to destroy her and reclaim his property. If that happened he would never regain all his powers. That was unacceptable.

"What about the other female, the one with the black hair? What is she?" Shar had been watching the other female with too much interest in the week they'd been watching Keelin Petronilla.

"She's mixed blood. I don't know what." But the couple times he'd walked past her in that club, he'd felt...off. Something about her had felt familiar, but not. He didn't like what he didn't know, especially since he wasn't in top form. "We will avoid her for now."

"What should we do tonight?" Now that their scouts were dead, Shar meant.

"We'll follow them and when she's alone, I'll send out another attack. A larger one with hunters. I want to see how powerful she is."

"What if the hunters kill her?"

"They won't." Not when he ordered them not to. Naram just wanted to test her powers, to see how well she battled. He had to be the one to kill her or he'd never get what he needed. When she was out of the way he'd eventually kill the rest of her kind or keep them as his slaves. As it should be.

CHAPTER FOUR

Keelin traced her finger along the stem of her martini glass, the nervous energy humming through her making her jittery. She couldn't believe what had happened in that parking lot. The demon thing was bad enough, but the fact that she'd started putting off the mating glow while kissing Bran; just no. Absolutely not.

She didn't want a mate. Not now and maybe never. And definitely not one like Bran who was all bossy, Alpha male.

She shifted against the leather seat of the private booth she was sitting in, trying to banish the reality of her situation, knowing it was useless. She wished she could escape him but until Finn showed up they were stuck waiting here at Bo's place.

Ophelia and Nyx were on the dance floor and Bran was...coming her way with a bottle of beer in his hand. He looked like a lethal predator stalking across the dance floor. More than a handful of females and some males turned to watch him move. He was like a beautiful piece of art, rough around the edges and a male you could never, ever tame. He didn't look like most dragon shifters in the physical sense, at least not his face. He was way too hard and so very masculine.

She tried to remain unaffected by him, but it was impossible. Especially now that she'd gotten such a wonderful taste of him. When he entered the enclave and tugged the heavy curtains closed, she started to push up from her seat. She didn't want to be alone with him. Okay, she did, but she didn't exactly trust herself.

"We're talking, Keelin. Here or out there." There was no room for argument in his voice as he stood there watching her. For some reason she found his dominance incredibly sexy.

"Fine, but you're sitting on that side," she said, pointing to the other side of the round table set in the middle of the semi-circle booth. Right now she needed a little distance between them, however much of an illusion it was. Because if he didn't want space between them, there wouldn't be any. Her animal side knew exactly who he was to her after that kiss and wanted a whole lot more.

Bran's green eyes narrowed and once again she was struck by the slight difference in his left one.

"Is something wrong with your eye?" she asked, frowning at him.

He stilled at her question before sliding into the booth across from her. His expression had gone carefully neutral as he watched her. "I didn't think you were cruel," he said quietly, a note of hurt in his voice scraping against her senses.

Her inner dragon pushed at her, angry at the shift in Bran, demanding she make things right. Keelin wasn't sure what she'd said though. "I...why would you say that?"

His head tilted to the side the barest fraction, as if he was assessing her. "I can't see out of my left eye. I was born this way."

She inwardly cringed at her callous question, wishing she could take it back. "I didn't realize or I would have never...I'm sorry," she finished lamely.

Surprisingly, he relaxed at her statement. "I thought you knew."

She shook her head, not sure what to say now.

He made the decision for her, launching right into a conversation of exactly what she *didn't* want to talk about. "Do you want to talk about what happened in the parking lot?"

She shook her head, her gaze trailing down to his full mouth. It was the only soft part of the male. And she still couldn't believe she'd just let him shove her dress up like that. She'd been so primed, so ready for him it jarred her. "I don't want a mate," she blurted.

"You sure about that?" he asked dryly.

"Just because my animal side makes a decision doesn't mean I have to be on board with it. I was stuck in Protective Hibernation for hundreds of years and before that sheltered to the point where I felt like a prisoner. I like my new life and I don't want to be trapped by an overprotective mate." No matter how sexy he was.

He snorted, the sound full of derision. "Right."

Her back straightened at his tone. "Right, what? I'm telling the truth."

He leaned forward a fraction, pinning her with his hard gaze. "I'm sure you are."

She felt like there was some underlying meaning she wasn't getting. She'd only been out of Protective Hibernation a little over a year and was still catching up on some things. She bit her bottom lip, hating the awkwardness that suddenly surged through her. While she loved her new freedom she sometimes cursed her parents for sheltering her for so long. Maybe if she hadn't been sheltered, she would understand whatever it was Bran wasn't saying aloud and she wouldn't feel like that weak, silly female so many in her clan thought her to be. Wanting to get away from him and the feelings he evoked inside her, she shoved her drink away and started to slide out of the booth.

"I'm also sure if I looked like my brother you'd feel differently." Now more than derision, there was pain lacing his words.

Her eyebrows drew together. What did his brother have to do with anything? "Your brother is mated to my friend."

"You know what I mean."

On a burst of frustration she slammed a fist on the table harder than she'd intended, making her drink skid across it. "No, I don't!" Stunned by her sudden display, she tamped her growing annoyance down. Something about this male brought out too many emotions, making her behave irrationally. Standing, she started to pull the curtain back but Bran was lightning fast.

For such a big male it surprised her how quick he was. He didn't touch her, but he stepped forward so that she had no choice but to press back against the table until she was sitting on the edge of it.

Leaning down, he caged her in, putting both hands on the edge of the table, his powerful body blocking her way. "You're not lying." Not a question.

"Of course I'm not. I barely understand this conversation." And being so close to him, inhaling that earthy, dark winter night scent that was all Bran was making her nipples tighten in anticipation of touching and kissing him again. Something she shouldn't be thinking about. She needed to remember how obnoxious and domineering he was.

"You're a confusing female," he muttered, still not moving.

Against her will, her attention fell to his mouth once again. All the muscles in her body pulled taut as she imagined that mouth on other places and she swallowed hard.

He inhaled suddenly and she knew he had to scent her desire. Stupid pheromones. He let out a low groan, one of his hands moving up to cup her cheek. For such a rough-looking male, he was surprisingly gentle. "Why did you take credit for killing the demons?" he asked softly, the question taking her by surprise.

"I didn't want you to get in trouble." There had been no other reason than that. She knew how complicated supernatural politics could be and he was an Alpha in another Alpha's territory. From what she'd seen Finn was fair, but still, something deep inside her hadn't wanted Bran to face any sort of punishment.

In response, his other hand slid up her leg, slowly, giving her time to stop him. Looking into his hard face, she didn't want to. She might not want a mate, but that didn't mean she didn't want Bran.

"You want me to stop?" he murmured.

She shook her head. "No, but I don't want a mate. Okay?" Her words came out shaky, but with an Alpha, or really any freaking male, she knew she needed to be crystal clear.

He murmured something that sounded like 'okay', but she couldn't be sure. Unlike the franticness from the parking lot, his movements were slow and controlled as he brushed his mouth over hers. She leaned into him, holding onto his shoulders for support as his tongue teased against hers.

As she did, his hand moved higher, his rough, callused fingers stroking up her inner thigh with determination. She was vaguely aware that she was glowing again but they were in the privacy of the booth. No one would be able to see them. And it didn't mean she was going to mate with the male, just…have fun.

When she sucked on his bottom lip, he groaned into her mouth, that wicked hand moving even higher until he teased the edge of her panties. Because her dress was such a tight fit, she couldn't spread her legs very far. The restrictive feeling was surprisingly erotic as he dipped a finger under the silky material, shoving it to the side until his middle finger grazed her clit.

She jerked against him, needing more.

His tongue flicked against hers, teasing in the same way his finger started teasing her clit. Soft, gentle, with just enough pressure to make her crazy. Heat flooded between her thighs as he started rubbing her sensitive bundle of nerves in an erotic rhythm. It should probably shock her that a male was being so forward with her so quickly, but this was what she wanted. No more living like a protected princess. And she knew Bran would never hurt her.

When he pulled his mouth from hers, she almost protested until he started feathering kisses along her jawline. The feel of his stubble rubbed against her skin, making her even more aware of him.

"I want to feel you come on my fingers." His voice was guttural, his words sending another shot of heat between her legs. "And on my tongue," he continued, dipping a finger inside her, as if testing her slickness. "But that'll be later."

Later? Her inner walls tightened around him, wanting more. She tried to find her voice, but he slid another finger into her wet sheath as he kissed his way back to her mouth. This time when he kissed her it wasn't gentle, but that hungry claiming once again.

Moaning, she tried to roll her hips against his fingers but he grabbed her hip, holding her in place as he thrust his two fingers inside her. Keeping them buried deep, he started massaging her clit with his thumb, using her moans as cues to how hard or how fast she liked it.

Her entire body lit on fire with his caresses. He shouldn't know how to please her so quickly, not when her former...lover, as in singular, had been so sadly lacking.

Her clit pulsed steadily, the need for release building inside her. It wasn't long until he found that perfect rhythm and her inner walls were clenching around his fingers tighter and tighter.

Letting her head fall back, she closed her eyes as her orgasm built faster and faster. Her heart rate and breathing kicked up and he must have sensed the change in her because he began stroking his fingers in and out of her while still strumming her clit.

The extra stimulation was too much.

When he grazed his teeth along the column of her throat, a low growl emanating from him, her toes curled in her heels. She let go of her control, her climax taking over as pleasure surged to all her nerve endings.

It pummeled through her in wave after wave, every inch of her sensitized as she wished they were both naked. She wanted to feel him pushing deep inside her, stretching her, giving her what she craved. Burying her face against his neck, she clutched his upper arms and inhaled his scent. That had just barely taken the edge off.

She wanted more. A lot more. And knew he must too.

Reaching between their bodies, she started to undo his belt but he instantly stepped back, withdrawing his fingers and all that delicious body heat as he did.

Confused, she stared at him. "Why are you stopping me?"

He shook his head once, the action sharp. "I don't...that was just about you."

"It should be about both of us," she whispered, not fully trusting her voice.

His jaw tightened, his green eyes flashing with some emotion she didn't recognize. He didn't respond though. But she understood Alpha shifters well enough. This had been about him dominating her, showing her the pleasure he could bring her with just a few strokes. Probably part of his plan to convince her to mate with him. How could she be so stupid? And there went her obnoxiously bright glow, dimming once again.

Dropping her gaze, she slid from the table, tugging her dress down as her heels clicked against the floor.

"Keelin—"

Straightening, she held up a hand, but couldn't look at him. "I get it."

He grabbed her hand, forcing her to look at him. "You get what?"

She struggled to find her voice as she stared at his hard face when the curtain pulled back.

Nyx's eyes widened when she saw them. She had a mixed drink in her hand. "Oh, I thought...should I come back?" She was already starting to let it slide back into place when Keelin shook her head.

"No." She stepped out of Bran's embrace, yanking the curtain open. "I'm just grabbing a drink," she muttered, hurrying past her friend on wobbly legs. Ophelia was making her way to them along with Solon and Jason, who must have just arrived.

Ignoring what she imagined was Bran's intense gaze behind her, and the fact that everyone could likely scent what they'd just done, she disappeared onto the dance floor, mixing with the crowd and getting lost. With her shorter height, even in heels, it was easy to disappear. She glanced behind her and when she didn't see him, she knew he couldn't see her.

Instead of heading to one of the packed bars, she made her way for the front exit. She wasn't going to wait around for Finn any longer. She could just fly back to the mansion and call or text her friends from there. She knew they'd understand and it wasn't like they were depending on her for a ride. And once she was in the sky pretty much no one could try to attack her and definitely not track her, so she wasn't worried about being alone. Besides, she was a freaking dragon. She could take care of herself.

As she stepped out into the cool night, she inhaled the fresh air, automatically glancing around for a place to duck behind so she could strip. She didn't particularly mind being naked in front of others but she knew Bo had cameras set up everywhere and didn't want to flash him or his security guys.

Before she'd taken two steps, she sensed Bran before she even scented him. As if her body was simply that attuned to the sexy male. "I'm heading to the mansion," she said without turning around, stepping out into the parking lot.

His hand clasped around her upper arm, firm but gentle. "Keelin, damn it—"

They both stilled at the sudden charge in the air. It was almost like a soft buzzing filled the atmosphere, growing louder and louder until... "What is that?" she whispered, automatically grabbing his hand and taking a step back. She might be a dragon and able to take care of herself in most situations, but she wasn't a warrior and something weird was happening. All the hair on her arms and on the back of her neck stood up.

Bran clasped her hand tighter, but instead of moving with her, tried to push her behind him. "I don't see...there." His body pulled taut as a dozen, no, two dozen male forms emerged from the vehicles in the parking lot.

But they weren't males or men. They were formed like men, as if mimicking their likeness, but they didn't have substance, their skin color a dull gray, their entire being monochrome. Even their clothes were all the same dull color and everything matched. They all wore loose black pants and T-shirts and their feet... Her stomach roiled. They didn't have feet, but were all moving forward on a mass of dark gray cloud-like substance.

Bran shoved her back fully now, moving them toward the door when it opened with a clang as it slammed against the outer wall. She didn't have to turn around to know it was Bo. His half-demon scent was embedded in her brain. She didn't know many of his kind and it was unique.

Even though Bran tried to keep her behind him, she managed to peer around his huge body. The mass of beings stopped, their lack of any movement preternatural. She couldn't tear her gaze from them. And maybe she was being paranoid but she could almost swear they were all looking at *her*.

But that couldn't be right.

"Give us the female," the beings said in one voice, sending an icy blade traveling down her spine.

Her blood chilled.

They weren't speaking in English, it was ancient Aramaic, which was creepy all by itself. As a Petronilla dragon, the gift of her clan was to understand any language on the planet. Right now she wasn't sure she was actually thankful for it. Not knowing these things wanted her might be better.

Bran stepped forward, but Bo let out an angry sounding snarl more feral, animalistic-sounding than human. He raged at them in the same language. "Who sent you?"

"Give us the female," they repeated.

Another snarl then he started chanting. She understood the actual words, but they didn't make sense in any context.

Until the things let out a united scream, the horror of the sound washing over her like jagged glass scraping against her bare skin.

She grabbed Bran around the waist, ready to pull him back when he turned and tackled her to the ground. Before they'd landed the scream stopped and a loud rush of wind rent the air. Keelin's hair blew back even as Bran crouched over her. Just as suddenly the wind died and black dust particles landed all around them.

"They're gone," Bo said, motioning for the two security guys who had come outside with him to go back in.

Bran smelled like fire and rage, his dragon clear in his eyes as he looked up at Bo. His jaw tightened as he shoved up and pulled Keelin with him. He drew her into her arms, tucking her tightly against his chest as he appeared to struggle to speak. Keelin couldn't be sure, but she guessed he was battling his dragon and if he let the leash off too soon it wouldn't be pretty. Despite what had happened between them inside, she didn't make a move away from him.

"What were those things?" she asked quietly, her gaze scanning the now empty parking lot. Well, except for the vehicles. A fine coat of black dust covered everything. She had some on her arms and legs but didn't bother wiping it off, mainly because she didn't think Bran would let her out of his grip for even a second.

"Hunter demons. Low tier." Bo answered her, but his gaze was on Bran, his expression wary, probably because he was worried the male was going to snap.

"What does that mean?" Dragons had kept to themselves for millennia and while they knew a decent amount about shifters and vampires, demons or half-demons were a whole other story.

Bo shrugged and started to wipe at the dust on his long sleeves. It came off easily. "Someone sent them. Someone powerful. I don't know of any beings who could have done that."

"You seemed to get rid of them easily enough," Bran said, finally speaking. His voice was tight but she felt the difference in him as he held her. He'd relaxed the tiniest bit, the action soothing her.

Bo snorted and ran a hand over his closely trimmed brown hair. Tonight it wasn't dyed any outlandish color and she wondered if this was the natural shade. "That wasn't easy so much as dumb fucking luck. Considering my heritage," he said bitterly, referring to his father she guessed, "I read up on anything related to the under-world I can get my hands on. I knew what those were and I took a chance."

"What else can destroy them?" Bran asked.

"Probably you two." His words were vague but she guessed he meant their dragon fire. Before she or Bran could ask another question, he continued. "What I want to know is why the fuck they wanted you."

Bran stiffened next to her and she realized he hadn't understood what they'd said. She looked up at him and for a moment was struck by the fierce possessiveness in his expression. "The only thing they said was 'give us the female'. Twice." And she wasn't going to lie to herself; it scared the hell out of her.

Without warning Bran picked her up, scooping his arms under her legs and back. She let out a short yelp but it had barely escaped her mouth before he kicked open the door to the club, Bo close on their heels.

The second they cleared the door she realized that the music was off and everyone was staring at them. Oh hell, did everyone know what had happened outside? The insulation in this place was good, but that scream would have ruptured her eardrums if she'd been human.

"Music!" Bo shouted and just like that a steady beat started up again and vamps and other beings were once again grinding on the dance floor.

In her periphery, she was aware of her friends hovering near the closest bar, but all her attention was on Bran who was staring down at her.

She had the irrational urge to reach out and trace her finger over his soft lips, to see if he'd suck her finger into his mouth, maybe bite down. But she couldn't tempt this Alpha, not if he was going to try to use her own body against her. Even if he didn't mean to do it intentionally, it would happen just the same.

A rumble emitted from him, his sapphire-green eyes glittering dangerously. "We're getting you the hell out of here. Out of town, out of—"

"Stop right there," Keelin snapped, wiggling in Bran's arms until he let her down. "We need to talk to Bo and Finn and figure out what the heck is going on. I'm not running simply because—"

They both turned at the sound of Bo letting out that now-familiar sound of rage, though much quieter than he'd been outside. Her dragon clawed to the surface, fear that more of those things had shown up. Her worry dimmed when she realized the source of his anger.

A tall, dark-haired male had his hand clamped around Nyx's upper arm and had pulled her close. The female didn't look happy about it. Clearly neither was Bo. He stalked off, heading in their direction, determination—and death—lining his face.

Before she could dwell on that situation, Bran turned her back to face him, a similar determined expression on his annoyingly sexy face. Oh yeah, she was in for an argument. Big bad Alpha was about to learn that there was no way he was going to run roughshod over her and move her out of town. No way in hell.

CHAPTER FIVE

Bo tried to tamp down his demon half as he stalked toward Nyx, but it was impossible. He hadn't fucked anyone—or wanted to—since she'd started working for him. For some reason she calmed his demon half and he had no clue why. All he knew was that when he was around her, he felt sane and wasn't constantly battling inside himself. And he wanted more of that.

Right now he felt anything but sane, however. Some asshole had his hand on Nyx and he was about to lose it in three, two...

The male turned at Bo's approach, his hand dropping to his side, but clearly not out of fear. The male was tall, handsome in an almost feminine way, with dark hair that looked as if he'd taken hours to style it. His expression was one of disdain as he looked at Bo. He wore a custom-made suit and looked out of place here.

"It's fine, Bo," Nyx said quickly to him, avoiding his gaze as she looked anxiously at the unknown male. "He's leaving."

"You have a week," the male said to Nyx, his gaze flicking back to assess Bo before he strode off, his head held high in an obnoxiously aristocratic way.

"Who was that?" he demanded, not caring that his demon likely showed in his eyes. Normally around her he restrained himself with no problem, but now…he felt restless. And so damn possessive of her it raked against his insides.

She flicked a dismissive hand in the air. "No one important."

Oh yeah, she was lying. "My office. Now." He placed his hand on the small of her back and despite an initial pushback, she sighed and let him lead her to the quiet hallway. He loved touching her to the point he'd basically avoided it since she started working for him. It was too dangerous.

Unlike most of the scantily clad patrons and employees at his place, she wore dark jeans, heeled boots, a freaking turtleneck and cardigan—and got hit on more than anyone who worked here. It was that prim, buttoned-up thing she had going on.

He definitely understood the appeal. He wanted to unwrap her, slowly, and savor every inch of the sweet female. She made him want to be *gentle*. It was a foreign sensation, but he couldn't deny it.

"Bo, seriously, I appreciate you looking out for me but he was just some jerk. I don't—"

He opened the door to his office and motioned inside. "Don't lie to me," he bit off. Whoever that male had been, he wasn't random to her. And Bo wanted to know who he was. Once they were inside, he shut the door behind them and motioned for her to sit.

Folding her arms over her chest, she collapsed in one of the chairs and crossed her legs.

"Do you want a drink?" He leaned against the front of the desk, looking down at her. He knew the position was dominant and he had no problem using his size to subtly get what he wanted—answers.

She shook her head and for the first time he realized how pale she was. Of average height, she had long black hair and seemed taller than she was because of her slender build. Her skin was normally peaches and cream but now there was a grayish tint to her face. Feeling like a shithead for the way he'd been trying to get answers, he immediately crouched in front of her and took her hands in his. They were ice cold.

"Who was that male? I can help you." He gently rubbed one of his fingers over the pulse point in her wrist. He wasn't sure exactly how to comfort a female, but he'd seen mated males with their females before and figured this was good. Plus it let him touch her, even if he knew he shouldn't.

"He's just someone from my past. That's all." At least she wasn't trying to lie to him again.

Unlike shifters or vamps he couldn't necessarily scent lies, but he sensed them most of the time. Like a vibe a person exuded. "He said you have a week. What did he mean?"

She stared at him with ocean-blue eyes he could drown in for so long he wasn't sure she'd answer.

"My family wants me to return home," she said simply.

He gritted his teeth. "Who's your family?"

Her jaw tightened and she shook her head. "It doesn't matter. I'm not going."

Trying a different tactic, he took a deep breath. "If I don't know what I'm up against, I can't help you." He rubbed her other pulse point with his thumb, savoring the feel of her soft skin. Everything about her was soft and impossibly sweet. It was just an essence she put off without even trying, part of who she was. From the moment she'd walked into his place he'd known she didn't belong. He'd also known he wasn't letting her go.

He couldn't.

Whenever he couldn't watch out for her, he'd always assigned one of his security guys specifically to keep an eye on her. He didn't want any of his customers hassling her.

Her pretty lips pulled into a frown at his words. "I don't need help—though I do appreciate it. You've been so kind already, I..." She let out a long sigh and withdrew her hands from his to rub them over her face. "I just want to live a normal life," she muttered.

"Tell me who that male was." Because Bo had the irrational urge to hunt him down and gut him.

She bit her bottom lip and shook her head. What he wouldn't give to be able to taste her.

"A former lover?" he asked.

She looked so disgusted at the question as she let out a delicate snort of laughter he knew she was telling the truth. "No. Just drop it please. I don't want to cause you any trouble here, so I'll just leave."

The way she said it made it sound as if she meant for good. His baser half roared, clawing at his insides. He kept himself in check. Barely. "Okay, so you don't want to talk about your past. I can live with that. Your family wants you to return home but you don't want to go, correct?"

She nodded.

"Will they continue to pressure you or hunt you down until you return?" he asked, completely guessing.

Nyx bit her bottom lip then nodded again.

"Do you need protection?" Because she would have it. From him personally.

"No." There was only the briefest pause before her answer, telling him what he needed to know. Not to mention he felt the shift in her, the lie.

"You're lying again." He moved closer, sliding his hands along the side of her seat until he gripped the back of the chair. Her breathing kicked up as he leaned toward her, his face inches from hers. Against his will, his gaze dropped to her lips and it took all his restraint not to lean in and nibble on them. He'd probably just freak her out though. Or worse, repulse her. She knew what he was and didn't seem to have a problem with him being a half-demon, but he was her boss. Nothing more.

And sweet, quality females like her didn't go for males like him.

"Bo." The sound of his name on her lips was a jolt to his system. She placed a tentative hand on his shoulder. Even through his shirt he felt her touch all the way to his core, burning him alive. "My family is fifty kinds of screwed up. On both sides. I'm not going to bring my troubles here. I'll just leave and—"

He let out a growl that surprised them both, stunning her into silence. "You're not going anywhere." Immediately he realized what an obnoxious ass he sounded like when Nyx's eyes narrowed.

She placed her free hand on his other shoulder, the sensation electric. For the first time since he'd met her, her gaze was challenging. It almost felt as if she was ready to shove him away and there was a subtle amount of power beneath those fingertips. Not for the first time had he wondered just what the hell kind of supernatural being she was. "Oh really?"

He should back down, but he couldn't force himself to do it. This show of fire from her stirred his inner demon. "*Really.* I watch out for my people." Okay, the truth was, he was watching out for her.

But her expression immediately softened at his words. "Bo."

"Let me do this."

"I can take care of myself." There was a thread of steel in her words he took note of, his demon side approving.

"Humor me then."

She removed her hands from his chest, crossed her arms over her breasts and shifted against the seat, but since he wasn't moving, there was nowhere for her to go. "It'll be better for everyone if I just leave. If my family knows where I work then they know where I live."

"Then you'll stay here."

"At the club?" Her cheeks tinged pink and he could imagine what she was thinking. She might not have ever been behind the red door, but she had to know what went on back there. And she'd have heard that he used to partake of that particular pleasure frequently in the past. For the first time in his long life he hated that part of himself.

Now that he'd said it out loud, he didn't want her anywhere near those rooms. "My house." The words were out before he could stop himself. When her luscious lips parted, definitely ready to protest, he continued. "My place is huge, you'll never see me, and more importantly, it's protected. No one will be able to locate you even if they use tracking spells."

Her eyes brightened at the last part and he knew he was close to convincing her. "I know you think I'm some kind of charity case, but—"

"I don't think that and this isn't the first time I've done this for an employee." A complete fucking lie. He'd helped employees before, sure, but he'd never let anyone into his home. Not even his lovers.

She relaxed a little more though. "Oh…Your place is really protected?"

He nodded.

"It would just be for a little bit. And I'll pay you. Money isn't an issue."

He'd guessed she needed her job about as much as Keelin did considering some of the expensive brands he'd seen Nyx wear, but hadn't questioned it. Bo still wasn't taking her money. Grunting a non-response, he stood and took her hand in his. "You're staying with me starting tonight?"

Her eyes narrowed the slightest fraction. "You phrased that as a question, but it sounds more like an order."

He didn't respond, figuring it was smarter not to.

Finally she lifted her shoulders. "Fine. Starting to-night. And thank you. I promise you won't even know I'm there and it'll be a week max. I just need to figure some stuff out."

Nodding, he reluctantly let her hand go. If he had anything to say about it, she'd be with him for more than a week.

He might not have a clue how to win over a female like Nyx, but he was definitely going to try. Because he couldn't let her go.

* * *

"You think I'm just going to tuck tail and run out of town because of some unknown threat? Why would I do that?" Keelin demanded as she tried to rein her temper in. Years of being treated like some weak female—because she'd let her family do it, damn it—pushed in on her.

"Because those demons specifically wanted *you*." Bran's voice was low, deadly, barely carrying over the thump of music streaming through the speakers and the sounds of people dancing and talking.

"So wouldn't it make more sense to stick around and figure out what's going on? If I run, they'll just follow. And Bo said that someone sent them so we need to figure out who that is and stop him or her or whoever."

"No, it would make more sense to leave and regroup. Plan an attack and figure out what we're up against."

Okay, so she liked that he said we, but still, she wasn't running. "I'm not going anywhere."

His sapphire eyes flared bright, his dragon peeking through for a moment before he rubbed a hand over the back of his neck. "You drive me fucking crazy."

"Good," she snapped. Because he made her insane. Just looking at him had her all twisted up inside. It was just physical, something she understood, but it didn't seem to matter.

"Good?" he growled.

"Yes. I know what you were trying to do back in that booth, Devlin." She couldn't bring herself to call him by his first name. It felt too intimate and she didn't want that at the moment.

"My name is Bran."

She continued as if he hadn't spoken. "If you think you can get your way simply because we have decent chemistry, you deserve to be driven crazy." She poked him in the chest once for good measure.

Taking her by surprise, he grabbed her wrist and brought her hand up to his mouth. He bit the tip of her middle finger oh-so-gently. "*Decent* chemistry?" His voice was all low again.

Her cheeks flamed at his words. "Figures that's what you'd focus on."

He grabbed her hip with his free hand and pulled her flush against him, letting her feel how much she affected him. For a moment she could pretend that it was just the two of them as their surroundings bled away into nothingness.

Until Solon, Ophelia and Jason strode up to them, their scents nearby reminding Keelin that she had more important things to worry about than her crazed hormones. She turned to face her friends to find Ophelia watching her and Bran with interest. Bran didn't let her go, still kept his grip tight and possessive. The most primal part of her liked that other females saw Bran this way with her. She wanted everyone to know he was taken. Even if that made no sense.

"Finn just texted. He can't get away but said to come back to the mansion. We're going to drive but if you two fly you'll be able to lose any potential tails," Solon said. "It should be safe."

"What about Nyx and Bo?" Keelin had seen her head back into Bo's office with him and they hadn't come out yet. She wanted to make sure her friend got out of the club and home safely, especially after everything that had happened tonight.

"I'm going to stay and wait for her. I'll let Bo know you guys have left," Jason said, his voice casual, but Keelin wasn't fooled. She was pretty certain the male was interested in Nyx.

"I'll make sure Keelin gets back to the mansion safely," Bran said before she could respond.

She dug her elbow into his stomach, not that it would do anything considering how built the male was, but she didn't like him just taking over. She also didn't feel like arguing with him in front of the others so she simply nodded. "We'll meet you back there soon."

Hopefully they could figure out what was going on and who was after her. She'd just started making friends and carving out a new life and didn't want to leave it all behind. In fact, she refused to. Now that she had a taste of freedom she would fight tooth and nail to keep it.

CHAPTER SIX

Finn leaned back in his office chair and rubbed a hand over his face. The male looked exhausted after listening to everything Keelin and Bran told him. If the Alpha wanted her to leave his territory, she wouldn't blame him, but she hoped he didn't. "Low tier hunter demons," he muttered. "I've never heard of that."

"Bo seems like he's willing to be open with information," Keelin said quietly.

Nodding, Finn didn't respond and Keelin figured he wasn't going to trust the half-demon to be his only source of information.

"I'll reach out to Justus," Lyra said from her perch on the edge of his desk. The Alpha's vampire mate was a couple inches taller than Keelin and blonde as well. She was much younger though at roughly ninety years old.

Still, she seemed light-years older than Keelin, her knowledge of the world clearly more vast. Unlike Keelin, she hadn't been sheltered.

"Who's Justus?" Bran asked.

Lyra shifted a fraction against the desk, glancing back at her mate before answering. "A male from my former coven. He was a Roman general so he's been around a long time. He might know something or know someone who does."

"Until we know more about what the demons wanted or who sent them, I've increased patrols around the city." Finn looked at Keelin as he spoke. "Just be smart when going to work. I'm not going to check up on you, but tell someone where you're going to be at all times. You should do that anyway. We all do here. It's the pack way."

"Okay." Keelin had no problem with that. She'd been doing it since she'd started staying here anyway. She liked the pack sense of responsibility for each other. It was exactly like her clan, they all watched out for one another. It was more or less a shifter thing.

Finn looked at Bran then and they seemed to have a silent conversation for a few long moments until finally they both sort of nodded and Finn spoke again. "You must be tired so I'll let you get Bran settled in. I've set him up in the room next to yours."

Keelin's first instinct was to say no but the Alpha had been so kind to her and her brother— something she'd never forget. For the way the male had taken care of Drake, Keelin would always be in his debt. And Finn looked so tired right now that she wasn't going to bitch about anything. Even if it rankled her that he'd placed Bran in the room next to hers. Well room wasn't really the right word, more like small apartment. All the rooms in the mansion were ridiculously spacious. "Thanks, I will."

Once they were out in the hall, which was thankfully empty, Bran said, "I should just stay in your room after what happened."

Snorting, she shot him an incredulous look and continued toward the end of the hall. "You'd like that."

"I *would*. So would you." He dropped his voice an octave, the sensuousness of it not lost on her. And he was so smug looking.

She couldn't deny that she'd love sharing a room with him, but she wouldn't tonight. They needed to lay out some ground rules and more than that, she needed to steel herself for the incendiary attraction between them. "I'm not going to deny that I want you, but if we..." she quickly searched for the right phrase, "...hook up, then that doesn't mean you have some claim on me."

Something in his demeanor shifted in that moment and she wasn't sure what it was. She motioned that they should turn left at the end of the hall.

"If we hook up?" he asked, his voice completely neutral.

"Well..." She knew he wanted her so why was he asking. Had she used the wrong phrase? No, she'd heard her cousins and other clan members use it before. It usually meant to engage in a sexual relationship.

Biting her bottom lip, she turned away from him and smiled politely at a male warrior who passed them in the hall. He gave Bran a curious look before nodding at her and continuing past them. When she looked back at Bran he was scowling. "What's that look?"

His green eyes flashed in annoyance. "Nothing. So, *if* implies you're thinking about it."

Sighing, she stopped in front of a wooden door. "This is you. And yes, I would like to…" She trailed off when another male turned into their hallway at the other end. "Can we talk in your room?" she asked quietly, not wanting everyone in her business. She'd learned early on that it was almost impossible to keep secrets here, but that didn't mean she planned to broadcast this conversation.

Bran opened the door wordlessly and ushered her in, his hand at the small of her back. He flipped on the light to reveal a masculine-looking room with big, wooden furniture. There weren't any personal items and the art on the walls were all black and white prints of wolves or the moon at various stages. Very fitting. Two doors were halfway open, one to a bathroom and another an Asian inspired sliding door to what looked like a walk-in closet. A suitcase and a duffel bag sat on a bench at the end of the king-sized bed.

"Do you want to sit?" Bran asked, looking oddly nervous as he motioned to a chaise near one of the oversized windows.

"No thank you." She just wanted to get this conversation over with, to lay things out between them so they were both on the same page. "How long are you planning to stay in town?" she asked, motioning to the bags.

He lifted those broad shoulders. "As long as it takes."

"You're here for a job of some kind?" Because he hadn't been exactly clear on that point.

"Yes." He wasn't lying, but it annoyed her that he wasn't giving her more information.

She pursed her lips together. "Well, what kind?"

He sat on the edge of the bed, his gaze on her intense. "I don't want to talk about that."

Keelin remained where she was closer to the door, liking the small separation between them. "Fair enough."

"Why are you fighting a mating? I thought all females..." He trailed off, getting that uncomfortable expression again. One she couldn't quite read.

She leaned against the door, wrapping her arms around herself. "You think just because I'm a female I should want to get mated? Like what, I've been dreaming of this day my whole life?" Like humans she'd read about who dreamed of big weddings. No thank you.

"Well, maybe. The mated females in my clan are all happy."

"And none of them had any issues or drama with their mates before they were mated?"

He snorted. "I didn't say that."

"Exactly. Look, my parents..." Who she so did not want to think about right now, but couldn't get them off her mind as she worried about when or if they'd officially risen from their Protective Hibernation, "...kept me more than a little sheltered." Translation: smothered. "I've never had any fantasies about mating. All my dreams were about freedom and now I've gotten a taste of it, I love it. This new world is great and while I would like to experiment with you—"

He lifted a sardonic eyebrow. "Experiment?"

Her cheeks flushed, but she continued. "I want to lay out some ground rules. Basically, just one. No mating will be in our future."

"I demand more than that. For the duration of our...arrangement," he said the word as if it offended him, "you will be intimate with me and me alone." A low growl rumbled from him, the sound deadly.

She understood the sentiment. The thought of him with another female made her inner dragon flare to life, ready to slice him to ribbons. "Deal. And you will only be with me."

He snorted, as if that was a given. The sound pleased her far more than it should.

"You don't get to tell me what to do or where to go or who I can talk to," she continued.

Bran rose from the bed, all sleek lines and deadly grace as he approached her. "I don't want to chain you down, Keelin. I just want to get to know you. Take you on a fucking date."

"Really?" So many of her clan members were familiar with dating and it was something she wanted to try. "I've never been on a date."

"Me neither."

There was no acidic scent to his words indicating a lie, but it was hard to believe. "Truly?"

"The females I've been with... Ah, never mind," he muttered.

Yeah, she so didn't want to go there either. She might not want to be mated, but she didn't need to hear about his history. "Then we will go on a date."

"Are you asking or ordering?" he asked, amusement in his voice.

"I believe I'm ordering," she said in her best, haughty princess voice, hoping he understood she was teasing. The thought of bossing this sexy, dominating male around was oddly arousing, even if it was an illusion. Bran would never let any female tell him what to do. But if they were going to get to know one another, she needed a male who she could relax around.

To her surprise, he grinned, the action softening his entire face so that he didn't look like an intimidating Alpha, but a sweet male who just wanted to take her on a date. "You're sexy when you boss me around," he murmured, crossing the last couple feet between them.

He was sexy all the time, she thought, but didn't say it aloud. She was certain a male like him didn't need his ego stroked any more. Taking her by surprise again, he placed both of his big hands on the door next to her head and leaned down.

She dropped her arms and immediately moved her hands to his chest. She tangled her fingers in his shirt. Without thinking, she pushed up from the door, stepping into the protection of his body. Her eyes grew heavy-lidded as she inhaled that dark winter scent of his.

When he leaned down, running his nose along her jaw and up to her ear, she shuddered, her nipples growing painfully tight at just that bare contact. Her experience was so paltry and she wasn't sure what, if anything, she should do next.

"I love your scent," he murmured, his deep voice soothing to all her senses even as her heart rate kicked up.

She started to slide her hands up his chest when he sighed and stepped back. His dragon was in his gaze as he watched her. "Go out on a date with me tomorrow—tonight."

It was well after midnight so they were in the early morning hours of a new day. She started to say yes when she remembered that Rhea had promised to train her that evening. "I can't, but I'm free tomorrow."

Jaw clenched tight, he nodded and stepped back fully from her. "I'll plan something for us."

She wanted to touch him again, to run her fingers, mouth and tongue all over that hard body. Now that they'd laid things out and he understood she wasn't looking for a mate they were free to enjoy each other. But she wasn't quite that brave. Not yet. Making the first move was hard and she knew she should probably just shove her shyness aside but couldn't make herself do it. In fact, her inner dragon refused to let her make the first move. Instead of doing what she craved, she reached for the doorknob behind her and tugged it open. "Okay, I'll see you soon then."

He just nodded, but the energy pumping off him was fierce and a little overwhelming. She knew if she stayed any longer she'd do something she'd regret so she stepped out into the hall and shut the door behind her.

Letting out a jagged breath, she hurried to her room on shaky legs. Throwing herself at Bran would be a mistake, maybe that's why her inner dragon had held her back. She might want the male desperately, but with an Alpha male she knew she needed to keep some boundaries between them. To make it clear that she could take him or leave him. That she was completely in control.

Even if that was the furthest thing from the truth.

* * *

It took all of Bran's control not to chase after Keelin like some trained puppy. Instead of doing what he wanted, he pulled his cell phone from his pants pocket and called his former boss.

August McGuire picked up on the second ring despite the early hour. "Yeah?"

"That shit you wanted me to look into... Does it involve demons?"

"Why?"

"Answer the damn question."

The male was quiet for a long moment. August was a Kodiak bear shifter hybrid, though no one knew what his other shifter half was or how old the male was. And Bran didn't want to know. He had enough secrets and knowing any more about his former black ops boss wasn't something he wanted to add to his knowledge base. There was a rustling on the other end then the sound of a door shutting. Finally August spoke. "Couple weeks ago one of my guys got a call from a contact. A dragon was found dead a couple towns from where you are now."

Bran's back straightened. "You're just telling me this now?"

"Why the hell do you think I sent you?"

Bran had assumed it was because August had known he was headed to Biloxi and wanted a favor. The male hadn't said a word about a dead dragon. "You don't have anyone else?"

"No dragons on my team at the moment."

Okay, that made sense. "What kind of dragon was it?"

"Moana. I've got official confirmation from someone in their clan, but the coloring's right anyway so we would've known."

"It was in dragon form?" Bran didn't bother keeping the disbelief out of his voice. It was hard to take down a dragon in animal form. Usually that only happened by another dragon and when it did, the victor dragon just burned the other one to ashes. There'd be no body left to find.

"Yeah. Female. One of my guys says that it looks as if she was being tortured in human form and her animal took over despite being confined to a space too small to accommodate her animal. Cage must have been spelled or something so she couldn't break it, but she still shifted, breaking a lot of bones. Not sure where she was tortured, but it wasn't where she was found."

Bran shoved back the annoyance inside him at the lack of information sharing even as he contemplated the new info. Moving a dragon while in dragon form was damn hard. Especially unseen. So if someone had moved the body from where she'd been originally tortured, that was...interesting. "You're such an untrusting bastard," he finally muttered.

If August had told Bran all this earlier it would have made a difference. Instead August had made it sound like he just needed a small favor.

"I wanted to see what you could find without any information from me. This isn't the first dragon to go missing. I wanted your ears on the ground."

Closing his eyes, Bran rubbed his temple and sat back on the edge of the bed. He shouldn't be surprised by his former boss, but it still pissed him off. The male had often sent him on missions with only half the information. It was like a test, probably to see if Bran was still on his game. "You're going to send me every scrap of info you have on whatever it is you want to investigate and you're going to tell me the final objective. I've got a lot of shit I'm dealing with, I'm in another Alpha's territory, and I'm doing you a fucking favor. I will *not* do this mission blind. You don't like it, find someone else." Because if this involved Keelin, even remotely, he needed to know everything in order to keep her safe.

August let out a loud, sharp burst of laughter. "I've missed you, Devlin. The objective is to figure out what the fuck is going on. A few dragons in the area have gone missing, all Moana. There were some strange carvings on the dead female so I'll email you the pictures. No one on my team knows and nowhere in any database can we find the origin of the symbols so I don't know if demons are involved. I don't know shit at this point. You're not the only one dealing with a shitstorm of stuff. This dragon thing is low on my radar but I know how quickly things turn around so I wanted someone I trusted on it before things escalated."

"Work that bad?"

The male grunted. "Same old politics. I'll probably retire next year."

Bran snorted. August had been saying that for as long as he'd known him. "I'll believe it when I see it."

"So why are you asking about demons?"

He ignored the question. "Send me what you've got and I'll see if I can get someone to nail down the origin of the symbols. Do you have a list of where the dragons went missing from, any other info about them?" Because dragons were so damn secretive he knew his old boss might not have that kind of info just yet.

"I'm working on it. You know any of the Moana clan?"

"No, but I'll reach out to their Alpha." From what Bran had heard their Alpha was a female and a good leader.

"Keep me updated." August disconnected before Bran could respond, not that it surprised him.

Tossing the phone onto the bed beside him, he laid back against the comforter for a moment and covered his face with his arm. Finding out about missing dragons was not a simple fucking favor. August had made it sound like there were some strange supernatural happenings going on in Biloxi and that was it. Just a quick little investigation, nothing more. Considering strange and supernatural tended to mix together like rum and coke, it wasn't all that odd. He didn't want to worry about anything else but courting Keelin, but if his own kind were missing... No way in hell was he letting that go unchecked.

* * *

Naram leaned back against the booth in Bo Broussard's establishment. It was potentially foolish to be here, but he wanted to know more about the male who owned it. Naram wasn't a demon, but he'd found demons could be very useful.

It was possible that the half-demon owner might want to strike a deal with him. And as the female dragon's boss, Naram could use the male very nicely for his own gain. He needed that blasted female and *his* bracelet.

"You want to get one of the rooms behind the red door?" The female vampire next to him traced a finger down his neck, her voice a seductive purr. She was fascinated by him, as so many females were. He knew it was because of his physical form and because she couldn't figure out what he was—and she wanted to try his blood.

He might let her drink from him but he hadn't decided yet. If she was a good fuck, he might. "Perhaps," he said idly.

She let out a huff of annoyance and shifted closer. "We can invite someone else with us if that's your preference."

He paused and looked at her, as if debating what she'd said. "What about the male who owns this place? Is he available for the evening?"

The female sighed and rubbed her breasts against Naram's arm. "I wish. He's picky about who he fucks and I heard he's off the market now anyway. I think he's fucking one of his new employees. He only likes females though, for future reference."

Interesting. Naram hadn't seen the male in the last couple hours anyway so he might as well indulge in some fun. His apprentice Shar was off on a recon mission and Naram deserved to enjoy himself after all his years in captivity.

He gave the nameless vampire female a smile he knew she'd find charming and leaned closer, grazing his lips across hers. "If you blow me right now we'll get a room."

Giving him a wicked smile she practically dove for his cock, not caring that the curtain for their booth was still open and that anyone could see them. The one thing he'd learned about vampires long ago was that they were hedonistic.

As she freed his cock and sucked him deep into her mouth, he closed his eyes and let his head fall back. It was good that some things hadn't changed.

CHAPTER SEVEN

One month ago

Keelin stiffened outside the swinging door to her kitchen. *He* was in there.

Again.

What was that male up to? It had been four days since she'd almost died and Bran Devlin had been hovering around her like some paid nanny ever since. It didn't matter that she'd politely asked him to leave. He just showed back up again.

Keelin was too worried to tell either of her brothers about his behavior. Bran was an Alpha and even though their clan had been welcomed onto Petronilla property, especially after helping save her and Victoria from that maniac, she wasn't certain how Drake or Conall would react to knowing the Alpha had been in her home so much. Unless they'd asked him to do it? Drake had been absolutely wrapped up in his new mate and though he'd come to check on Keelin, she couldn't blame him for wanting to do nothing but stay indoors with Victoria. And as Alpha, Conall had been putting out all sorts of fires that came with being head of a clan. Especially after the shitstorm of discovering one of their own was so treacherous.

Steeling her backbone, she pushed the heavy kitchen door open to find Bran at the stove. Cooking.

She blinked. "What are you doing?" she asked, then felt stupid because it was pretty clear.

He flicked a glance at her over his shoulder, eyed her from head to toe in a clinical manner that had her bristling. Darn that man, he seemed to think she needed his babying. "Cooking for you. Should you be out of bed?"

"Should you be in my kitchen?" Inhaling the rich scent of coffee, she decided to ignore him as she went in search of the heavenly brew. Being able to brew coffee so quickly was something she liked about this modern world. As far as she was concerned, modern conveniences were awesome. Especially indoor plumbing and coffee makers, thank you very much.

"I can bring you breakfast in bed." His voice was quiet, soothing and managed to rankle her because she found him incredibly sexy and he seemed to look at her like she was a cousin or sister to take care of. For a brief moment days ago she'd thought maybe he saw her with male interest but that must have been her imagination.

"I'm fine, but thanks. I've been getting out the last three days."

He grunted, his broad back still facing her as he shook his head. Though she couldn't see his face, she knew he was frowning.

"Where's Conall?" she asked when he didn't respond. She pulled out her favorite coffee creamer from the refrigerator and added a little to her mug.

"Dealing with some upset clan members I think."

"Oh." She bit her bottom lip and sat at the island on the opposite side from where he was by the stovetop. A little distance was a good thing right now. Her inner dragon was feeling off-balance around the male and she wasn't sure why. She knew she was fully healed so it couldn't be that. "Look, it's not that I don't appreciate you cooking because it's very nice, but why are you here?" She was beyond surprised that her Aunt Alma hadn't taken over like she normally did. The female was like a second mother to Keelin.

Bran shrugged. "You need someone to take care of you. The sausage is done, how do you want your eggs?"

She gritted her teeth at his words. She didn't need anyone to take care of her, but... she was really hungry. "Over easy, please." She still wanted to ask him about what he'd been doing here the last couple days since it was clear he wasn't interested in her sexually. And she hated that she wished he was. The male was impossibly sexy, not that she thought she stood a chance with an Alpha.

The sound of her front door opening made her stiffen until she scented her brother. Seconds later Conall entered the kitchen, his expression exhausted but calculating as he looked at Bran. The two Alphas nodded at each other in greeting but didn't say anything. Her brother didn't seem surprised to see him here. Okay, so her brother must have enlisted him to be her nanny. Just great. She rolled her eyes and took a sip of her coffee, savoring the wonderful taste.

"What the hell is this I hear about you moving to Biloxi?" Conall demanded of her, apparently not caring that they had an audience.

In her periphery she saw Bran swivel from the oven to look at her. She ignored his presence as best she could and smiled sweetly at her brother. "You heard right so I'm not sure what your question is. I'm leaving at the end of the week."

Bran let out a rumbly growl, making both of them turn to look at him. His green eyes flashed angrily, though one of them looked a little cloudy. She wondered if he'd gotten hurt when out looking for her and Victoria. Before she could dwell on it, Conall growled too.

Freaking males.

"Is that really the best idea right now?" her brother asked, his face a mask of calm, though she knew it was just an illusion. She could sense the tension in the room it was so palpable.

"It's the best idea I've ever had. It's not like it's permanent, I'm just getting away for a little while. I need this, Conall. Please don't fight me on it." Because after all she'd dealt with from her parents, Conall had always been the constant in her life. She couldn't deal with him if he didn't support her.

Sighing, her giant of a brother shook his head and rounded the island, wrapping an arm around her shoulders and dropping a kiss on her head. "I'm going to miss you," he murmured.

"That's it?" Bran's question startled both of them as he dropped the spatula onto the counter behind him. It wasn't that he shouted. If anything, his question was deceptively quiet, but she sensed something dark and wild in him and didn't understand it.

"Devlin," Conall said just as quietly, a similar kind of undercurrent pulsing off him as he stepped away from Keelin and fully faced the other Alpha.

She didn't understand what passed between them, but whatever it was, it wasn't settled when Bran turned back to the stove suddenly. Keelin tensed, knowing that his action could be taken as a grave insult. He'd just turned his back on Conall while on Conall's land. Alphas didn't do that.

To her continuing surprise, Conall took a seat next to her and looked as if he was fighting a grin. "Why don't you whip me up some eggs too, Devlin? I like over easy." And that was definitely laughter in her brother's voice.

"You'll get scrambled. And I hope you like shells in it," Bran said without pause.

Okay, she didn't understand what was going on between these two, but she didn't much care. In just a few short days she'd be free from the overprotectiveness of her clan and would be living in a new city and hopefully making new friends. All with the blessing of her brother.

This was perfect. No one was going to take her shot at freedom away from her.

* * *

Present day

Keelin set her phone down on her bed and frowned. She'd tried calling half a dozen cousins from her clan and none of them had answered. That was definitely not good.

She didn't want to jump to conclusions, but the only thing she could think was that her parents were truly awake from their Protective Hibernation and no one wanted to confirm it. Or worse, they knew her parents were on their way here and didn't want to tell her.

Her stomach pitched at the thought. Not that she cared if they came. Let them. She was finally standing on her own two feet. But the truth was, a confrontation was the last thing she wanted. It would get ugly, things would be said and, just, ugh, no thank you.

She wasn't even calling her cousins because of that though. Glaring at her phone she thought about calling Ophelia, but knew the female would likely gossip to the rest of her pack. And she couldn't call Nyx because it was clear in the month she'd known her that the female had no freaking experience with males.

That left Gabriel. The wolf pack's Guardian was brutally blunt and she really liked him. She quickly dialed him and was pleased when he picked up on the second ring.

"Hey, Kee. What's up?"

"Not much. Where've you been the past couple days?" She hadn't seen him around the mansion at all and that wasn't like him. Especially since another Alpha was staying here. He was normally all snarly if there were any perceived threats to the Alpha or anyone else in the pack.

"Out of town. Work."

Ah, then he was doing stuff for Finn and there was no way he'd tell her what about. Fine with her, she just needed answers. "You're a male."

He snorted. "Last time I checked."

"What are the rules for shifter males when hooking up with a female?"

There was a long pause, then, "Uh, what?"

"You know, like official, well, *rules*. What do I need to know when hooking up with a male that I don't plan to mate? Are there things I should or should not do?" She was certain she'd made things clear with Bran, but she wanted to be prepared and not give him the wrong idea that their sexual relationship would lead to more. Because it most certainly would not. She wasn't even sure if he wanted more, but males could get so possessive.

"I've only been gone a couple days! Who the fuck... Oh, right, Bran's in town. Shit, Keelin, you can't just hook up with him."

"Why not?"

"Because I saw the way that male looked at you in Montana," he said as if she were brain damaged.

"That's not a sufficient answer. Now tell me the rules!" This conversation was embarrassing enough, she didn't want to drag it on for longer than necessary.

"I... I can't even believe I'm having this conversation," he muttered. "Okay, with a male like Bran there are no fucking *rules*. I guarantee he wants to claim you so if you decide to hook up with him—and don't use that term, we're too fucking old for it—then all bets are off. He's going to try to convince you to mate with him."

She shook her head even though Gabriel couldn't see her. "No, we've discussed things. He knows where I stand and he hasn't said a word about mating. I just want to make sure I don't break any unwritten rules."

There was another long silence. So long she looked at her cell phone screen to make sure they hadn't been disconnected. Finally he spoke again. "Are you a virgin?" His words came out as a horrified whisper.

"No," she said through gritted teeth, feeling her face heat up. She'd had sex, albeit boring, unmemorable sex. "I just haven't slept with a shifter before." Because her one and only lover had been a weak human. If she'd slept with a shifter her mother would have killed him. Probably. She hadn't been willing to take the risk.

Gabriel let out a relieved breath. "Oh, good. Okay, then don't worry about anything else. You've told him the score. You only want him for his body. End of story."

"You don't have to make it sound so bad."

"It's true, isn't it?" There was a note in his voice she couldn't quite read.

"No, not exactly." What she knew of Bran she liked. Well, when he wasn't trying to run roughshod over her with his bossiness. But even that felt as if it came from a good place, as if he just wanted to protect her.

"But you don't want anything long term?" Gabriel persisted.

Her inner dragon clawed at her, telling her to shut up, but she said, "Correct. I just want to have fun." Maybe she wanted to get to know Bran a little more, but she didn't admit it out loud.

"Then keep things light between the two of you. Just sex and fun."

That sounded easy enough. "Okay, and that'll work?"

"Fuck no. He's an Alpha, but that's all I can give you. Just don't be surprised when you end up mated in a couple weeks."

She narrowed her eyes in annoyance. "Gabriel, you are a horrible source of information."

"I just call it like I see it. Good luck and please do *not* keep me informed on what goes down between you two. Look, I've gotta go," he murmured, ending the call before she could respond.

She glared at her silent cell phone. He'd been no help. Maybe she should ask Ophelia after all. The healer was older than Gabriel anyway and she seemed to keep all the males in the pack in line. They all seemed a little terrified of her. Keelin would just need to convince the female not to blab to everyone.

When her cell phone started ringing she nearly jumped. For a brief moment she contemplated not answering it since it was Conall but knew she needed to. "Hey."

"They're awake," Conall said without preamble.

Just like that, the bottom of her stomach dropped out. But just as quickly pure joy surged through her that her parents would be reunited with the son they thought had been taken from them forever. She could only imagine how they must be handling everything. "Have they seen Drake?"

"Not yet. He and Victoria are on their way back from Oregon now."

"How are mother and father taking the news?"

"Overjoyed and...worried about you." Her brother sighed and she could imagine him rubbing his hand over his face tiredly. "Well, father thinks it's good you're out on your own but mother wants to know where you are and who you're with."

"You didn't—"

"No. They don't know where you are, just that you're safe. However, you know someone in the clan will break eventually and tell them what you're up to."

"What do they think of all the technology?"

He snorted, the sound so purely her brother it made her smile. "Mother called it a passing fad, but she likes the indoor plumbing."

At that Keelin laughed too, something in her chest rattling loose at the thought of seeing her parents again. She truly loved them and knew they would die for her, but she couldn't go back to the way things had been. For a moment she thought about telling Conall what had happened at Bo's club but decided against it.

He would just worry and the truth was, she wanted to handle this crisis on her own. Or at least without her clan's help.

* * *

Bo glanced up from reading his text at the soft footfalls on the winding staircase of his home. He swallowed hard at the sight of Nyx striding down the stairs, looking like a princess or angel. He nearly snorted at the thought. She couldn't be that or she wouldn't be here with him.

Her long black braid lay over her left breast which was unfortunately covered by a slim-fitted turtleneck. What the hell was up with her and turtlenecks? And why the hell did they get him so hot? Tonight it was a royal blue one and sleeveless, showing off toned arms. Instead of pants she wore a skintight leather skirt with silver studded skulls covering it that reached her knees, and four-inch heels. The heels alone were dangerous considering how often she seemed to run into things, but the entire outfit was slightly different than her normal attire.

A mix of naughty and nice.

His cock throbbed and he hoped she didn't glance down at his crotch. Or maybe she would and put him out of his misery. Yeah, right. A guy could hope though.

"You look different," he said as she reached the bottom of the marbled entryway.

"Thanks, I think. Cynara gave me this skirt. Said I should mix it up. You think it'll help with tips?" she asked, twirling once, a grin on her face.

Bo just grunted, making a mental note to ask Cynara what the hell was wrong with her, though he already knew the answer. Cynara was after him to make a move on Nyx. Nosy bitch.

"Can I ask you something?" Nyx's heels clicked as she approached.

"Only if I get to ask you something in return." Because he was through being subtle. He wanted to know more about her family and why they wanted to take her away from him. Whether that was their intent or not, at the end of the day, his demon side just knew someone wanted to take her. That wasn't going to happen.

She bit her bottom lip and his cock jerked as he imagined the feel of that lush mouth wrapped around him. Finally she nodded. "Okay. Is Cynara your sister?"

He stilled at Nyx's question, surprised she'd figured it out. They had the same rapist bastard of a father but different mothers so they didn't look similar. "Half-sister. How did you know?"

Nyx lifted a delicate shoulder. "Just a guess. The way you two banter and you let her get away with anything. Plus you talk to her differently. It's the way Rhea and Solon from the Stavros pack act with each other."

"They're not related."

"I know, but they act like brother and sister. I don't have any examples to go on with my own family so it was just a guess."

Bo wasn't sure how he felt about anyone knowing personal information about him, but deep down he didn't worry about Nyx using that knowledge against him. Even his demon side trusted her, and that was a rarity. "No one else knows."

Her big blue eyes widened. "Oh, I won't say anything, I was just curious." Then she gave him one of those sweet, shy smiles that made him feel like a complete monster for wanting someone so innocent. He also wondered just how damn innocent she was and how much it would take to get her naked and under him. "Now it's your turn to ask a question."

"Why does your family want you back?" If he knew maybe he could figure out just what the hell type of supernatural being she was.

Her smile and the light in her eyes dimmed and he wanted to punch himself in the face. Or maybe the nuts. Anything to make this erection go down.

"They think they can force me into marriage."

An ancient Greek vase on a pedestal a few feet away exploded into a hundred pieces. Nyx gasped and swiveled, her eyes growing wide as the pieces froze in midair. Bo rolled his neck once, trying to ease the tension as he mentally ordered the pieces back together.

When she looked back at him, her pretty face was a mask of confusion, but at least there was no fear. "You don't have to worry, they won't make me. They can't."

He was fairly certain she misunderstood his reaction, which was fine with him. If she knew how fucked up he was over her, she'd have too much damn control over him. He held out an arm to her, ready to get the hell out of here and head to his club. "You sound sure of that."

She linked her arm through his, her long, elegant fingers resting on his forearm. He inhaled her sweet scent, trying not to be so obvious that he looked like a perv, but it was hard not to shudder at the feel of her touching him. However innocently. "My father's side likes to ignore my mother's heritage. In doing so they forget I'm more powerful than all of them." Her words were said as fact without a trace of arrogance.

He opened the front door since his Mercedes was already waiting. His other three vehicles were in his garage, but the Mercedes was classic, understated and more importantly, had bullet-resistant windows and magic-resistant spells on it. He wasn't taking chances with Nyx's safety. The scent of blooming magnolia trees filled the air as they stepped outside. He loved the scent of the Gulf Coast this time of year. After all his years on the earth, it was one of his favorites. Probably because it reminded him of his mother, who he missed every day. "That's an interesting piece of information. Why tell me that?"

"I trust you, Bo." She smiled at him again, so open and trusting he didn't know what the hell to do with the feelings that exploded inside him.

She shouldn't trust him. He was a monster who wanted to do wicked things to her. He'd make it perfect for her, make her crave him so she never wanted to walk away.

"You trust me enough to tell me what you are?" he asked.

Her grin turned cheeky. "I agreed to answer one question. If you want to know that, we're going to bargain for it."

Bo could think of a lot he'd bargain just to know a shred of information about the innocent yet sensual woman holding onto his arm. "Bargain?"

She nodded and for the briefest moment, her gaze flicked to his mouth before she glanced away, her cheeks flushing a faint shade of pink.

Oh, hell. He couldn't be sure what she was thinking, but if she was remotely interested in him... Bo tugged the car door open for her with more force than necessary. He couldn't think about that now.

He had a full night of work and other shit to take care of. He could worry about his plan to claim Nyx later.

CHAPTER EIGHT

"This baby is a little heavier because of the silver-coated bullets, but it's a beauty." Solon picked up the next weapon he'd laid out on the table to show Bran, holding it out as if he was showing buried treasure.

Bran hid his smile at the other male's enthusiasm. Finn had sent more warriors out on patrol tonight because of what had happened at Bo's club last night. Since Keelin had said she couldn't go out with him tonight—and he couldn't sit around waiting for her like a pathetic adolescent—he was going to scout out some areas in the city before meeting with the Moana Alpha in a few hours.

"If you start making out with that thing I'm leaving," Rhea muttered, arms crossed over her chest as she looked at Solon, though the adoration in her face was clear.

Bran had seen them interact on more than one occasion—and the female was a truly impressive warrior, having taken down a dragon by herself—and he was certain Rhea viewed Solon as a little brother.

Solon frowned at her, his dark eyes flashing in annoyance. "He asked to see my weapons."

"I don't think he wanted you to start stroking your newest one and calling it 'my precious'."

Bran couldn't help but laugh as the male grumbled and tucked it into one of his shoulder holsters. Like a switch flipping, humor fled his body as he scented Keelin. He turned toward the entrance to the training room and two seconds later she appeared in the doorway.

Dressed in all black—skintight pants and a tank top that should be illegal—her gray eyes widened in surprise as she took in the three of them and another four warriors at a neighboring table quietly talking among themselves. Bran had heard his brother's mate Fia call Keelin one of the great beauties of the dragon race and it was true. Dressed in what he considered battle gear, Keelin was a wet dream come to life. Her long blonde hair was pulled back in a tight braid against her head, the first time he'd seen it like that. All she needed was a couple weapons in hand and she'd fit right in with the warriors down in the training room.

"Keelin," Rhea said, breaking away from them before Bran could find his voice. "I totally forgot to tell you. Finn's got us doing extra patrols so I can't train you tonight. I'm so sorry."

"Train?" Bran asked, catching up with Rhea, his shoes sinking slightly into the training mats as he crossed the floor toward Keelin.

She flicked him an unreadable glance. "Rhea's showing me some physical defense moves."

Keelin was a dragon. A deadly force. He started to ask why, but after she'd been shot and nearly tortured by her cousin—and nearly killed—she must want to be able to defend herself from other supernaturals.

Her cheeks flushed pink and she looked at him as if embarrassed. "She's just teaching me about modern weapons and stuff," she continued, even though he hadn't responded.

Rhea started to say more but Keelin glared at her, making the other female's mouth snap shut in surprise.

"Come on, Rhea, we've gotta go," Solon said, striding past them, loaded down with hidden weapons. The male dropped a quick kiss on Keelin's head as he passed, making Bran's dragon flare to the surface, clawing and snarling, but he managed to lock his beast down.

For now. Wolf shifters were naturally affectionate and it was clear many of them had taken a liking to Keelin. He couldn't act like an ass because of a friendly overture.

"I'm really sorry, Kee. I promise to make it up to you this week," Rhea said.

Keelin shook her head, smiling. "It's okay."

"You coming Bran?" Rhea asked.

He'd planned to head out with them, but... "Nah. I'll let Finn know when I leave though." As everyone started leaving the training and weapons room, Bran nodded at the mats. "Is she teaching you about weapons only or are you physically training?" Because her dress code indicated they were, and if anyone was going to be teaching Keeling hand-to-hand, it was him. No one else was touching her, and especially not another male.

Surprising him, Keelin glanced down at her intertwined hands, as if embarrassed. "She's teaching me self-defense in human form too."

"Why are you embarrassed?" he asked.

When she met his gaze her embarrassment was even starker. "You obviously know about what happened to me since you were there," she said, her voice filled with disgust. "Before that, before we even got to Montana, we were all attacked on the way there."

"By the Veles clan?" He'd heard about it.

She nodded, her lips pulling into a thin line. "One of the Veles dragons attacked me. We were both in human form. He was so much stronger than me and I couldn't shift with all the stress. Everything happened so fast and..." She swallowed hard and for a moment he saw shame in her eyes. Not being able to shift under stress wasn't exactly rare, at least for a non-warrior, but it was clear she was angry at herself.

"He hurt you?" His voice was raspy and hoarse, fear slicing through him without reprieve. He'd heard about the incident but hadn't realized Keelin had been hurt.

She shook her head. "No, but he tried to rape me."

Fire burned the back of Bran's throat. That hadn't been what he'd expected at all. "He's dead?" Because if he wasn't, that male was on borrowed time. Keelin straightened suddenly and inhaled, likely scenting his fire. Damn it. He toned it down.

Her head tilted a fraction to the side as she studied him, but she nodded. "He's dead, but it doesn't change the fact that I want more training. I can't always depend on my shifter side to protect me, especially if I'm attacked by another dragon. I'm not a warrior and I need to know everything I can about self-defense."

Bran nodded in agreement. "That's smart."

She seemed surprised by his statement, her eyes flashing that silvery color. "You agree?"

"Of course. If you want I can help train you tonight. Just tell me what you and Rhea have been going over and we'll start there. I can even show you how to flip a supernatural male onto his back." If he got to touch her while training, that was just a bonus.

She placed her hands on her hips, her expression unbelieving. "Even an Alpha?"

He'd let her flip him onto his back any time she wanted if it involved her riding him soon after. "Yep. You're small so people will underestimate you. You can use that to your advantage in any battle. Flipping someone or taking them off guard isn't enough but once you've stunned someone enough to push them off balance, you have options." Keelin seemed pleased by that.

"Thank you," she said quietly, her arms loosening at her sides.

"For what?"

"For treating me like an equal." She headed for the nearest mat, her movements lithe and as quiet as any predator he'd ever seen.

Her words were interesting and something he filed away. He was starting to understand the female more. She said she didn't want a mate, but what she didn't want was to be in chains or treated like she was weak or less than anyone. Bran would never to do that to her. He'd just have to show her.

As she stood there, bouncing from foot to foot on the mat he wondered if she was a little nervous. He hoped not because of him. "Tell me what you've learned so far."

"Mainly we've gone over every weapon known to man. I honestly probably won't ever need to use them and they feel a little offensive to my dragon, but Rhea is very thorough."

Bran understood. Their animal natures were separate but at the same time dual. Using a weapon when they were living, breathing weapons made no sense to their animal side.

"Other than that she's taught me how to get out of bad situations when I'm in human form. It's only been a couple weeks and only when she can fit me in to her schedule so I have a lot to learn."

"So all defense?"

"Precisely."

"Okay, tonight we'll do something with simple offense. And I wasn't kidding about you flipping a male. You're actually the right size for this move."

She smiled at him again and he wondered if she had an issue with her size. She was smaller than any dragon he'd ever met but to him she was perfect. He loved the way she fit right up against him.

"If you wanted to attack me in human form, how would you do it? Without your fire." Because some creatures, not just dragons, could protect themselves from dragon fire. It was always temporary spell stuff, but she was right, she needed every weapon in her arsenal. He tensed, straightening his stance readying for an attack. He doubted she could hurt him, but he wanted to see her technique, if she even had one.

Looking impossibly unsure she bit her bottom lip. "I don't know how I'd do it."

"Oh." He immediately relaxed and took a step forward, ready to show her some surefire moves when she pounced, moving lightning fast and ramming into his middle in a tackle.

She'd taken him off guard and her follow through was decent, but he instinctively grabbed her and flipped her onto her back, covering her body with his as they slammed against the mat. If she'd been a true enemy there were half a dozen ways he'd end her life now.

That was the farthest thing from his mind as his gaze dipped to her mouth. The feel of her under him had his entire body going rock hard. Their bodies were perfectly aligned for raw fucking, something he shouldn't be thinking about. But it was damn hard not to. He rolled his hips once, his erection impossible to hide. She sucked in a breath and her eyes went heavy-lidded as she watched him.

Though he wanted more than anything to lean down and capture her mouth, making sure she could protect herself was more important than anything. He met her fiery gaze again, completely ensnared by this female. He cleared his throat, forcing himself to get his shit together. "Acting innocent or weak is smart," he said, impressed by what she'd just done. "Now I'm going to teach you how to actually take down an opponent."

About an hour later Keelin's body was damp with sweat as adrenaline pumped through her. If only she could flip the obnoxious male in front of her. But he'd stripped off his shirt and she was finding the sight of his bare, oh-so-muscular chest a distraction. It was affecting all her senses, both visual and sensory because every time she touched him, her brain went haywire.

"You can do it," he insisted, watching her with those green eyes, a mix of lust and frustration in his gaze.

She figured he was annoyed with her for not flipping him yet. He'd shown her the move too many times to count and she understood the dynamics, but every time she slid into his body and embraced him she wanted to wrap her legs around him and kiss him senseless. She blamed her inner dragon.

"Again." There was a bite of authority in his voice as he practically growled at her.

Letting out a growl of her own, she rushed him. The second her arms entangled around him she had to bite back a groan. She knew what she was supposed to do but his dark scent invaded her senses as she wrapped one arm around him. Instead of finishing the final few steps, she inhaled deeply, feeling almost drugged by that scent.

"Damn it, Keelin." He didn't bother flipping her this time.

"I know I can do it," she said, feeling the need to defend herself. "I don't think that's the problem."

Hands on hips with no shoes or socks on—he'd taken them off almost immediately—he stood a few feet in front of her, the mat slightly depressing under his weight. "What's the problem?"

"You. All shirtless and stuff. My dragon won't let me fight you." Oh, God. It was so embarrassing even admitting it. She needed to spar with someone else to test out her theory.

"Huh." He watched her then, his expression curious—and a tiny bit smug. "I believe that."

"Yeah?"

He nodded, that sexy gaze dropping to her mouth and the scent of his lust filling the room. She had a feeling he'd been holding off until now but had apparently decided to let his control slip because that scent was so overwhelming she was ready to strip right there. "Every time I flip you onto your back I don't feel like I'm training you."

Before she could respond she scented someone else nearby. Turning toward the entrance she smiled when she saw Spiro, one of the warriors entering. He had on sweatpants and nothing else. "Hey, Spiro. You're not out patrolling?"

He shook his head. "I was on the day shift. Have you guys seen a black hoodie with a wolf on the front lying around here?" he asked, heading for a cluster of rowing machines.

"No... Hey, would you mind sparring with me for a sec?" she asked, ignoring the way Bran stiffened next to her.

Spiro glanced over from the workout machines, an amused expression on his face. "You want to spar?"

"Bran's taught me some new moves and I want to try one out."

Spiro looked at Bran, then her, before bending down to pick up a discarded hoodie tucked behind one of the rowers. "Why don't you wait until Rhea's back?" There was something in his voice that rankled her.

Keelin crossed her arms over her chest. "Why?"

Looking uncomfortable, Spiro rubbed a hand over his dark hair. "She's a female."

"And you think you're stronger than Rhea?"

"I didn't say that and no—but don't tell her that—it's just, I don't want to hurt you."

Feeling insulted, Keelin pasted on a smile and remembered everything Bran had taught her. "I understand. It's okay if you don't want your ass kicked by a female. I get it."

Spiro stiffened then rolled his eyes. "You're not baiting me that easily."

"Let him go, Keelin," Bran murmured. "I don't think it's a gender thing. He's just afraid of *dragons*."

That was apparently the right thing to say. Spiro dropped the hoodie and stalked to the middle of the mat. "All right. Show me what you've got." His body was coiled tight as he faced off with her.

Keelin looked at Bran and raised her eyebrows. She could tell he didn't want to, but he stepped back, moving off the mat and giving them space. When she looked back at Spiro she smiled sweetly. "You'll have to bear with me. I'm still trying to get some of the mechanics of these moves down."

And that did it. He relaxed just as Bran had done earlier. Except this time she knew what to do. Using her supernatural speed, she rushed him, using her dominant side to swoop in and semi-tackle him. Instead of tackling, however, she stepped fully into his embrace as he tightened his grip around her. Twisting, she punched her hip into his crotch and swiveled at the same time in a fluid pivot. As she did, she bent and just like Bran said, tossed Spiro on his ass.

I did it!

As he hit the ground she let out a little shout of victory and did a fist pump—then yelped as Spiro grabbed her ankle, knocking her to the ground. Before she could move, he was on top of her. All the air whooshed from her lungs until a blur of movement knocked Spiro off her.

Snarling, Bran had Spiro flattened, face down, his canines descended and the distinct scent of fire tinging the air as he leaned close to the male.

"Bran, get off him!"

Spiro wasn't moving, but he wasn't injured either. He'd gone still in that preternatural way shifters and vamps could, the faint whisper of his breathing the only sound he was making. "I wasn't trying to hurt her," he said quietly. "I thought we were supposed to be sparring."

Bran looked at Keelin, his expression fierce and all she saw in his eyes was pure dragon.

"It's okay. I'm okay," she murmured, keeping her voice as low as possible. She wasn't exactly scared by this display, but she was worried. For Spiro's safety.

He blinked, his gaze turning human again. Frowning, he looked down at Spiro then let the male up before moving to stand protectively in front of Keelin.

The shifter muttered something about just wanting his 'damn hoodie and crazy dragons' before stalking from the room.

The moment the male was gone Bran turned to look at her and ran his hands up and down her arms, as if searching to make sure she was okay. His callused palms were warm and she wanted to feel them everywhere. For a moment his fingers grazed over her bracelet and it seemed as if he wanted to say something.

But her vision shifted, the edges turning fuzzy until Bran's face blurred, just as before with that creepy demon.

What was happening to her?

Keelin tried to shake her head, to stop whatever was happening but was sucked under for a moment as images flashed in front of her. Bran was mostly naked with shreds of clothes falling off him as if he'd maybe half shifted then stopped. His expression was murderous, his face streaked in blood. "You motherfucking traitor!" he shouted, fire exploding from his mouth at another huge naked male also covered in blood.

The fire flowed around the male, not touching him, but that didn't stop Bran from attacking with a...sword. A sword? The male had dark hair and tattoos covering his chest. His eyes sparked red.

What was happening?

"Keelin!" Bran's worried voice cut through her thoughts as the images faded into nothing.

That was when she realized he'd pulled her tight against him. She ran her fingers up over his chest, resting them lightly against his hard muscles. His heart rate was out of control. Jarred from her vision, his embrace calmed her in a way she hadn't expected. The strangest sense of possessiveness welled up inside her after what she'd seen. Because she understood on a deeper level that the vision had been real. "Are you okay?" she demanded, smoothing her hands over his skin.

He stared at her as if she'd lost her mind. "Me? What about you?"

"I'm fine." Or she felt fine. "Why?"

"You spaced out or something. Your eyes glazed over and you weren't responding. Did that fucker hurt you?"

"Who?"

"Spiro," Bran gritted out.

"He barely touched me. I... I just had the strangest vision of you and some other male." Not caring what he thought, she stepped closer, wrapping her arms around him. She needed to know he was okay. She quickly relayed what she'd seen right down to the male's red eyes, even though she felt a little foolish, wondering if maybe she'd lost her mind—and was surprised when Bran went immobile, watching her almost warily.

"Who was he? Did he hurt you?" She wasn't sure why she was so worried when Bran was standing right in front of her, but she couldn't seem to help it.

"That male is dead."

"You called him a traitor."

"I did," he said, clearly being obtuse and not expanding for her. "Is that the first time you've had a vision like that?"

Keelin wanted to talk more about what she'd just seen but Bran seemed to be shutting her out so she didn't push. Something told her the male wouldn't break under torture so there was no point in questioning him. For now. She started to instinctively say yes to his question but shook her head as she remembered the night before. "No. The same thing happened with one of those demons at the underground fight club. It was really brief, but disturbing." After she described what she'd seen the night before, Bran went more still, if that was even possible.

Just as quickly, his expression turned thoughtful. "What did the female look like?"

Closing her eyes, Keelin forced herself to remember every little detail. When she was done describing the woman, she opened her eyes to find Bran pulling his cell phone from his pocket. After a few quick swipes, he pulled up a screen and held it out to her. There was a picture of a woman under the bright red word CLASSI-FIED but she ignored that little tidbit—for now—and focused on the female. The woman was alive and smiling in the photo.

"That's her." Keelin looked at Bran as he slipped the phone back into his pocket. "Who is she?"

"A dead Moana dragon." Before Keelin could think of a response, if there even was one, he continued. "I've got a meeting with the Moana Alpha in two hours and you're coming with me."

CHAPTER NINE

"There's more activity than normal tonight," Shar said, stating the obvious to Naram.

Naram frowned, watching from their perch on the roof of a house a block over from where the Stavros mansion was. He couldn't see the actual mansion or onto the grounds because there were so many trees and a surrounding wall, but he could see shifters leaving the residence through the gate. They were being subtle about it, so they wouldn't draw any attention by potentially nosy humans. Though Naram doubted that would be an issue. He'd done some digging and the pack's Alpha had been buying up most of the real estate in this historic neighborhood. It was all under shell corporations or different names, but over the past few months he'd bought almost every house that came up for sale so that most were now unused. Which meant no neighbors. Smart move, one Naram could understand. His own private residence was far from any prying eyes.

Naram and Shar had been watching them ever since they discovered the female dragon living in Biloxi. "Let's move closer." Naram placed a hand on Shar's shoulder as he spoke and transported them a block over.

He only traveled this way when he had to because it was a huge drain on his powers. Once he'd regained all his strength it wouldn't matter but until then he was careful with how much energy he expended. Especially since the dragon blood he'd been drinking was almost gone. Even with the ritual carvings he'd been cutting into the dragons to increase the power of the blood, it wasn't enough. Nothing would be enough until he had that damn bracelet.

Directly across the street from the mansion now, they stood cloaked on the sidewalk. Cloaking himself and Shar was difficult and the downside was that they couldn't speak. He might be able to make them appear invisible but he couldn't hide their voices. And if someone touched him or Shar, his cloaking would fall. It was the downside to magic. There were always limitations no matter who you were. Especially since he didn't have his talisman anymore. He wondered if Keelin even knew what she possessed on her wrist.

When the gate opened again he was surprised to see the female dragon in the passenger seat of an SUV, the male dragon driving. They seemed to be having an animated conversation as they steered out of the gate— which closed almost immediately behind them.

Making a split-second decision, he followed them. The chance of stumbling upon her like this was a sign from the gods. He was meant to follow her and possibly even kill her tonight. And reclaim what was rightfully his. His father had wanted to make life difficult for him, to put so much of Naram's power in that damn talisman. He'd wanted to teach Naram a lesson, to remind him that he needed to hold onto his power and not take it for granted. Well his father was an obnoxious ass. All he'd done was weaken Naram.

Soon all his troubles would be over and he would finally regain all that was his and take his proper place in the world. First he needed to kill the male to get rid of his most obvious obstacle. Once the male was out of the picture then he could eliminate the female. He hoped.

Her grandmother had been too strong for him, but she'd only managed to imprison him, not kill him. That had been her ultimate mistake. She should have sent him to Hell, but for some reason she'd been worried he would escape. He didn't understand why since he had so many enemies there. Enemies who would love nothing more than to see him in chains and tortured for eternity. They were all simply jealous of his heritage.

Her folly was his gain because now he was free and no one was ever locking him up again. Grasping Shar's shoulder again, he used his power to flash the two of them from stop to stop, keeping the two dragons within his sight. He needed to see where they were going in order to keep up with them.

The farther out of the city they drove, the more his powers waned. Still, he was glad the other two weren't flying. It would have been impossible to follow them in a timely manner. Or even at all. While he'd used the bracelet to originally track her, it had been vague enough to get him to the general area of the city. Now that he was in the same central area as Keelin, he couldn't track her as well.

He didn't like the direction they were headed in. The farther west they went, the closer they crept into Moana territory. They had to know it too. Why would these two dragons head into another dragon clan's territory? Did they know he'd been taking the Moana dragons?

No, no one should know. He and Shar had been working alone, only summoning demons when he need-ed assistance. Of course those scouts the other night had been foolish and cocky, trying to play with Keelin before they incapacitated her, telling her they wanted to kill her. If they hadn't been so stupid they might not have been incinerated by the male dragon.

By the time the SUV stopped they'd been traveling almost an hour. Naram wasn't certain what city they were in now, but they were on a quiet stretch of beach with no neighbors for a mile on either side. The dragon couple pulled up to a quiet, two-story beach house raised off the ground.

Maybe this was a lover's tryst? There didn't appear to be anyone else around, not even humans anywhere that Naram could see. Just lots of bright stars overhead, the heady scent of the Gulf on the other side of the house and the two dragons getting out of the SUV.

Keeping his and Shar's cloak in place, he waited to see what the couple would do. After a few moments they got out then entered the home. He waited another solid minute to make sure they didn't leave again before flashing him and Shar back to their base of operations. Naram didn't want to leave but he had to recharge or he'd be useless.

He had three drugged and unconscious Moana dragon shifters in human form in cells, though two were near death. Taking a bag of blood he'd syphoned from one of them, he quickly drank it. He needed the strength before he could do anything else.

Sweetness burst over his tongue and down his throat, the surge he got from the blood overwhelming. He always felt invincible after getting a taste. Maybe he'd drink from Keelin before he killed her. His cock stirred as he thought about how sweet her royal blood would be, how potent.

"What are we going to do?" Shar asked, his arms over his chest as he leaned against the far wall of the dungeon.

"Summon Akkadian demons and have them kill the male. I'm tired of playing safe."

Shar nodded his agreement. "The Akkadians are already angry at having been locked away after their brief foray into freedom."

"I know." It was why he was choosing them. Akkadians typically preferred to fight one-on-one, but he was going to order them to attack as one unified battalion. He needed the male dead so he could go after the female and this was the perfect opportunity. They were away from that pack and the club she frequented. No one was around to help them.

CHAPTER TEN

One month ago

Keelin paused as she heard the sound of her bedroom door opening before peeking out from her walk-in closet.

Bran Devlin and all his annoying sexiness was standing in her doorway looking surly and good enough to eat.

She stepped out fully from her closet and placed her hands on her hips. He'd just made himself right at home the past week. "What the heck are you doing in my bedroom again? You know I'm not recovering anymore." The male was making her and her dragon side edgy. She might be sheltered but she knew his behavior wasn't normal. Males from other clans, or people in general, didn't just show up unannounced in other people's bedrooms and homes.

"Why are you moving to Biloxi?" he demanded, completely ignoring her question.

"Excuse me?"

Growling—actually growling at her—he took a step into her room, tension radiating off him in thick waves. "You will be unprotected by your clan."

131

She stepped forward too, wishing she had shoes on so she wouldn't be so dwarfed by the male. Who did he think he was, to question her decision? "I'm sorry, I'm unclear on how that's any of your business. I'm also unclear on why you're in my room."

Those beautiful sapphire-green eyes flashed brightly. "I want to court you. And you should not be going to Biloxi alone."

Beyond surprised she dropped her hands from her hips. "You want to court me?"

His head tilted to the side a fraction as he watched her. "That can't be a surprise to you."

Well, it was. Sort of. She'd suspected he might be interested but he'd hovered around her the past few days, acting more like a nanny than anything. She decided to just ignore what he'd said, much like he'd ignored her questions. "I *am* going to Biloxi."

He turned all growly again and for some insane reason she liked the sound of it. Her nipples tightened at the sound as heat flooded between her thighs. What was wrong with her? This stupid caveman act should not be turning her on.

"Why are you leaving the protection of your clan?"

Her eyes narrowed. "You think I need protection?"

For a moment he paused, looking as if he suspected this was a trick question. "Dragons should be surrounded by their kind."

"So you don't like other shifters?"

"I didn't say that." He rubbed the back of his neck, the muscles in his arms flexing as he did so. "Are you going to respond to my request to court you?" His whole body pulled taut and he cleared his throat, suddenly seeming nervous.

"You didn't actually request anything," she murmured as nervousness slid through her. Why would an Alpha clan leader want to court her? Her dragon battered against her, clawing at her, telling her to step closer to the male. Just as she'd been ordering her the last few days. For some reason whenever Keelin was in his presence, she wanted to rub up against Bran like a feline in heat. It was insane. "But I'm not interested in a relationship. With anyone."

He narrowed his gaze, as if he didn't believe her.

She continued before he could respond. "I'm leaving today and nothing will change my mind. Thank you for the offer to court me, but..." She shrugged, unsure how to continue. No male had ever offered before and she had no experience with this type of situation. She was surprised he hadn't talked to one of her brothers first. Of course, according to their customs he wouldn't, he'd just go for what he wanted. It was how dragons were. And she actually liked that he'd come to her first, even if his timing was bad.

Instead of responding, he stalked to where some of her bags were and picked up two of them. "I'll take your bags downstairs," he growled because apparently that was all he was capable of doing.

Her nipples tightened even harder at the sound and she inwardly cursed her response. Frustrating male. She had everything planned out and getting involved with a possessive male was not in the mix.

No matter how sexy Bran was.

* * *

Present Day

"This is where we're supposed to meet the Alpha?" Keelin looked around the empty beach house as they stepped farther inside. She couldn't scent anyone in the house and knew Bran couldn't either. Otherwise she doubted he would have entered the home. His senses were probably even more attuned than hers since he was an Alpha.

Bran's entire body was tense as he followed her gaze, scanning the empty home. There wasn't even furniture inside. "Yes."

"Is this normal for Alphas to meet like this?" She hadn't been out of Protective Hibernation long and in the past her parents had never involved her in anything, let alone Alpha meetings. Her brother had kept her pretty involved over the last year but she'd never been to a meeting like this with Conall.

"Yes and no."

"That's helpful," she muttered, falling in step with him as he headed down a hallway.

"Cloak and dagger bullshit is typical and meeting in a random place like this *can* be typical. Since I've never met with her before, yes, this is normal enough. If your brother asked to meet me in an abandoned home, I would think twice."

"Why?"

He shot her a quick look as they entered a huge kitchen. "Because it would likely be a trap since we already have a relationship. An obvious trap, but..." Trailing off, he lifted his shoulders, continuing to scan everything in the room like a predator searching for prey.

"Oh." A sliver of tension slid through her as she looked around the bare room. A wall of windows overlooked the ocean, the three-quarter moon and stars illuminating the water and beach perfectly. No one was on the beach, not that she'd expected to see anyone this late and this far from any main tourist attractions.

As he scanned out one set of windows, she tried not to stare too hard. In profile to her, everything about him was hard and defined. He'd never be considered beautiful—he was too raw and primal looking—but that very hardness on him was a beautiful thing.

"Why didn't you attack Spiro after you'd knocked him on the ground?" Bran suddenly asked, the new topic taking her off guard as he turned to face her.

"Ah..." She felt stupid giving the real answer, but decided not to lie. He'd know anyway. "I was so excited about taking him down I didn't really think that far ahead." She might be a dragon but she didn't go around attacking people for fun.

Bran just nodded, thankfully not making her feel stupid. "If it had been a real battle, once you'd gotten him on the ground you should have gone for his throat, which I know you know. So anytime in the future, if you can decapitate someone that's always the best option. You could use your fire to weaken or distract someone by blinding them. Then slice their head off with your claws if you have them down. Or just incinerate them if they're not protected from dragon fire. Or—"

"I get it," she murmured. When he raised an eyebrow she half-smiled. "I know what to do, that's not the problem." The only time she'd ever felt the need to commit true violence was when she'd learned that her brother Drake had been sacrificed to Hell as a young boy. That he'd been ripped from her family with no one to protect him. She'd have razed entire cities to the ground to get to him if that's what it would have taken. That scared her a little, knowing that if she was pushed, she'd let her most primal instincts take over.

"Then what is?"

"I don't know." She liked learning different defense moves but she also understood that she'd never truly know how well she could do until tested in a real situation. The problem with that was that she tended to panic instead of letting her dragon side take over and protect her.

He leaned against the island in the middle of the room, his pose casual, but she noticed that he turned his back to the refrigerator and wall, giving him a complete view of any window so that no one could sneak up on him. Always watchful. "Explain it to me."

She leaned against a countertop opposite of him, exposing her back to the windows. She knew if they were attacked Bran would protect her. "For the most part I stress out when faced with violence. I don't know why." Okay, maybe she knew a little.

He raised a dark eyebrow. "You sure about that?"

"At the risk of sounding like a whiny human who blames things on their parents... I think a lot of it boils down to how sheltered I was. Seeing the underground fights has been fascinating and a little jarring to all my human senses. Maybe it's wrong, but I find I kind of liked watching. At least my dragon side does. At the same time when faced with violence myself I sometimes freeze." It disturbed her a little how much the fighting fascinated her dragon side while her logical, human side fought it.

He snorted. "You're not desensitized to it like most supernaturals. Or humans even."

"Exactly." Which was good and bad. "So, why are you in Biloxi? That picture you showed me said it was classified." She could change the subject just as quickly as him.

Bran didn't move, but there was a subtle change in him as he watched her. "I thought the reason I was here was obvious."

"Do you mean because of me?" Asking that left her feeling exposed even if she'd made it clear that things between them were just about having fun.

"I *am* here because of you."

She narrowed her eyes. "That's not the only reason." He didn't respond, his silence annoying her. So she decided to push while they were waiting for the Moana dragons to show up. "Why do you have something with the word classified on it? Unless there's a secret dragon organization I don't know about, that's from one of the world governments. I'm guessing US since we live here."

"By definition classified implies—"

She rolled her eyes. "I know what it means. Tell me why you have that document."

"I can't." His expression was carefully neutral and there was no give to his statement.

"Fine. Are you here for another reason other than me?" With supernaturals you had to be really specific sometimes. Otherwise they could answer vaguely, implying one thing without actually having to lie.

"Yes."

"Are you investigating something specific?" He had to be. With that picture he'd shown her and the fact that Finn was letting him stay in his territory, there had to be a really good reason.

He paused a moment then gave a sharp nod. "Yes."

"For someone?"

Sighing, Bran rubbed a hand over the back of his neck. In that moment he looked so exhausted she couldn't help the pang of sympathy that twisted inside her. "It's complicated."

Tightening her jaw, she turned away from him, looking out the window. That classified document he'd shown her had to be somewhat of a big deal. So she knew she shouldn't expect him to tell her where he'd gotten it or who he was working for—if he even was at all—but some part of her she didn't want to acknowledge felt irrationally hurt that he was keeping her in the dark. She didn't care if it was an emotional reaction and stupid considering they weren't even in a relationship.

She sensed him before she ever heard him move. His big hands settled on her hips, his chin coming to rest on the top of her head. That masculine scent of his wrapped around her, making her thoughts once again go haywire.

"Keelin," he murmured, sliding his hand around her waist in a possessive embrace. He tugged her close so that her back was against his chest.

She'd changed before they left earlier so she was wearing a thin coat over a top and jeans but it didn't matter how many clothes were between them. She could feel his heat sear straight through to her. When she looked up at the window in front of her she could see the reflection of his glowing eyes and realized her body was starting to put off that soft gold light again.

Though she wanted to be annoyed with herself for the physical reaction she simply couldn't help it. Her stupid dragon had decided that this was her mate even though Keelin disagreed. Aaaand, she shut down all those thoughts when he leaned down and nipped her earlobe between his teeth. He felt so good wrapped around her like this. When this meeting was over, she planned to get very naked with the male.

"I want to ditch this fucking meeting," he growled, tugging on her ear.

She arched against him, wanting exactly the same thing.

His grip around her tightened but as he did she scented... sulfur? She started to turn in Bran's arms when he turned instead and shoved her back, a growl leaving his throat.

She swiveled, sensing that danger was close. Stepping out from behind him she froze at the sight of an Akkadian demon who'd seemingly appeared out of nowhere. Because neither she nor Bran had heard it. Her senses might not be on par with his but she wasn't weak and Bran definitely should have scented it before it got into the house. Or heard it.

And this thing was definitely Akkadian. She might not have ever seen one before but she knew from Drake what they looked like. Besides, she'd have known anyway after reading about them in various supernatural history books.

The being staring at them was at least seven feet tall with short, thick horns sprouting from its head. She could tell it was male because of its jutting appendage—which it was casually stroking. *Disgusting.* Bile rose in her throat as she took in the rest of its reptilian skin and clawed hands and feet. Glowing crimson eyes landed on her and the creature made a growling/howling sound that caused all the hair on her arms stand up.

For once her inner dragon was ready to shift, no questions asked. But Bran hadn't made a move. He seemed to be watching the creature, waiting for something. The urge to shift, even in this room which would be too small to contain her larger form, was strong.

"Bran," she said quietly, needing to hear him say something. Anything.

"Go out the back door and shift." A soft order.

She wasn't leaving him. The very idea scraped against all her senses, repulsing her. She simply couldn't go without him. "No."

Before he could respond five more Akkadians appeared as if from thin air, one popping into existence after the other. What. The. Hell.

Fire burned the back of her throat, her body readying for the change.

As the demons let out what she knew was a battle cry, Keelin opened her mouth and sprayed fire, the need to protect Bran and herself overwhelming as the flames released from her. The two demons she hit full-on in their faces screamed, the stench of sulfur permeating the air. Next to her Bran did the same, his fire all-consuming as he jumped over the island, diving at them.

She started to move too when five more appeared, closer to her. Her heart jumped into her throat as they advanced like a military unit.

Before she could attack, Bran jumped at her, lightning quick, his arm snagging around her waist. She didn't think to fight him as he tugged her close. It took all of a second for her brain to compute what he was doing. Curling into him, she kept her head down as he gripped her tight and dove through the nearest window.

Glass shattered around them as he shouted, "Shift!"

For the first time in pretty much ever she let her dragon take over without thought. Cool night air rushed over her as Bran released her. The magic of the shift surged through her as she would have tumbled over the edge of the balcony. Instead of plummeting, she soared into the air, ordering her natural shield into place so no one could see her. She snapped her wings out and flew toward the ocean before banking left. She turned back to the house, gaining rapid speed.

She couldn't see Bran and would have panicked, but then saw a burst of flames erupt from the air, blanketing the balcony and over a dozen Akkadian demons below.

Taking his lead, she swooped down from the opposite direction and released her own stream of fire at the swarming demons. There were so many of them she couldn't understand where they were coming from.

She'd seen a Hell Gate before so that wasn't it. Those things had simply *appeared*. That had to be strong, dark magic. She'd worry about that later.

Annihilating these things was all that mattered now.

Diving in a freefall, she let out another stream of flames at the bottom of the home, catching the gaunt, humanoid creatures trying to run toward the road.

Adrenaline rushed through her as she let her animal out to play, taking out demons left and right until finally the house was in flames and there was no sign of them anywhere. As they'd been killing the demons she'd been able to guesstimate Bran's location but now that the beings were dead she couldn't see him anymore.

Taking a chance, she landed on the beach and shifted back to her human form. When she did, she let her natural shield drop. Though her heart was pounding wildly in her ears, she glanced around, looking for any signs of life.

When she didn't see anyone; not Bran, demons or even a stray human, she headed back up the sandy incline. Thankfully the houses on this stretch were far apart but someone would eventually see the flames and call the fire department.

A whoosh of air above her blew her hair back before she heard Bran land in the sand next to her. A moment later there was a slight flash of sparkling color as if he was dropping his shield and shifting at the same time. Then he stood in front of her, naked, beautiful and furious. Not at her though.

"Are you okay?" he demanded, hurrying the ten feet toward her, moving faster than she could blink.

She nodded and looked him over. She hadn't felt any glass slice into her when they'd dived through that window but her shift to dragon had been so instantaneous they'd have both healed during the shift. Still, she drank him in hungrily with her gaze, needing to make sure he was all right. "I'm fine, what about you?"

He grunted and tugged her close, his body coiled tight as he glanced at the burning remains of the house.

"How did those demons appear like that?"

"I don't know." His voice was grim. "I need to check out the house to make sure they're all dead. Did you bring your cell phone in with you?"

"No." It was still in the car and she hadn't burned the vehicle so unless Bran had it should still be fine. And they'd at least have a change of clothes.

"Wait here and—"

She stiffened next to him and pulled out of his embrace. When his gaze automatically fell to her breasts she gritted her teeth. "I'm going with you."

He started to argue so she turned and headed up the incline. She didn't have the energy for an argument now. When she breached the top of the sandy hill, her eyes widened. Yep, the house was toast. If the Moana dragons had owned it they might be pissed. "Hey." She turned suddenly to Bran to find him scowling down at her. She ignored it. "Do you think the Moana clan set us up?" From what she knew of their kind it didn't make sense considering their clan was the most peaceful of all dragons, but it didn't mean they weren't treacherous.

"Anything's possible," he muttered, clearly not happy she was going with him.

Keelin placed a hand on his forearm. "If I'm with you, you can watch out for me but if you leave me on the beach I'm unprotected." She figured appealing to his protective nature would win her points.

His lips pulled into a thin line. "We both know you're coming with me no matter what I say."

"I'm glad we're both on the same page. Come on. Let's check for those beasts and put some clothes on. It's chilly." His gaze dipped once again down her entire body, making her nipples tighten. Ignoring his effect on her, she linked her arm through his and tugged. "Come on."

When they made it to the wood walkway, they both paused at the top of the stairs, looking around at the dunes for any lurking attackers. Keelin couldn't scent anyone and she hadn't seen anyone flee when she'd been in the air. But after the insanity of those things just appearing...yeah, she was going to be sleeping with one eye open.

As they reached the end of the walkway she heard the flapping of multiple wings overhead, but couldn't see anything. Her inner dragon rose to the surface again, ready to protect her.

Bran tensed too, shoving her behind him in that dominant way that should probably annoy her, but she found she more than liked. She wasn't a warrior and she wasn't going to pretend like she was. Reaching back, he pulled her close so that her chest was flush against his back as they scanned the sky.

"Can you cloak yourself?"

She did it without thinking. "Done."

He did the same, though she could see the faint out-line of him, as if she was looking at a transparent, wa-tery outline. Without a word, he started moving forward. She stayed right on him.

"I mean you no harm," a female voice called out just before a woman revealed herself near the rubble of the burning house. She walked in their direction over the soft grass, unabashed in her nakedness.

Bran dropped his cloak so Keelin did too. She couldn't be sure but she guessed the female was the Moana Alpha. Tall, lithe, with bright cobalt eyes that were even more vivid against her bronzed skin and es-presso colored hair, she looked and walked like a queen. Keelin instantly fought her stupid feelings of insecurity as the female's gaze roved over Bran with appreciation as if she had every right in the world to look her fill at him.

"Tell your people to reveal themselves." Bran's voice was hard.

Keelin didn't hear flapping anymore and she could scent others. After the woman flicked her hand in the air, three males revealed themselves. All perfect speci-mens of the dragon race just like their Alpha. Tall and muscular with bronzed skin that gleamed under the moonlight. And they all had the same cobalt eyes as their Alpha. When two of them looked at Keelin, their gazes clearly interested, Bran stiffened but didn't say anything.

BEYOND THE DARKNESS | 147

No one was saying anything which was a little strange. Everyone was just staring at each other. *Naked.* Keelin wrapped her arms around herself. Was this how Alpha meetings normally went? They all just stood around and said *nothing*? If so, it was weird. "Can we get this little meeting started?" she blurted, nerves taking over. Because she wanted to put some freaking clothes on. Nudity didn't bother her around Bran or her own clan, but the three males were all looking at her now with far too much interest.

The female's gaze snapped to her, as if seeing her for the first time. Which obviously wasn't the case. Her blue eyes narrowed before they flicked back to Bran. "Why did you destroy one of my houses?"

"We were attacked by Akkadian demons," Bran said.

True surprise rolled off all four of them. "I'd heard there was a problem with them months ago but that it had been taken care of."

"Obviously not." Bran's voice was wry. "Did you have anything to do with the attack?"

Keelin guessed he was just testing her since the female's surprise had seemed real.

Now the female looked pissed. "You come onto my territory and accuse me of such a thing?" Oh yeah, she had the haughty Alpha thing down pat.

"I didn't accuse you of anything."

The female didn't respond, just looked at Bran again, her gaze sweeping over him as if he was a piece of meat from head to...crotch. Then back up again.

Keelin nearly yelped when she felt her claws starting to extend into her palm. Surprised, she forced her body under control. She really wished they could just get on with whatever this meeting was about. Bran had been annoyingly vague, just informing her that she was going with him. And she really wanted to contact Finn and let him know Akkadian demons had been near his territory. She felt a lot of loyalty to the male. Plus she and Bran needed to talk to Bo and see if he knew what the deal was with those things appearing so quickly. If he didn't know, she planned to call her new sister-in-law, Victoria. Keelin didn't want to involve her if she didn't have to, but the woman was brilliant and read all sorts of obscure texts so she might know something. The adrenaline surging through her now was out of control and she wanted to shout at these two to get on with it because she had stuff to do.

Finally the female looked at Keelin again, her gaze curious. "Since Bran is apparently too rude to introduce us, I'm Nalani."

Keelin nodded politely, manners drilled into her from a young age. "I'm Keelin Petronilla."

At that, Nalani's eyebrows raised. "I thought you looked familiar. You bear a striking resemblance to your mother."

"You've met her?" That meant this female was seriously old.

She nodded. "Centuries ago. She is very strong." That was apparently all she was going to say on the matter because she turned back to Bran. "My clan has a home not far from here. We will have the meeting there. The humans will notice this fire soon so we should go. One of my men can drive the vehicle out front. I assume it's yours?"

"It is and I will drive it myself." There was no give in Bran's voice.

Nalani flicked a lock of her long, dark hair back over her shoulder. "Fine. One of my men will go with you." Just like with Bran, there was no give in her voice either.

Jaw clenched tight, Bran nodded, but his entire demeanor was hard. Without looking at Keelin or touching her, he motioned that she should walk ahead of him.

She felt strangely hurt that he wasn't touching her or claiming her in front of the other female, but she didn't say anything. Just headed toward the waiting SUV. Even though she had a dozen questions she knew she wouldn't be able to ask them. Not if they were going to have a freaking shadow in their vehicle.

She really wanted to get to the bottom of whatever had just happened. Because demons appearing like that out of nowhere, was insane.

CHAPTER ELEVEN

Naram wanted to scream at the sky. He was too weak, however. And if he did, he'd reveal himself to the nearby dragons. Across the street from the burning beach house, he stood on an empty lot overgrown with grass.

He'd wasted so much energy—so much blood—on those stupid fucking demons. He'd sent them directly into the home in a surprise attack. Using his gift of magic he'd done what only two types of beings could do. He'd released those demons without using a Hell Gate.

Now he would pay for the expenditure of energy. Even if he'd had all his powers back that type of action would have drained him. But since he'd used magic and the assistance of dragon blood, he was useless.

It would take him a day or two to completely recover. Time he shouldn't have to waste because of the incompetence of those demons. As it was he was barely keeping his eyes open. The blackness of sleep beckoned to him and he needed to return to his shelter so he'd be protected. His castle was his only safe haven. His entire body felt like one giant bruise.

"Perhaps it's a good thing," Shar murmured, low enough for his ears only.

152 | KATIE REUS

"How?" Even talking took too much energy, but he didn't want to reveal that to Shar. He liked the young demon well enough, but he also understood that Shar followed him only because of what Naram could give him. There was no mercy for the weak in this world. If he proved an incapable leader Shar would leave him.

"You expended a lot of energy," he said quietly, mirroring Naram's own thoughts. "Even if they'd killed the male there's no guarantee we would have been able to take her on. Not if she was in her animal form. So Akkadians aren't useful to us but you'll find another way. Perhaps a binding spell or a form of dark magic to restrain her."

"That is...a good point." He tightened his jaw, trying to hide his slurred speech. His muscles were starting to tremble as blackness crept in on him. In his weakened state he wasn't thinking clearly, but the male was correct. Being so drained he wouldn't have been able to defeat her anyway. Not unless she'd been truly weakened by the Akkadian demons.

He thought about what Shar proposed, but a binding spell on another supernatural being, especially one as strong as a dragon, was exceptionally difficult. Impossible really. But that didn't mean he couldn't use other dark magic on her.

Naram just needed to figure out her weakness, what would work on her. Because everyone had a weakness. He would find it, then destroy her. And take back what belonged to him.

* * *

Keelin glanced around the open pool area of the mansion the Moana clan had taken them to. The cabana they were under had striped gold and bronze curtains billowing in the light breeze and someone had brought them a bottle of champagne. As if this was some sort of social visit. The place was impressive though and Keelin could appreciate the art she'd seen on the way in.

The Alpha had been telling the truth, it wasn't far from the home they'd just burned to a crisp. If she strained she could just hear the sound of sirens in the distance. Probably because of the fire.

Now she and Bran were sitting on what she guessed was custom-made outdoor furniture. The heavy wood seats with plush cushions were comfortable and the type of material that would weather any storm. Not that she cared.

The Alpha female was still keeping them waiting. It had only been ten minutes since they'd arrived but it felt rude. She couldn't help but wonder if it was intentional.

"Power play?" Keelin murmured to Bran, who sat directly next to her. It could be the only reason the stupid female was doing this.

He snorted, his laid-back pose casual and deceptively unassuming. They'd chosen a loveseat under the awning to sit on together and he'd thrown his arm around the back of her seat. He still hadn't touched her, not since they'd left the burning house, and she wasn't sure why. He shouldn't be angry with her for any reason so that couldn't be it.

She didn't know how he could be so relaxed when they had stuff to do. Since that Moana dragon had rode with them on the way here they hadn't been able to communicate much with the Stavros pack. Though she had sent a mass of texts to Finn telling him exactly where they were going. So if the Moana clan attacked them, his pack would tell her and Bran's clans and there would be hell to pay from a whole lot of people. Still, they needed to let Finn know everything else that had happened.

When Bran squeezed her shoulder she looked over in surprise, even as she felt immense pleasure from that soft touch. "What?"

"Let's go. This is bullshit. They need my help, not the other way around." He started to stand but just as he did, Nalani emerged from the sliding glass doors of the house—topless.

Seriously? She wore a long skirt of some sort of mesh material that was completely sheer, gold bangles on her wrists and ankles so that she jangled every time she moved, and no freaking top. That was just obnoxious. Keelin wondered if she was doing it for Bran's sake. With such a beautiful female displaying herself she couldn't help but feel insecure. And pissed.

"Don't get up on my account." Nalani waved a dismissive hand in the air.

"I'm not. We're leaving." Bran's voice was hard and unforgiving. Keelin had never heard that tone before but it sent a shiver down her spine.

Keelin inwardly smiled that the female's breasts didn't seem to be a distraction to Bran.

Apparently his tone had the same effect on the other female. She straightened and picked up her pace, her breasts moving as sensually as she did. Keelin hoped Bran wasn't checking the female out but refused to look at him.

"Please stay." Nalani held out her hands in a peaceful gesture. "I had clan business to attend to. I wasn't trying to be rude." Her words sounded sincere but Keelin wasn't sure she bought the excuse.

Something about this female rubbed her the wrong way. Of course that probably had a lot to do with the way Nalani had been checking out Bran, and now was flaunting her bare breasts at him.

He paused but sat back down. This time his demeanor wasn't casual, but that of a predator poised and ready to strike. "How many of your clan are missing?"

The other Alpha sat too. "Four, but one is dead, as you know, so I've lost five."

Bran hadn't discussed much on the phone with her because the Alpha female had been resistant to talking at all. Now that he'd met her he found himself impossibly annoyed at her rudeness. "Do you know anything about the carvings on the dead female?" he asked, wanting to take her off guard. Bran hadn't revealed specifics of what he knew on the phone, just that he knew dragons were disappearing and that he wanted a meeting.

Her blue eyes started to glow as she watched him. "We don't know the origins of them. Not even me so they must be truly ancient. Now tell me how *you* know about them." It was subtle but he heard the razor's edge of authority in her voice.

Bran wasn't telling this female shit. He shrugged. "I make it my business to know when my kind are being threatened. What can you tell me about the ones who have gone missing? Habits, places they liked to visit, anything important."

"Why should I?" she demanded.

He shrugged. "You don't have to. I'm here because I want to help but if you won't share information, I'm gone. No skin off my back."

Her jaw clenched, her eyes flashing bright blue. "You're just as obnoxious as your father was."

Bran's father had been obnoxious, arrogant and extremely powerful so that wasn't exactly an insult. "What's your point?"

"You just expect me to share information with you in return for nothing?"

"Not nothing. I hope to help discover who's taking your clan members."

"For what end?"

"What the hell do you think? To fucking stop them." Like he needed to explain himself.

To his surprise, the other Alpha half-smiled and leaned back against her cushioned seat, seemingly more at ease. "Good. I have a file on each missing dragon I will have one of my men send to your email." She looked toward the back of the house. "Now," she continued. Though he couldn't see anyone, he knew her warriors were lurking nearby. He scented at least a dozen. "One of my clan members sent a message to August McGuire about my dead clan member. I'm assuming he's the one who sent you?"

It took a lot to surprise him, but her question did. Next to him Keelin shifted restlessly, but he kept his focus off her. He'd been forcing himself not to touch her or make any outward possessive gestures since the moment the Moana dragons had arrived. He wasn't sure that he trusted them yet—or ever would—and didn't want them to know Keelin meant so much to him. It could make her a target if they wanted to hurt him. Because seeing Keelin hurt, especially because of him, would gut him.

"You know August?" he asked, refusing to commit one way or another.

"I know of him. If I hadn't wanted him to find my female, he wouldn't have." That deadly edge was back, the power rippling off her fiercely.

He hoped he never had to find out which of them was stronger. He'd fought in enough battles and he hated fighting his own kind. Their lives were precious enough and it went against his nature.

"The female who was killed...was she involved with anyone? Have any ties to demons?"

Nalani paused for a moment but shook her head. "She wasn't mated or seeing anyone. Not seriously anyway. She slept with whoever she chose, mostly humans. She found them amusing. And she liked to frequent the half-demon's club in Biloxi."

Bran kept his expression neutral. "Bo Broussard's club?"

She nodded. "Yes."

That was interesting but could mean nothing. As far as Bran knew Bo's place was the only supernatural-only club in the area. There were a lot in New Orleans but that was an hour and a half away.

"I'm acquainted with Bo, as is Keelin," he said, nodding to her. "If it's acceptable to you, I'll show him the pictures of all the missing dragons you send me." He'd be doing it anyway but figured he should show some good will and let her in on it. Bo would have many contacts, as well as the Stavros pack, and Bran was going to use every resource at his disposal.

"Thank you. I've done enough research on the half-demon that I don't think he would be involved in anything so treacherous as taking dragons. He enjoys his life. And I don't think he's powerful enough anyway."

Bran nodded, agreeing. The half-demon was powerful but incapacitating a dragon shifter was difficult, especially if they were of the warrior class.

She cleared her throat then, her gaze flicking curiously to Keelin, then back to him. "I've heard there are talks of alliances between dragon clans."

It wasn't a question but he was under the impression she was asking something. "Yes. My clan and Keelin's have been working together and will continue to do so."

"You have also been talking with the Stavros pack." Now her gaze switched completely to Keelin. "*You* live with them."

So the Alpha had known who Keelin was before she'd introduced herself earlier.

"At the moment." Keelin's answer was succinct, her body language making it clear she was uncomfortable.

All the more reason for them to get out of there. He'd gotten the information he'd come for.

The female nodded once, her expression still unreadable as she turned that laser-like focus back on him. "I don't scent that you two are mated." The bold statement was clear she referred to them being mated to each other.

"We're not." *Yet.* Because Bran had every intention of locking down the female next to him. Originally it had been a purely primal reaction to her, something he didn't fully understand, but now that he'd gotten to know her, Bran wasn't walking away from Keelin. He cared way too much for his own sanity.

Next to him Keelin went impossibly still, her scent becoming completely unreadable. His inner dragon clawed at him, not liking the distance she was putting between them, not understanding her reaction.

Nalani nodded, more to herself than him. "I'm looking to form an alliance. A strong one." Her fingers trailed almost absently between her breasts, the action probably meant to be sensual. Her intent was very clear. She was looking to mate with another clan's Alpha.

He gritted his teeth at the display. She could look and tempt all she wanted, but he was interested in only one female. He hated that she was pulling this shit in front of Keelin. He didn't think she was being disrespectful to Keelin on purpose since they hadn't made public claims on each other, but he still didn't like it. Bran stood, needing to get him and Keelin the hell out of there. "We have leads to follow up on, but I thank you for your hospitality."

Keelin and Nalani stood at almost the same time. Both women smiled politely at each other and murmured equally polite goodbyes, then Nalani asked Keelin if she could set up a meeting with the Petronilla Alpha. Keelin, to his amusement, was very vague with her answer, refusing to commit to anything, her expression hard, the sharp glint in her bright eyes unmistakable.

They were escorted back through the house to the front where his SUV was still parked. The long wraparound driveway led to an iron gate, much like the one the Stavros pack had. This property was just as private and screamed of wealth. Like most dragons, the Moana clan clearly had high living standards.

Even though he knew they weren't alone, not truly, once it was just the two of them by his SUV, he said, "I think we should head to Bo's club."

"Do you?" The bite of sarcasm to her question took him off guard. Before he could answer, Keelin started stripping. His dick immediately hardened as she revealed perfect pink nipples and full rounded breasts. But she barely glanced at him.

Wait... "What are you doing?" he demanded as quietly as he could, not wanting to draw any undue attention to them.

"I'll fly. You can fucking drive by yourself," she snapped, stalking away from him and shifting before he could say a damn word.

He'd rarely heard her say the word fuck so he knew she was pissed but he couldn't understand why. Maybe it was because Nalani had been half-naked? But it wasn't as if he'd been staring at the other female. And it wasn't as if he could have asked their host to cover up. Though every possessive fiber of him wanted to stalk after Keelin and follow he knew he couldn't show any sort of weakness in front of the Moana dragons he had absolutely no doubt were watching them. If he chased after her they'd note it. Until he was mated to Keelin he couldn't let these unknown dragons be privy to anything that could possibly harm her.

A strange sensation of joy surged through him as he watched her shift. She was so fucking beautiful it almost hurt his eyes. Her jade wings glittered under the moonlight, her sleek body a burst of diamond-colored scales that twinkled riotously. She looked over her shoulder at him, her gray eyes glowing with barely concealed rage. She snapped her jaw at him once before launching into the sky and disappearing completely from view.

Damn it. He jumped into the SUV, knowing she'd beat him to the club in her dragon form. He didn't want her unprotected and he was going to get to the bottom of whatever her problem was. Which he was pretty sure had to do with the half-naked Alpha he couldn't have done anything about. Fucking females.

CHAPTER TWELVE

Keelin couldn't stop the rage pulsing through her. For the first time in memory she actually had to rein her dragon side in from breathing fire at anything and everything. But mainly at Bran. Leaving him behind had been the best decision.

He could just drive himself to Bo's and hope she was there when he arrived. If he would even care. She couldn't believe the way he'd basically ignored her that whole time.

And she didn't care that she'd told him she just wanted things casual between them. He'd put no claim on her, had acted as if she meant absolutely nothing to him in front of Nalani. That beautiful, perfect-looking dragon who'd dared to flaunt her perfect, bare breasts at Bran and made all Keelin's primitive instincts rush to the surface. Was she being irrational? Maybe. Probably. *Yes.*

She didn't care one bit. Her dragon side wanted to claw him to shreds and her human half was in complete agreement.

The female Alpha had been practically naked and he'd done nothing to signal that he was with Keelin. No small touch on her back, leg, nothing.

The back of her throat burned with the need to release her fire, but she held back, knowing that if she
slipped the leash she might not be able to contain herself.

The flight to the club was over far too soon, but she
felt better once she arrived. Keeping her cloak in place,
she circled the area a few times. When she was certain
she was alone except for the security guy smoking by the
front door, she landed near the outskirts of the parking
lot so she'd have enough room and shifted to her human
form. Only then did she let her cloak fall.

Normally she'd change before heading inside but in
her escape from Bran she hadn't brought her clothes or
her phone. As she walked to the front door, the vampire's eyes widened with surprise and a heavy dose of
lust as he watched her approach. She was still too annoyed to care about his blatant interest. He'd been with
Bo for a few years from what she'd heard but she'd only
worked with him a couple times.

Forcing herself to take a deep breath and be polite,
she gave him a sweet smile she didn't feel. "Can I borrow
your shirt?"

"Yeah, sure, of course." He stumbled over his words
as he practically ripped the plain black T-shirt over his
head and handed it to her. "You need anything?" he
asked as she tugged it over her head. His expression was
oh-so hopeful.

Vampires had a different scent than shifters. It was
still primal but less earthy. Right now she just cared that

she had something to cover her naked body with. Shaking her head, she said, "No, but thank you. Is Bo working?" He normally was, but not always and she wanted to talk to him.

"Yeah, but he's dealing with some employee shit. I think someone's getting fired," he whispered.

Keelin raised her eyebrows, then nodded and headed inside. Bo was pretty laid back about things so unless someone stole from him, hurt someone, was seriously out of line with the customers or employees—or did something to Nyx—she couldn't imagine him letting someone go lightly.

Inside things were busy but seemed normal enough. Nyx was at a high-top table talking to a group of females who seemed to be hanging on her every word. Nyx was blushing at something one of them said, then she nodded and headed for the bar. She paused when she saw Keelin, her eyes widening as she made a beeline for her.

In bare feet she was a lot shorter than Nyx who was wearing ridiculously gorgeous heels tonight. "Hey, are you okay?" Nyx asked, taking in the borrowed shirt and bare feet.

Keelin nodded, barely able to contain the annoyance bubbling inside her. When Bran got here she was going to ignore him, see how *he* liked it. "Yeah. Stupid night, that's all."

Her friend frowned and glanced down at her attire. "Cynara's got extra clothes in Bo's office. I'm sure she wouldn't mind if you borrowed something."

166 | KATIE REUS

"Where's Bo?" Because she so wasn't interrupting him if he was firing someone.

"Behind the red door. I think something bad happened." Nyx bit her bottom lip and looked over her shoulder, though it was too crowded to see past the high-top tables and multiple dance areas to where the door was.

"Okay, I'll ask Cynara then. Thanks."

"No problem, just let me know if you need anything, okay?"

She nodded, some of her earlier steam fading. "I will."

After checking with Cynara she headed to Bo's office and found a few different sets of Cynara's clothes in one of the closets, all of which were incredibly revealing. Even with their height difference, the clothes would all fit. Sort of.

In the end she chose a leather dress that was truly ridiculous. It was more like lingerie than anything but all her lady parts were covered. Barely.

The front of it was all black laces criss-crossing down in a V that dipped past her navel to just above her mound. The back laced up too, with the only actual leather material running along her hips up to her ribs and the sides of her breasts. Keelin wondered where Cynara bought this stuff. Maybe she had them custom-made because Keelin had never seen anything like this anywhere. And she'd done her fair share of shopping since waking from her Protective Hibernation. Cynara even had shoes which were a size too big but the three-inch heels fit well enough. Since the straps wrapped around her ankles they stayed in place.

Once she was out in the club, she found the security guy and gave him his shirt back. He didn't say anything, just stared at her so she took that as a good sign. The dress was revealing and she was going to work it tonight. Let Bran see how it felt when she ignored him.

A popular song thumped through the speakers, making her want to dance. But first, she was grabbing a drink. Or three. On the way to Cynara's bar, Nyx sidled up to her and slid her arm through one of hers. "I've already had four males and three females offer to buy you drinks. Those females," she said, with a very slight nod to the right, "have been hitting on me all night and asked if the two of us would like to join the three of them behind the red door."

On the outskirts of the high-top table seating, three females all with long, black hair and Asian features smiled and raised their martini glasses when Keelin looked over. She could see their animals in their gazes and guessed they were feline. She smiled back. "Does Finn know those cats are in his territory?"

Nyx laughed as they continued threading their way through the growing crowd. "Yeah. They made sure to tell me they'd already talked to the Stavros Alpha and were just passing through. They're snow leopards."

Keelin raised her eyebrows. "I've never seen one before." They were so rare and for three of them to be in one place was pretty cool.

"Me neither. They're really nice and really horny. I'm sure they won't have a problem picking up someone tonight, though females seem to be their preference. Now tell me what's going on with you. For real."

"It's too much to explain. Just…males are stupid." She sounded like a petulant adolescent but didn't care.

Nyx snickered. "No kidding. A bunch of Stavros packmates are here tonight. I don't think just to party, but they're at one of the private booths if you want to join them."

"I do. Send over a couple bottles of Bo's best champagne." She had the money and tonight she was going to spend it. Deep down she wondered if Bran would even care when he got here. He'd made it clear what he thought of her in front of that female. Keelin shoved the hurt away as best she could.

Her friend just smothered a smile and nodded. "Sure thing."

* * *

Bran's mood was black by the time he made it to Bo's place. He'd wanted to ditch his SUV completely and fly but knew it would have been stupid.

Almost forty-five minutes later he was finally fucking here. The more time he'd had by himself the more he wanted to know what Keelin's deal was. He didn't understand her anger at all. It wasn't like he'd asked that female to prance around half-naked and he hadn't looked at her more than he had to.

The parking lot was packed so when he stepped inside he wasn't surprised the place was full. Scents of sex, alcohol, perfumes, and a dozen other things accosted him at once. There were a lot of shifters here tonight. Not just wolves either.

Before he'd taken more than five steps two females who looked alike enough to be related approached him. Wearing matching plaid Catholic schoolgirl skirts the size of band-aids and tops that looked like bras, they both smiled at the same time. It was creepy.

Knowing he would come off as a dick, he didn't care. Before they could touch him or say anything he bared his teeth and growled, letting his dragon show in his eyes.

Simultaneously they flashed their fangs and flipped him off before turning around and flashing their ass cheeks when they swiveled away in search of someone else.

When he saw Bo talking to a female with purple hair behind one of the bars, he started making his way to the two of them. Bo spotted him and nodded in acknowledgement so Bran parked it by the end of the bar and waited until the half-demon made his way to him. Bo ducked under the hatch of the bar, his expression as grim as Bran felt.

"What's up?" Bo asked.

"We need to talk."

"Can it wait? Tonight's insane." He looked ready to murder someone.

Bran shook his head. "It won't take long."

"Fine. My office."

"Where's Keelin?" Bran asked, scanning the place, unable to see past the throng of people crammed onto the dance floor. He desperately wanted to see her, but needed to get this shit over with so she could have his full attention.

"At a booth with a bunch of the Stavros pack."

His inner dragon was immediately soothed at the knowledge. She was protected. As soon as he got this conversation over with Bo he was finding her.

Once they were alone in his office, Bo leaned against the edge of his desk, not bothering to walk around it. "I'm not trying to be rude, but fucking talk."

Bran had no problem getting to the point. "Dragons in the area are going missing." Because fuck it, if his kind were coming out of the closet so to speak, he wasn't going to hold back anything. Besides, this half-demon knew about them.

Bo still seemed surprised though, the scent rolling off him true shock. "There are more in the area than you and Keelin?"

"Yeah." And the half-demon wasn't getting more information than that. At least not yet. Bran retrieved his tablet from where he'd tucked it into the back of his pants. He turned it on and pulled up a couple of the files Nalani had sent him. Swiping his finger across the screen he placed the pictures of the missing dragons on the screen then turned it around. "You know any of these individuals?"

Bo shifted uncomfortably against his desk and nodded. "They've all been in here before. They're *all* dragons?"

"Yep. What can you tell me about them?"

A scent came off the male Bran couldn't pin down. Bo cleared his throat. "Well, I've fucked two of them." Okay, that was embarrassment rolling off the guy. He pointed out two pictures of dark-haired females. "We had a threesome but it was casual for all of us. Those females liked to have a good time. Can't believe I didn't know they were dragons," he muttered.

"What did you think they were?"

He shrugged. "Felines. It's not like they shifted or anything and I knew they weren't vamps or Stavros pack."

"Anyone else who works for you fool around with any of them, male or female?"

"I don't know, but I'll ask. Discretely," he added.

"I want to know anything and everything about them that you or anyone could remember. Who they left with, dates, anything. No detail is too small."

Bo nodded then tapped his earpiece. "Hold on," he murmured to Bran. He must have some sort of blocking system because Bran couldn't hear what the person on the other end was saying.

But it was easy enough to read Bo's body language. The male stiffened and turned away from Bran. "Get her

172 | KATIE REUS

off the stage. Now," he murmured. "I don't care what she says. Fucking do it." A deadly growl rumbled from the male before he turned back to Bran, his expression stiff and his eyes flashing amber.

There was something off about the male's whole posture and it set Bran on alert. He immediately stood. "Who were you talking about?"

Bo cleared his throat. "What?" As if he didn't understand the question.

Without thinking Bran grabbed Bo by the throat and slammed him down onto the desk. The half-demon's eyes flashed brightly and Bran knew his dragon was in his own eyes. Bo didn't struggle or attempt to get out of the hold, just glared at him.

"Talk!" Bran demanded. Then realized he was squeezing the guy's throat. Fuck. He released it, feeling like an out of control adolescent and stepped back, his breathing jagged, his heart about to burst through his chest. That fucker had been talking about Keelin. He just knew it.

Bo sat up and adjusted his shirt, looking annoyed more than angry. He cleared his throat. "First, I'm going to tell you that I have one room open behind the red door. Number eight. Use it with your female. Second, don't fucking kill anyone. Third, do *not* destroy my club or you and I will come to blows. My magic only goes so far with cleanup. Fourth, Keelin's dancing with some guy on one of the platforms—"

Bran was gone, burning through the office door without thought. He vaguely heard Bo cursing behind him but he ignored it. Sprinting down the hallway he managed to open that door instead of incinerating it.

Because he was saving all his fire for the fucker who thought he could touch his female. There was no way Bo would have reacted that way if the guy hadn't been touching Keelin. Dancing and touching went together.

The vision in his one good eye blurred and it took all his self-control not to shift right in the middle of the club. There were half a dozen raised platforms in the back area of the club. But it was blocked by a shitload of people and a wall that acted as a barrier to that part of the establishment.

Not willing to deal with shoving through everyone, Bran let out a roar, not caring who knew what he was. The earsplitting sound reverberated through the club and the music quieted. "Get the fuck out of my way!" he snarled, stomping through the crowd that now split a perfect path, giving him a wide berth.

He knew he looked like a complete fucking lunatic. He didn't care.

It would have been easier to simply destroy everything in his path, but he managed to control himself. Just barely. He hurried past the private booths, all of which had the curtains drawn back now so people could stare at the crazy shifter. Fuck all of them. When he stepped around the walled area blocking the back he immediately spotted Keelin.

And nearly lost his shit.

She was climbing down off a raised platform that she'd apparently been dancing on. Some guy had his hands on her hips and was helping her.

What she was wearing...his dick instantly got hard at the sight of her. He'd seen her naked, but still, seeing her like this was hot. That wasn't a dress, it was... Hell if he knew what it was.

She pushed the guy next to her away when she saw Bran, her gray eyes flashing with just a hint of unease— and annoyance. The entire room had gone quiet and he was vaguely aware of some Stavros pack members near Keelin on the wood dance floor, though everyone had stopped dancing.

Feeling almost possessed, he stalked across the room, not surprised when everyone cut another path for him. Out of the corner of his eye he saw the male she'd been dancing with run out of the room. The predator in him wanted to give chase, but he let the fool go. The music had been turned down and Bran spotted a DJ in the corner, but the room was dark with colorful lights flashing over everything.

He had eyes only for Keelin.

The closer he got to her, the more annoyed she seemed to get. She put her hands on her hips and glared at him. The movement of her hands made her pseudo-dress pull taut, the laces stretching over the full mounds of her breasts, pulling back just enough so that her nipples were almost popping out.

Nipples he'd only seen when she'd been about to shift. Soon he was going to kiss and taste them. Because she was *his* alone and they both fucking knew it.

"What the hell do you want?" she rasped out in what he was certain she meant to be a demanding voice but came out almost a whisper.

"You."

Pure anger flared in her eyes. "You don't get to have me!"

He tried to speak but couldn't make his voice work no matter how hard he tried. Aware of far too many eyes on him, he did the only thing he could think of to give them privacy. He scooped her up and threw her over his shoulder, caveman style.

"Hey!" She pounded on his back so he slid his hand up the back of her thigh, under her dress, as he turned and headed out of the room and toward the red freaking door.

She was completely bare, the feel of her smooth skin making his cock even harder. He dug his fingers into her ass cheek and she stilled immediately. Just touching her soothed his anger. He was still furious she'd let some asshole touch her, but with her in his arms he could breathe and think straight again.

In the distance he heard Bo order the DJ to turn the music back up but he ignored everything and everyone as he cupped Keelin's soft skin. She felt so damn good. Knowing he was risking her wrath, he slid his thumb in between her legs, dancing dangerously close to her folds.

He was going to imprint himself on every cell in her body, make sure she knew she belonged to him.

Her fingers dug into his side as he reached the red door, but she didn't tell him to stop. She didn't say anything, but her arousal teased his senses, the scent enough to bring him to his knees and beg just to taste her. Someone opened the door and he found himself looking at an amused vampire on the other side.

Bran bared his teeth and stalked past the guy. The hallway was plush and he recognized some paintings as originals of an up and coming painter who specialized in erotic art.

"Bran, maybe we should—"

"Enough," he growled, putting an end to whatever she wanted to say.

He ignored everything, his boots silent against the gleaming floor as he made his way down to door number eight.

He could barely hear the club outside the door and once he entered the room, he couldn't hear anything but the sound of his and Keelin's breathing. Talk about some serious insulation. Good. He didn't want anyone privy to what he and Keelin were about to share. She was his and his alone and he planned to show her how important she was to him.

The room was opulent, all golds and creams with flameless candles on every flat surface, giving the room a romantic atmosphere. Not at all what he'd expected. It was the equivalent of a five-star hotel room, though he was certain there were toys and other things in the heavy armoire by one of the walls that had things he wouldn't find in a hotel.

Though he hated to let her go, he set her on her feet before him. The second her heels hit the ground, she shoved at his chest, her expression livid, eyes narrowed. He didn't move.

"What's the matter with you? Why would you do that in front of everyone? You can't just manhandle me like that." Her voice shook and her cheeks were flushed a delicious pink as she took a step back from him. That rise in color spread down her neck and over her barely hidden breasts. God, he just wanted to shred those laces with his claws and reveal all of her. "Quit staring at my breasts," she hissed with a soft stomp of her heel.

His gaze flashed to hers. "Why? They're mine." The bold statement tore from his lips, his inner dragon in complete agreement. He was a fucking Alpha and tired of pretending he didn't want to claim her. She might think this pull between them was casual, but it wasn't for him. He wanted her for his mate and not just because of fucking biology.

Her full lips parted, her eyes widening in pure surprise. Just as quickly that surprise shifted and she let out a huff of annoyance. "Did you actually just say that?"

He took a step toward her, untamed energy like he'd never felt before pulsing through him. "Why'd you leave like that? And why the fuck were you grinding with some other male, dressed like this?" He couldn't actually be sure that she had been but it was a guess.

When her cheeks tinged a bright crimson and she glanced down he knew he'd been right. "You acted like I meant nothing to you," she finally said, her voice low, shaking with emotion. If he'd been human he might not have heard her. She looked back up at him and the hurt in her gaze did him in. Shit. All the anger he'd been feeling dissipated.

"Keelin—"

Swallowing hard, she shook her head. "It was *humiliating*. You didn't even put your arm around me or on the small of my back or...anything. I know how possessive you are and I don't care if it sounds stupid, but you acted like I was no one to you."

"You're not angry because she was walking around half-naked?"

Keelin blinked in true surprise. "You had no control over that. Don't get me wrong, I didn't *like* it." That anger was back as she said the last part.

He was an idiot. Risking her rejection, he took a step closer so that barely a foot of space was between them. He wanted to touch her so badly, but resisted. Because if he started something, he wasn't stopping. And he wouldn't be stopping tonight but first they needed to talk. Apparently. He hated talking when they could be doing more important things. "I wasn't sure what their true intentions were and I didn't want them to know you mean so much to me. It would make you an instant target."

Her eyebrows pulled together as she stared up at him. "You acted like an asshole to protect me?"

"I didn't... Damn it, yes. But I wasn't trying to act like one. I need you safe, Keelin."

"You just let an entire club full of supernatural beings know I mean something to you." Her expression turned wary then, as if she'd decided what he'd just done negated what he'd said about his earlier behavior.

"Because you let some male put his hands on you." The words came out as a growl. He grabbed her by the hips and tugged her against him so that she could feel his erection against her stomach. Screw keeping his distance. He needed his hands on her.

Her fingers splayed over his chest and he hated that there was any clothing between them. "We were just dancing."

"Yeah, with you dressed like this," he growled, a pop of anger resurfacing. He hated that he'd hurt her, but he was still pissed some asshole had touched his female. He wanted to rub his scent all over her so no male would come near her.

"Like what exactly?"

"Sex."

Her lips pulled together in a thin line and she didn't deny it. How could she when her dress looked more like lingerie. Hell, it probably was.

"With no fucking panties," he continued, letting one of his hands stray down to the hem of her dress right in the front. Instead of shoving the dress up, he let one of his claws extend and split the material, careful not to touch her skin. He sliced all the way up to the laces and kept going. They popped free one by one, splitting right in the middle until he reached the last one.

The dress fell open, hanging loose on her body.

"That's not my dress," she whispered, her eyes wide, the arousing scents she was throwing off potent and sweet. Her body started glowing, the soft gold filling the room in a bright, beautiful light.

"Did you let that bastard touch you?" He didn't know why he was asking. He should just let it go. But some dark part of him needed to know as he devoured her with his eyes, desperate to get his hands and mouth all over her. Now he finally understood why his brother was so fucking pussy-whipped over his mate. Females made you insane. But he knew Keelin was worth it.

She hesitated. "My hips."

"Not these?" he asked, sliding his hands up over her ribs and side until he cupped the full mounds of her breasts. They were surprisingly heavy, her nipples hardening against his palms. He hated that his fingers were calloused, that he could mar her soft skin in any way.

But she shuddered and arched her back at his touch, her eyes going heavy-lidded. She still hadn't answered so he pinched her nipples lightly, needing her full attention. Her eyes flew open, her breath hitching in her throat.

"Did he?" he demanded softly.

She shook her head, her gaze falling to his lips. When she licked her own, he didn't fight his groan. He wanted to capture her mouth now, hard and demanding, but he held back. Instead, he placed his hands on her shoulders and slowly turned her around. A giant mirror was on one of the walls—the one next to the huge bed they'd be using very soon—and he wanted her to see herself. To see how utterly beautiful she was in his arms.

He looked like a thug next to her, but he didn't care. Her long blonde hair fell down around her face and breasts in waves. Her peaches and cream skin was flushed pink everywhere, her gray eyes glowing an incandescent silver. Sliding his fingers under the leather straps at her shoulders, he pushed the ruined dress off her until it fell in a heap at her feet. Soon he was going to bury his face between her legs.

Leaning down, he nipped at her neck, then earlobe, his gaze on hers in the mirror. He slid a hand over her stomach and down to her mound. He cupped it possessively and was pleased when she sucked in a breath at her unmistakable wetness. "This is mine too."

She swallowed hard again but didn't respond. More importantly, she didn't argue.

But it wasn't enough. "Say it." He needed to hear the words. Needed to know she wanted him as much as he wanted her.

She held his gaze, stared back at him in the mirror, her eyes dilated with arousal. "I'm yours."

It felt like a giant fist reached into his chest and squeezed his heart. Bran inhaled deeply, letting her scent and her words flow into him. The hand at her mound tightened as everything male in him bellowed in triumph. She was his and by the time they left this room she'd know it in every cell of her body.

CHAPTER THIRTEEN

When Keelin's hand slid down over his, essentially cupping herself over his touch, Bran's dragon rippled beneath the surface just like when he'd first met her in Montana. She made him crazy, made him understand how a male could give up everything for a female. Deep down he knew he'd do anything for her. It didn't matter that they were still getting to know one another. Everything about Keelin called to him.

Unable to stop himself, he raked his teeth against her neck again, knowing he was playing a dangerous game. She wasn't ready to mate, his teeth shouldn't be anywhere near her neck.

She moaned and her eyes drifted shut as she bared her neck to him. Damn it, no. The way she made herself vulnerable with him meant she trusted him.

He wouldn't take away the mating choice from her. He couldn't do that and live with himself. His damn dragon had other ideas.

"Will you touch yourself for me?" he whispered next to her ear.

He watched her in the mirror, not surprised when her eyes flew open. He sensed her apprehension and not for the first time he wondered if she was a virgin. The thought of her with any other male made him crazy, but at the same time the thought of being with a virgin was terrifying. He was barely civilized half the time. He was not the male to take her virginity. When she didn't respond, he continued. "Are you a virgin?"

She shook her head, but he sensed her apprehension still, pushing against the surface. That bright gold glow dimmed a fraction. *No!*

"Are you nervous then?"

Her shoulders relaxed a fraction as she nodded. "Yes," she whispered. Her honesty humbled him.

Even though he'd originally brought her in here ready to fuck raw and hard he realized they'd be doing things differently tonight. He was surprisingly okay with that. Because he wanted Keelin anyway he could get her. Pathetic? He didn't care.

"Will you stroke your clit so I can watch?" he asked, his gaze clashing with hers in the mirror. The sight of her in front of him, completely naked and open to him, with him behind her, bigger, stronger and so damn brutal-looking—it made him want to be gentle for pretty much the first time ever. And this moment was more important than ever, because it was with Keelin.

Instead of responding audibly, she squeezed his hand, silently telling him to move. He did, but only sliding it higher to cup one of her breasts. As he did, she slowly started stroking herself, watching him intently.

Her breathing increased as her finger moved slowly, unsure at first. Watching her like that made him desperate. A low growl built in his throat at the sight.

When he started teasing both her breasts, rubbing his thumbs over her nipples, she let her head fall back against his chest, becoming more at ease. Even with her heels on she was so much shorter than him. He loved watching her like this, wanted to remember this forever.

Mesmerized by her stroking, he nearly jerked away from her when he realized the ceiling and every other surface in the room was coated with a pale gold flame. It wasn't burning them and it wasn't high, only an inch or so. Just as it registered for him, she saw the flames in the reflection of the mirror and froze.

Keelin turned in his embrace, her eyes supernova. "What—"

"It's me." His brother had told him this could happen when or if he ever mated. Bran hadn't been sure he believed him but it was clear he'd started the mating process. Something he'd already known, but seeing the actual manifestation of how his clan mated made him even more determined to claim her. To protect her from anyone and anything.

"Is this part of the Devlin clan's..." She trailed off, clearly not wanting to say the words. Because mating was apparently off-limits.

In a thousand fucking years he never thought he'd want to settle down but now that he'd found the right female he hated that she was so damn resistant to mating. How could she not feel the pull that he did? He wanted to crawl out of his damn skin.

"Yeah," he rasped out. "Don't worry though. I won't..." Now he couldn't finish the thought. But he wouldn't bite her. It didn't matter that they were both showing signs of the mating with her glow and his fire, until he bit her while he was inside her, he couldn't solidify their link. And he was through talking. He needed to watch her come for him, then push inside her and make her his.

Cupping her mound again, liking that she was now facing him, he slid a finger inside her with no warning. She was so slick, so wet. And would taste amazing.

"Oh," she moaned in surprise, leaning into him, her fingers sliding up his chest in a way he was coming to crave.

Even if he was still clothed. That was about to change soon too. Crushing his mouth over hers, he grabbed her by the hips and walked backward to the giant bed. Bigger than a California king or even the custom-size beds dragons tended to get, he'd never seen anything so big—which told him this was likely for multiple partners.

He snarled at the thought of sharing her, the sound ripping from him as Keelin's legs hit the back of the bed. At least he couldn't scent anyone else in this room. Bo must keep these places beyond clean.

"On the bed." He knew he probably sounded like a domineering asshole but those were the only words he could force out.

She didn't seem to mind, her breathing shallow and the scent of her desire overwhelming him as she continued to move backward. The pale gold fire covering the bed opened up for her, flickering all around her, but not touching. His cock ached as he watched her stretch out in front of him, her long hair falling around her face and breasts in waves. He couldn't wait to fist her hair and pull her head back so that she bared her neck to him— no, damn it. He had restraint.

Moving quicker than he ever had, he stripped naked before crawling onto the edge of the bed. When he met her gaze he realized she was staring at his erection. She looked nervous.

Frowning, he stayed where he was, still crouching, even though every fiber in him wanted to take her. He reached out and gently picked up one of her ankles. Slowly he started removing the heeled shoe. "What are you thinking?"

"That you're huge," she blurted. Her cheeks turned pink and he knew she wasn't trying to stroke his ego.

He slipped off the first heel then moved to the next, savoring the feel of her soft skin against his palms. She said she wasn't a virgin and he believed her but that didn't mean she'd been with shifters before. Because most dragons were big, especially the males. "Have you ever been with one of our kind?"

Those cheeks went from pink to crimson as she shook her head. "Just a human."

He nearly swallowed his tongue at the way she said 'a', as in singular. Fuck him. He couldn't help primal pleasure that punched through him knowing he'd be her first shifter. And her *last*. No one was going to touch his female. He was going to make sure she enjoyed this so much she'd never want to leave his bed.

He was going to have to go a hell of a lot slower than he'd planned. His cock throbbed almost painfully between his legs. Well tough shit for him.

Discarding the second shoe, he moved in between her legs, thankful that she easily spread them for him. Even her legs were slender and delicate-looking. Every inch he moved closer, the stronger her scent of desire grew and the brighter her own light illuminated the room.

He crouched down, dropping his head to her inner thigh, breathing in the heady scent of her arousal. His mouth watered. "Lay back." A soft order.

She hesitated for a moment before letting herself fall against the silky cover. He nipped the sensitive skin of her inner thigh and she jerked, her hips rolling. Smiling against her leg, he moved higher.

She skated her fingers through his short hair, digging into his scalp. Oh yeah, he didn't want her to let go. Unable to wait any longer, he moved fully between her spread thighs, sliding his hands up the inside of her legs as he moved. Without warning, he ran his tongue along her wet folds.

She jerked against him, maybe in surprise or just pleasure, letting out the sexiest moan he'd ever heard. He wondered if that human had ever kissed her like this or if this was her first time. He licked her again, savoring her taste and wondering if he'd ever get enough of her. She was fucking perfection. He'd never imagined he'd be with a female like her. Now he couldn't imagine being with anyone but her.

"Bran." His name tore from her lips as he continued stroking and teasing. Hearing his name on her lips made him even more possessive than he thought possible. He slid a finger inside her, not surprised by how tight she was. She was so damn slick he knew he'd have no problem sliding right into her tight body. And he was the one turning her on so much.

His balls pulled up tight at that thought, but he was making sure she came first. Because it didn't matter how many lovers he'd had in the past, he knew that once he got inside her, he wouldn't be as long as he wanted—not the first time. It was one of the reasons he hadn't let her touch him in that booth yesterday.

Flicking his tongue over her clit as he started stroking two fingers in and out of her, he grinned when he felt the tips of her claws scrape against his scalp. The bite of pain was welcome, letting him know she was losing control.

"Faster," she demanded, her voice hoarse.

He increased his pace and the pressure of his tongue until her inner walls clenched tighter and tighter, the ripples of her orgasm starting.

"Bran!" she shouted and tore her hands from his head as her back arched against the bed. He heard the sound of ripping material as she writhed against his face and fingers, the slickness of her pleasure coating his fingers.

"You're mine," he growled against her, unable to stop the words from escaping.

As her orgasm punched through her, he withdrew his fingers and crawled between her legs. Though her eyes were half-open and she was coming down from her high, she reached for him, clutching his shoulders and pulling his face down to hers.

He cupped her face between his hands as he positioned himself between her legs. Slowly, he pushed past her folds, trying to give her time to adjust.

"Do it," she ordered, her breathing out of control, as if she couldn't wait to feel him inside her.

Unable to wait any longer, he slid into her, the feel of her tight sheath almost too much for his barely-there control. Slanting his mouth over hers, he began pumping into her with no damn finesse. He'd wanted to be gentle, but she wrapped her legs around him and dug her heels into his ass. Urging him, harder and harder.

It was too much. Everything about her was too damn much. He could feel his flames licking higher around them but ignored everything except the sensuous female beneath him.

Her breasts pressed against his chest as he slid his hands into her hair, cupping her head. The need to hold her, to dominate her, it was so fucking overwhelming he could barely breathe. He'd never understood the mating frenzy before, could barely understand it now. All he knew was he needed this female more than he needed his next breath. And he wanted her to need him the same way.

He reached between their bodies and tweaked her clit. She pulled her mouth back from his, her expression pure bliss as he felt her begin to tighten around him once again. Because of pleasure he was giving her with his body.

Bran lost it. Tingles raced up his spine and his balls pulled up tight as he buried his face against her neck. He desperately wanted to bite her, but held back. Barely. He inhaled that dark winter scent, knowing it would be imprinted on him forever. This female, their first and definitely not last time together, would always be with him.

His canines extended, the urge to bite, to mark, intense. When his climax punched into him, he grabbed her hips, knowing he'd bruise her and not caring. He wanted her to carry his mark and if she wouldn't carry it on her neck, in her scent. At least for now. The scent was only temporary, but soon she'd accept him. He'd just have to convince her.

The pleasure seared all his nerve endings as he cried out her name. It was too much and not enough. It would never be enough. Inhaling her scent, he nuzzled against her as his orgasm began to fade and as she slowly stroked her fingers down his back.

"That was amazing," she murmured. "I never really imagined..." she trailed off and though he wanted to hear the rest of her thought, he didn't have the energy to ask.

He wasn't sure how long they lay there intertwined, with him just breathing in her sweetness, but eventually he realized he likely weighed a ton. Rolling off her, he fell onto his back next to her and before he could pull her to him she was cuddling against him, running her fingers over his chest as if she couldn't get enough. His fire and her glow had dimmed now that they'd finished making love, but he knew it would be back, probably as soon as they started up again. He didn't plan to wait long.

"That was amazing." Her voice was a whisper against his skin. "Is it...always like that?" Her hesitation slayed him and when she looked up at him he saw how vulnerable she was making herself.

It humbled him that she trusted him enough to open herself up. He cupped her cheek, stroking his thumb against that satiny skin as he shook his head. "It's never been like that for me. You're fucking perfect."

She smiled at his words and lay her head back against his chest, her body molded right against his. Right where she should always be.

"I'm just sorry your dragon is so hell bent on mating with someone as fucked up looking as me," he murmured, keeping his voice light even though he wasn't joking at all. God, everything about her was perfect. It was no surprise she was so resistant to mating with him. He couldn't blame her, even if it sliced him up inside. Dragons were such a beautiful species but he'd gotten screwed in that department. Not that he'd ever cared before. All that shit was superficial. In his former job he'd seen ugly deeds committed by such beautiful people.

To his surprise, she snorted and smacked his stomach. "Bran Devlin, you're the sexiest male I've ever met. If you want me to stroke your ego you're out of luck." Then, to his utter fucking surprise, she slid her hand lower and grasped his already hardening cock before looking up at him. Her smile was an erotic mix of uncertainty and wickedness. "But I don't mind stroking this."

Her sincere words rolled through him, flooring him. But he lost all thought as she stroked once, twice—He pinned her flat on her back again, pushing his cock into her tight grip. Tonight wasn't over by a long shot.

And this thing between them wasn't ever going to be over. No way in hell. He wasn't letting her go.

* * *

Bo pulled the last of the cash from the biggest bar's cash register and shut the drawer. Everyone, except security, his employees and those still behind the red door, had left.

Even if he hadn't heard Nyx's heels clicking along the floor, he would have been aware of her approaching before he saw her. He was just that attuned to her or something. Whatever it was, when she sat at the bar, her arms crossed over her chest, he was surprised she seemed more confused than fearful. All the vamps in the club were leaving in droves and he'd decided to close up early.

"Okay, so be honest, what the hell is going on because that's not a light show. Is it?" she asked, looking up at the ceiling where a pale gold flame coated every inch of it and the walls. When she met his gaze she simply looked perplexed.

It wasn't burning anyone and it wasn't hot, but the vamps had decided not to take a chance. And Bo had sent Cynara home just in case the fire turned real. She was half-vamp, half-demon so he didn't think she'd be affected because of her demon side, but he hadn't wanted to take a chance with his sister. Fire was incredibly deadly to vamps. He'd told everyone it was just magic, but no one had really believed him. Which was fine with him. Even though he'd never closed early before he didn't mind doing it now. It meant he could spend more time with Nyx.

"I honestly don't know."

Her blue eyes narrowed. "You have an idea though."

He wasn't sure how she always seemed to know when he was holding something back. A grin tugged against his lips. He glanced around to make sure no one was within earshot before looking at her again. "This is a guess only, but I think it has something to do with Keelin and Bran. Dragons mate differently than any other shifter on the planet."

"You think they're mating?" she whispered, eyes wide.

He shrugged. "They're fucking at least." Although there was no way Bran didn't want more. There was no doubt after his display earlier.

To his delight, Nyx's cheeks flushed pink. The female was so innocent sometimes it killed him. "Oh. Well I guess that's not surprising. I can't believe he carried her off like that. It was so, so... caveman."

Bo snorted and started dividing up the bills in front of him. He'd have done the same damn thing in Bran's situation. Hell, he might not have been as civilized. Bo was just glad the male hadn't burned the place down. When they were hunting a mate, shifters usually didn't care who got in their way.

Right about now, he understood that attitude. Though he didn't plan on taking Nyx behind the red door. He wanted her in his home, in his bed where he'd never taken another female. And they'd have days and days of privacy because he wanted her all to himself, wanted to show her so much pleasure that she'd be exhausted with it.

"You're not surprised?"

"No." He thought about just leaving it at that, but looked up at her, pinning her with his gaze. "If my female was grinding on some other male I would have done worse."

Nyx's eyes widened. "Really?"

Against his better judgment, his gaze dipped to her mouth, his thoughts straying to an image of Nyx spread out and naked on his bed, looking up at him with those wide, beautiful eyes. "Yep. Provoking some types of males, shifter or not, can be dangerous."

"You would never hurt a female." Her words were soft, but he heard the unspoken question there.

He didn't like that she even needed to ask. He might be half-demon but he'd been raised by a human mother. "Never. But that male wouldn't have been so lucky if he'd had his hands on..." Bo wanted to say 'you' so fucking badly, but he held back. He had to play things right with Nyx. She was too damn sweet. "My female," he finished before returning his attention to the money.

Nyx didn't say anything after that and that was fine with him. Some days he thought she might understand what he wanted from her, but others she seemed so oblivious. He was starting to get edgy. Males and females had been flirting with her all night. That wasn't exactly new, but it didn't mean he liked it. All his protective instincts had flared to life. Instincts he'd never had until now. And feeling protective of his sister was way different than how he felt about Nyx. "How were your tips?"

"Fantastic." He glanced up to find a big grin on her face. "Those snow leopards were incredibly generous. And a little scary."

He stilled at her words, his body growing taut. "Did they threaten you?"

She blinked in surprise, then grinned, shaking her head. "No, I don't mean scary like that. I just mean, out of my league, uh, sexually." Nyx broke his gaze, looking at the bar behind him. "They wanted to take me to one of the rooms and were pretty explicit with what they wanted to do to me," she said in a rush, meeting his eyes again, her embarrassment clear.

He dropped his hands behind the bar so she wouldn't see him clench them into tight fists. "Were you interested?" He knew she wasn't, but the thought of anyone embarrassing her infuriated him.

She shook her head immediately. "It was flattering, but no way. Even if I was interested in females, three at once? I can't even imagine." There went that blush again, making his cock harden immediately.

He had no doubt what those shifters had wanted to do to her because they probably wanted the same thing as he did. Except he'd never share. That was something he had in common with the majority of shifters. At least when it came to Nyx. He would never share her with anyone.

He was almost certain she was a virgin too. Something that had never appealed to him before. But the thought of being Nyx's first? He rolled his shoulders, easing his demon back down. Yeah, that thought got him way too excited.

CHAPTER FOURTEEN

"What if they don't like me?" Victoria shifted nervously against the passenger seat next to Drake. Their private jet had arrived early and instead of bothering anyone in the Petronilla clan they'd just rented a vehicle.

It was five in the morning and even though Victoria knew Drake's recently awakened parents would have been more than happy to pick them up, she also knew that they couldn't drive. That had been Drake's excuse for not alerting them or anyone else, but she knew the real reason was that he was nervous to see them. He'd been kidnapped from his clan and sacrificed to open a Hell Gate at the age of twelve almost fifteen hundred years ago. His entire clan thought he'd been killed and had mourned him. Only recently had he been released back into the world and his parents had been in Protective Hibernation. To say they were dying to see their child was an understatement. But Victoria knew her mate was incredibly nervous about the meeting. He was still adjusting to this new world and for so long he'd thought his parents had abandoned him. He hadn't actually said but she wondered if he was still trying to come to terms that they hadn't.

"They will love you. *Everyone* loves you," he growled, as if he thought that was a bad thing.

She laughed lightly. "Well that's not true, but you're biased." For the past week they'd been visiting the Devlin clan to spend time with one of his oldest childhood friends and Drake had been acting like a rabid dragon to any male who looked at her. He'd always been protective, but his behavior had been extreme, especially for him. She finally realized that he wasn't on his home turf and surrounded by way too many of his own kind that he didn't know. His dragon side hadn't been able to let his guard down. She'd been extra affectionate and they'd had a ridiculous amount of sex but even that hadn't soothed him. Not that it was a jealousy thing, it was a protective thing because Drake knew she was his.

So when they'd gotten the news that his parents had woken up, she'd been doubly thrilled to return to their new home in Montana with his clan.

"It's okay to be scared," she finally said into the quiet of the vehicle. They were so close to his clan's gated land. They owned a huge ski lodge in Montana but the clan members all lived in their own little village. It reminded her of a winter wonderland and she absolutely loved running around in her wolf form in the snow. The change was huge from living on the Gulf Coast.

Drake glanced at her, his gray eyes flashing silver for a moment. "I am *not* scared."

Snickering, she reached out and grabbed his large hand. "I didn't mean to offend your big, bad alpha self."

At her words, he smiled, his expression relaxing. "I'm just ready to get home. And...yes, I'm nervous. What if... they don't like *me?*"

The question coming from him seemed ludicrous. From all accounts his parents had mourned his loss greatly, his mother starting a war with another clan when he'd gone missing. But his kind of fear was normal. She squeezed his hand and brought it up to her lips. "They're going to love you. In fact, I guarantee they never stopped."

Drake just grunted and turned his attention back to the road. The rest of the trip was in silence. Once they reached the gates Victoria called Conall even though Drake didn't want her to. Sweet Lord, he really was nervous.

Her new brother-in-law answered on the first ring. Not surprising since he was the Alpha and always seemed to be on call. "Hey, V. Everything okay?"

"We're just pulling up to the gates."

"Your flight wasn't supposed to arrive for a couple hours." She could hear the frown in his voice.

"Yeah, well, we're early."

"You should have called, I would have picked you up." He actually sounded hurt, which made her feel bad.

"Blame your brother." She looked at Drake, who frowned. "Yeah, I'm throwing you under the bus for this one," she murmured.

"Come to my house. My parents are here. I will wake them at once." Conall disconnected before she could respond.

"Did you hear that?" she asked.

Drake's knuckles were clasped around the steering wheel so tight they'd turned white. "Yes."

"It's going to be okay, I promise." Victoria hated seeing Drake upset, especially after everything he'd been through. Thrown into Hell so young, betrayed by someone he loved and trusted, only to escape fifteen hundred years later into a world so much different than the one he'd lived in before.

"I know. Thank you." He reached for her hand now, linking his fingers through hers as they drove down one of the quiet streets.

Huge homes dotted up the side of the snow-covered mountainside and not for the first time had she thought that it looked like something out of a postcard. She'd never need to go to Switzerland because their clan's land was the picture of it.

The energy humming through both of them was almost palpable as Drake parked in front of Conall's home. Similar to the high iron gate at the front of the property, there was also one around Conall's two-story place.

Victoria jumped out before Drake could round the vehicle and open her door. He wrapped his heavy arm around her shoulders when he reached her, pulling her tight against him before he pushed open the gate. It fell quietly back into place as they strode up the long, stone

walkway. She couldn't be sure, but she was almost positive they were being watched. Drake must have sensed it
too because he stiffened and looked to the left. She followed his gaze to the oversized windows of one of the
sitting rooms.

She couldn't see inside because of the reflective material on the glass but she would bet money his parents
were in there waiting. Watching.

The door opened before they'd reached the top step
and a tall, blonde woman who was a taller, slightly older
looking version of Keelin stood there, her dark, penetrating eyes filled with tears and a fierce maternal love.

Victoria hoped Drake would understand as she
smoothly slid out of his embrace, knowing his parents
would want to hug him. The other woman didn't even
glance at her, just rushed forward and wrapped her arms
around Drake, full-on sobbing. Drake murmured something Victoria couldn't understand and rubbed the
woman's back. No longer awkward or stiff, his voice was
rough. Not wanting to intrude on such a private moment, Victoria hurried through the door to be faced
with Conall and a male who was definitely Drake's father; Dragos senior.

The three males all looked so much alike it was stunning. Drake's father was probably six feet five, just like
Drake. With dark hair, and gray eyes gone silver in that
moment, he was a slightly older version of Victoria's
mate. And just as fierce.

Conall wrapped his arm around her shoulders, tugging her close and kissed the top of her head. "Can't believe you didn't call," he muttered.

She nudged him in the side. "You try saying no to him." Because Victoria found it pretty much impossible. Drake had her wrapped around his finger.

Chuckling, he held out a hand and said, "Victoria, this is my father, Dragos. Father, your oldest son's mate."

Victoria loved the formal way the Petronilla clan members sometimes spoke. They were all centuries or in some cases, millennia, older than her so it made sense. Her palms were actually damp as she stepped away from Conall and held a hand out to the huge male.

To her surprise, he scooped her up into a giant hug and squeezed tight. "My son told me how you saved Drake. My mate and I are forever in your debt."

Well, she hadn't actually saved him. She'd killed his bastard of a cousin who'd betrayed and sent him to Hell but Drake had saved all of them by destroying all those demons escaping from that Hell Gate. Her mate was truly amazing. She didn't think now was the time to explain that though. She tried to answer but Drake's father was squeezing her so hard she couldn't get any words out.

"Dragos, let the poor girl go. She's so small you will hurt her." At the sound of an admonishing female voice the grip around Victoria loosened immediately.

At five feet ten, she'd never been called small before, but compared to most dragons she guessed she was. Victoria landed on her feet only to be pulled into another hug by the blur of motion that was Drake's mother. Luckily the female didn't squeeze her too hard. "We are so pleased to meet you. So, so pleased that our son has found such happiness after such tragedy." Her words were muffled against the top of Victoria's head but they were going to make her cry.

Out of the corner of her eye, Victoria saw Drake's father pulling him into an embrace and she couldn't help it, tears started streaming down her cheeks. When his father made a choking sound that came out a lot like a sob, her throat tightened as she held back more tears. Her mate had thought he'd been alone and unloved for so long and now he had everything returned to him.

She glanced over at them and saw Drake's face in profile. His eyes were closed and she could tell he was fighting a ton of emotion himself. He'd learned at a young age to protect himself so she knew he was going on instinct.

When the female let her go, Victoria wiped at her tears and smiled at Drake's mother. They hadn't been officially introduced but she knew the woman's name was Arya. "I'm so excited to meet both of you. We got here as soon as we could." She'd actually told Drake to just fly ahead in his dragon form but he'd refused to leave her so they'd flown by airplane instead.

As she spoke, Drake moved quickly to her side, wrapping his arm around her in that familiar protective way she loved. She also figured he was using her as emotional support. His posture was stiff but she scented how pleased he was. It was something she'd never smelled before but the sweetest spring rain scent rolled off him. "I know it's early and... Victoria and I haven't eaten," he said awkwardly. He did that often, just said seemingly random things, but she understood what he was trying to convey.

"Neither have we," his mother said, looking at him with such love it was a punch to the solar plexus. "Maybe Conall will cook for all of us? I find I do not like those automatic ovens."

Conall snorted good-naturedly. "I'll cook, but first I'm making coffee."

As they all headed into the kitchen, Victoria nudged Drake and nodded toward his mother. She hoped he understood her meaning as she slipped out of his embrace again. The male's mother had lost her oldest child and Victoria could easily see how much the female wanted to be next to him. It was clear the father did too, but since the initial embrace he was just as stiff and awkward as Drake was.

So Victoria hurried over to Dragos and hooked her arm through his, taking the male by surprise as they walked down the hallway. "I want to hear about Drake as a child."

The male grinned such a paternally proud smile it sliced right through Victoria. Behind her she heard Arya telling Drake what a fine male he'd turned out to be.

Victoria inwardly smiled and forced herself not to start crying, even if they would be tears of joy.

After an hour of talking, drinking coffee and eating, Victoria could finally see Drake starting to relax. It was clear his parents were proud of the male he'd become. When her cell phone started ringing, she frowned because she recognized the ringtone. It was still really early in the morning. Her jacket was hanging on the back of the swivel chair at the kitchen island. By the time she pulled it out it was on the third ring.

"I'm so sorry, normally I would never be this rude, but this is really early, especially for Keelin to call so—"

Arya straightened in her seat. "My daughter is calling you?"

"Well, yeah."

"Is she all right?"

Victoria flicked a glance at Drake who just shrugged, before looking back at his mother. "I'm sure she is. Sometimes she works late so she's probably just getting off and forgot what time it was." It was possible anyway.

Now the female frowned. "Work? Where is she working?"

"Mother." Conall's voice was hard, taking Victoria by surprise.

Her phone had stopped ringing but she slipped off the seat. She needed to call Keelin back.

"Do not answer that question, Victoria," Conall ordered.

Victoria had no idea what was going on, but she was *not* getting in the middle of whatever it was. She avoided looking at Arya, feeling the female's penetrating gaze on her. It was too early for family drama. "I should call her back," she murmured to Drake.

Her mate nodded and excused them both, coming with her because he didn't like to let her out of his sight even for a moment. She so loved the male.

"You think everything's okay?" Victoria whispered as they exited into the hallway.

He nodded. "Yes, but Conall hasn't told them where she's living and we are not to tell them. I forgot to mention it to you. Keelin wants her space for a while."

Victoria's eyes widened. "Oh, wow. I feel like such a jackass now. I shouldn't have said anything at all."

"You didn't know." Drake shrugged in that casual way of his and she was glad that he seemed more like himself. He nodded down one of the hallways and she knew where he was leading them. Her favorite room, Conall's library. Before she could respond the phone started ringing again.

Victoria answered immediately, holding the phone up to her ear. "Hey, Kee. Is everything okay?" she asked as Drake held open the door to the library.

The female groaned. "Yes and no. I slept with Bran and it was fantastic. I can't believe I never knew sex could be this amazing."

Next to her Drake growled, and Victoria cringed, knowing he'd just heard his little sister say she'd slept with a male. "Um, before you go any further you should know that I'm with Drake and he just heard that."

The female just groaned then sighed. "That's okay. I'll tell you all about that stuff later. There's so much going on here right now that I'm not sure who to talk to."

"Is Bran with you?"

"No, he's getting us food but he'll be back soon. He knows I'm calling though."

"So what's going on?" Victoria hadn't heard anything from her packmates and she talked to at least one of them every day.

"Demons attacked me outside of Bo's club and then Akkadian demons attacked me and Bran last night. And it wasn't a normal attack either. Those things just appeared out of nowhere. As in, out of thin air. With no Hell Gate as an entrance. Have you ever heard of that happening?"

Victoria's stomach twisted at what the female was saying. That seemed almost unimaginable. Akkadian demons were horrific creatures who wanted nothing more than to destroy this planet. "No. Neither has Drake," she said when he shook his head, his frown deepening.

That didn't mean Victoria didn't know where to start looking. She'd been researching the creatures for the past few months and had already known a good bit about them before anyway. If Keelin needed her, she was going to do everything in her power to help. "Why

don't you tell me everything? And start at the beginning."

CHAPTER FIFTEEN

Keelin tossed her phone onto the heavy dresser next to the giant bed and stretched her arms over her head. She was glad to have filled Victoria in on everything. If anyone could help her it was that brilliant female. But the truth was, Keelin wasn't nearly as concerned as she should be about the demon attacks.

She was way too caught up in Bran Devlin. The very sexy male who was currently off grabbing food for them. After last night—well, this morning—she was deliciously sore and starving. He'd been completely insatiable and if she was being honest, so was she. She hadn't been able to get enough of him after that first time.

He was so generous and sweet in bed it had taken her off guard. The demanding, dominating, possessive part of him hadn't been a surprise at all. And truthfully neither had the generous side of him. But when he'd made himself vulnerable to her; that had been shocking. Not that she'd let on she realized he was being serious when he'd been disparaging of his looks.

On one level she could understand because as a whole, dragons were exceptionally beautiful. She'd always felt like a bit of a freak because of her small stature compared to everyone else. Standing out among her kind wasn't something she liked. So she could imagine Bran didn't like it either. Still, he was so well, *male,* and absolutely magnetic she couldn't actually see that he'd have insecurities. Not when that Alpha from last night had made it clear she wanted an alliance and more with Bran. Keelin was certain females probably threw themselves at him.

That thought made Keelin's claws come out. Literally. She winced when she sliced through the silky gold sheets again. They'd have to change them. Again. The room and en suite were incredibly well stocked with anything they might need. Including some very interesting toys and gadgets, some of which she wasn't even certain how to use. And she was too embarrassed to ask Bran. He definitely had more experience than her, that much was clear.

When the door opened she started to tense until she scented him. Her male. That abrupt thought made her frown until Bran stepped inside with a covered tray. The half-smile he gave her made a rush of heat flood between her legs.

His eyes flashed bright green with lust before settling to their normal color. Even though he'd told her that he could only see out of one eye it was difficult to tell other than an occasional cloudiness in one.

"Did you talk to Bo?" she asked, her hand straying down between her legs, wanting to tease him. He loved watching her touch herself and she was going to indulge him as much as she could.

Bran let out a low growl and set the tray on the nearest flat surface before prowling toward the bed. "Yes," he said, stripping off his shirt. "He's going to reach out to some contacts."

"Have you contacted Finn yet?" Because she still hadn't informed him about the Akkadian demons.

When Bran paused on the edge of the bed, his jaw tightening, she knew he hadn't. "I'll call him later," he muttered, moving to shuck his pants.

"No way. I just called Victoria and told her everything. We need to tell Finn now."

Bran cursed and grabbed his phone out of his pants pocket before he finished stripping them off.

Keelin continued stroking herself, knowing it was making Bran crazy. His cock was thick and hard against his abdomen as he had a brief conversation with the other Alpha. She nearly laughed at the way he was speaking, so clipped, his voice strained as his gaze zeroed in on the juncture between her thighs. Eventually the call ended and he set his phone down next to hers, still never taking his eyes off her.

"You're teasing me on purpose."

"Of course," she murmured. Then, feeling bold, said, "I looked in that armoire."

He stilled, his entire body and all those hard lines and muscles pulling tight. "And?"

"There are some interesting toys in there." She tried to sound sultry or seductive, but failed, barely getting the words out. A male like Bran had a ton of experience and she wondered if he'd want to use toys.

"Do you want to use any?" She couldn't read his tone or expression.

He'd know if she lied so she went for honesty. "No."

Pushing out a ragged sigh, seemingly in agreement, he crawled onto the bed. He moved in between her legs and batted her hand away from her mound to replace it with his own. He covered her mouth with his and began stroking her wet slit with a very talented finger.

"Seeing you touch yourself makes me insane," he murmured.

"I can tell." His fire and her light filled the room, coating all the surfaces again. There was no way either of them could hide their attraction to the other. Not that she wanted to.

Chuckling against her skin, he nibbled along her jaw. "If we were mated—"

She stiffened at his words and was glad when he stopped talking. She didn't want to hear whatever it was he planned to say. Even though she was starting to care for him so much it scared her, she just couldn't think about mating. Couldn't think about anything past this amazing experience they were having together. She didn't want to lose her independence.

Pulling back, he looked down at her, his expression fierce. "Afraid to talk about it?"

"Bran," she started, placing her hands on his shoulders and smoothing her fingers over him. He'd know if she lied, so she tried to think of a way to evade the answer. She wanted to clutch onto him, wrap her legs around his waist and let him impale her. What she didn't want to do was talk.

"You're mine, Keelin." There was a possessive edge to his voice that sent a thrill down her spine.

She couldn't lie to herself, she liked the sound of it. "Bran—"

"Say it."

"I don't want anyone else but you." That was the truth and all she was willing to say right now. She knew how forceful Alphas were and unlike her mother or someone like Rhea, she wasn't a warrior. And she was terrified that if she mated with a male like Bran she'd lose her independence. She'd just gained it, so it was too scary to think of losing it again. She wasn't Alpha mate material anyway. She wasn't a warrior in any sense of the word. And she didn't want to be. What the heck were their dragon sides thinking, choosing each other?

He let out an angry sounding growl and shoved off the bed. Before she could mourn the loss of him or ask what he was doing, he stalked to the heavy gold-framed mirror. To her surprise he lifted it off the wall. She watched his muscles flex as he moved back to the bed.

She pushed up onto her knees and wrapped her arms around herself, watching as he set the thing against the headboard. "Why?" she whispered, not trusting her voice.

"You're going to watch me fuck you, watch me take you from behind and know you're mine. Fight it all you want, sweetheart, you are *mine*."

Raw heat surged through her at his declaration. Before she had time to analyze her reaction, not that she was sure she wanted to, he was on her, covering her body with his bigger one, his mouth devouring hers in a crushing kiss.

Keelin moaned into him, loving his display of dominance as she wrapped her arms around his back and dug her fingers into it. He rubbed his thick length against her slit, teasing it over her clit, but refused to penetrate her.

The sensation was so erotic her nipples pebbled impossibly tight. She arched into him, rubbing against him like a feline in heat and not caring. She just wished he'd thrust into her, but every time she tried to maneuver to make him, he grabbed her hips and held her in place.

It frustrated and turned her on more than she thought possible. Her inner walls contracted impatiently, demanding he hurry up.

"Bran!" She grabbed the back of his head and tore his mouth from hers. "Do something."

The grin he gave her was completely wicked. Taking her by surprise, he flipped her over onto all fours so that she was facing the mirror. He hadn't been kidding about watching.

Her face heated up as he straightened behind her. With massive shoulders, a muscular body that made her wet just thinking about, and too many nicks and scars covering him, telling of a hard warrior's life, he was the perfect male specimen. And he wanted her. That thought sent another rush of heat between her legs.

He gave her another one of those grins, clearly scenting her desire. She didn't care because she scented his too. Spicy and overwhelming, it had her scooting back and trying to make him do what she wanted.

"So impatient," he murmured, running a hand down her spine and butt. He didn't stop, but kept moving lower until he reached between her legs. He slid not one, but two fingers into her and let out the sexiest growl.

Pleasure spiraled through her at the feel of him.

Grasping onto her hip with his other hand, he slid his fingers back inside her. "So fucking wet. All for me. Say it."

"You know it's all for you." She met his gaze in the mirror, mesmerized by the masculine picture he painted.

He looked as if he wanted to say more, but couldn't find the words. Instead he fisted her other hip and did what she'd been waiting for. With one hard thrust, he was inside her, stretching and filling her in a way that made her entire body light on fire.

His gold flames reached higher around her body as he began thrusting, his expression hard and fierce as he slid in and out of her. The fire teased the ends of her hair but didn't burn, just seemed to caress her.

Abruptly he thrust hard, pushing deep inside her and staying there. Her inner walls clenched around him, needing more friction. He slid one hand from her hip until he reached between her legs and tweaked her clit. When he started teasing, she clenched around him tighter and tighter. She was so close to climaxing.

Because of the angle of their bodies and her breasts, she couldn't see him stroking her clearly in the mirror, but she saw enough. Watching that determined expression cross his face as he brought her pleasure is what pushed her over the edge.

Her orgasm slammed into her, just as intense as all the others she'd had last night and this morning. Her nerve endings tingled with the sharpest awareness as she let her head fall forward.

Bran slid his arm under her, his forearm between her breasts and his hand around her neck, fingers wrapped gently and forcing her to look up. The move took her completely by surprise. "Watch." He nipped her ear after the soft order.

She stared at him in the mirror as he continued thrusting, her climax almost too intense to bear. To her delight, he found his release too, even as he continued strumming her clit. Finally she swatted his hand off, unable to take any more, her body falling limp in his arms.

Slamming into her one last time, he pulled her body tight against him, the heat of his release warm inside her. He raked his teeth against her neck, his gaze bright in the mirror as he watched her.

She swallowed hard, trusting him not to mark her, effectively mating with her against her will. The crazy part was, her inner dragon was clawing at her to let him—beg him to make that mark. But she couldn't.

Letting out a soft growl she thought might be a little frustrated, he nipped her earlobe enough that she felt the sting. "Deny it all you want, sweetheart," he said, loosening his grip and slowly withdrawing from her.

Even though it was clear he was annoyed with her, he turned her and pulled her into his arms, feathering kisses over her face and lips. "We've got to head out to meet Bo in a bit but shower with me first."

She grinned against his mouth as she linked her fingers behind his neck. "Was there a question in there?"

He lightly pinched her butt. "No. Shower. Now." Then he hoisted her up so that she had to wrap her legs around him and slid from the bed.

Times like this she found she loved his bossy, dominating side. She just wondered if they could find a balance where she didn't have to lose who she was. As soon as she had the thought, she shut it down. She couldn't start playing that game and doubting herself.

CHAPTER SIXTEEN

Victoria scrunched her nose when she picked up her mug of coffee and smelled it. Cold. Gah, how long had she been sitting here reading over these books? Setting the mug back down on the desk where she sat in Conall's huge library, she stretched her arms back over her head.

She glanced over at the sound of the library door opening. Her heart rate kicked up a notch. It was Arya. She'd been really sweet when they'd first met but after she'd discovered that Victoria knew about Keelin's whereabouts she'd been hard to read. Not cold exactly, but reserved. And the female wasn't supposed to be here. Drake was spending time with his parents, just the three of them, and Victoria had taken advantage so she could research for Keelin.

Unfortunately she was coming up with a big pile of nothing. Well as far as the Akkadian demon thing. She thought she might have a lead on the visions Keelin was having and the carvings on the Moana dragon. Bran had sent her a picture and while the markings were obscure, she was pretty sure she'd nailed something down. And it wasn't good.

Victoria smiled at Arya, a tall blonde, a truly stunning woman who could be a supermodel if she wanted. Her cheekbones were ridiculous and those dark eyes missed nothing.

Thankfully Arya smiled back. "Hello, Victoria. I brought you coffee," she said, holding out two steaming mugs. The female moved like a true predator, like someone thousands of years old and skilled in all sorts of combat. "Drake said you could probably use a refill."

She stood and rounded the desk. "Thank you but you didn't have to do that. I know you all are spending time together."

Arya just gave her a small smile and handed one mug to her before sitting on the edge of another desk with papers, notebooks and books strewn about. Victoria wasn't exactly neat when she was researching. When she realized Arya wasn't about to leave, she lifted the mug and murmured "thanks" again before moving back to her seat.

"What are you working on?" Arya asked, her eyes shrewd.

Oh, she knew very well. Or at least guessed this was about Keelin. And the truth was, Victoria needed the help. She wouldn't be betraying Keelin by being honest with Arya and the female would want what was best for her daughter. As long as she just didn't tell the female where Keelin was she wouldn't feel bad. Besides, this was bigger than that anyway, especially with those demons reemerging again.

"Something for Keelin." It was clear her honesty surprised Arya.

"Will you tell me?" The maternal concern she saw in the woman's eyes was real.

Sighing, she tugged the rubber band holding her hair in a ponytail free, letting her hair down. She was starting to get a headache. "I can tell you a little and I think I need your help."

"Is my daughter in trouble?" She pushed up from the desk and moved a heavy, tufted chair so that it was across from Victoria's desk.

Victoria avoided confirming or denying outright. "She needs some help. She was with...someone and Akkadian demons appeared out of nowhere. It wasn't a Hell Gate entrance, but thin air was more like how she described it." Victoria winced at the rage-filled expression on Arya's face. She knew—or hoped—it wasn't directed at her. Ignoring the female's reaction, she continued. "This is going to sound crazy but I think I might have found a reference for the type of beings that could—"

"Gods and demigods." Arya was matter-of-fact.

Victoria blinked. It had taken her forever to find that in research and this female just knew. Oh, she would definitely be using Arya for information in the future. "Yes. So...it's true then? I guess I wasn't certain if they were even real."

"They are but they live on a different plane than this one. The gods grew tired of humans back when I was a young girl. And when I went into Protective Hibernation nothing had changed. They haven't been around for thousands upon thousands of years. I've never had any interaction with one. Demigods, yes, gods, no."

Momentarily stunned, Victoria leaned back and rubbed her hands over her face. "Wow. Okay." She tried to regroup with the knowledge that the references she'd read were actually *real*. She felt as if her reality had just shifted in a huge way. "I guess it makes sense. Demons and half-demons are real. And God is real." She nearly snorted at herself. Considering she existed and was mated to a dragon shifter, she should be able to believe in damn near anything. But still, this was pretty wild. There were gods and demigods too.

Arya nodded. "You are correct."

"So how do gods and demigods fit into this equation?"

"Different religions." A simple, concise answer.

One Victoria didn't have time to question further. At least not at the moment. She would go back to that later because the nerd inside her was going to have a field day with questioning Arya. "So would you say you think it's unlikely that a god released Akkadian demons?"

Arya nodded again. "Yes. I can't imagine gods bothering themselves with humans or shifters. They have little to prove and truly, care nothing for this plane. They are... snobbish assholes, I think is the right phrase."

"From what I've read demigods are created in multiple ways but the most common is from a mating with another non-god."

"Correct. They occasionally sleep with humans but more often than not they'll choose a supernatural being. Not dragons though."

That was interesting. "Why not dragons?"

Arya smiled, the sight truly terrifying, for her predator lurked in her gaze as she spoke. "Because some of us can destroy them."

Well that was interesting. And yes, *scary.* She read something about winged creatures and gods and planned to go back to it later. It might have been a reference to dragons. Victoria so wanted to ask more questions but forced herself to stay on track. Keelin needed her help. "So let's say a demigod did this. Would there be a reason for a demigod to target Keelin or dragons specifically?" Okay she was on dangerous ground here and knew it. This was the woman's daughter and it was abundantly clear how overprotective the female was about Keelin. Well, all her children really. But Victoria needed answers for her friend so she had to play with fire just a little.

"Has someone targeted my daughter?" Arya's eyes went pure dragon, her brown irises completely eclipsed by a sapphire-green animal who was not happy.

"Someone is targeting dragons in the area Keelin is living." Not a lie so the female wouldn't scent it. Victoria was definitely going to have to choose her answers correctly or risk pissing off this powerful woman.

Arya's mouth pulled into a thin line as she looked at a spot over Victoria's shoulder, deep in thought. Suddenly she paled, all her focus on Victoria once again. "My mother imprisoned a demigod thousands of years ago, when I was a child. She didn't send him to Hell because she'd been weakened too much, but the imprisonment should have been enough. I..." Cursing, the female stood, rubbing her hands down the front of her black slacks in a nervous motion. "He promised retribution on all the females of her line. Victoria, Keelin is too weak to be on her own right now. She's not a warrior. If this male is after her I have to know where she is." Panic thrummed through her words and Victoria almost broke.

"She's been having visions. She told me that she's been seeing strange things when she looks at people. It's only happened a couple times but each vision has been dark in nature and true, as far as she knows."

The Alpha's eyes bled back to human, the scent of her surprise almost strong enough to knock Victoria off her feet. "You are certain?"

She nodded. "Keelin has no reason to lie to me and besides, I don't think she even knows how to lie." Victoria cleared her throat, hoping a quick change in subject would slightly distract Arya. "A dragon was found dead, killed, with carvings on her body. From what it sounds like the female was tortured in human form but then shifted to her dragon form. The carvings seemed to have stayed even after the shift, and I found something..." She searched her desk and pulled out one of the pictures she'd printed out before sliding it over to the woman. "I could be wrong, sometimes these references are so vague, but these carvings seem to be a power spell of sorts."

Frowning deeply now, Arya nodded. "Yes. The carvings are from an ancient people, older than me. Power spells such as this can be used for a variety of things but not many beings would know how to use them. Used on a dragon, the simplest answer for why is that it increases the potency of the blood for drinking."

Victoria hated that she was right. Whoever had carved into the dead dragon was obviously a monster, but still, she hated being right.

Arya was silent, seemingly digesting everything Victoria had told her. Victoria needed to learn more about demigods and their weaknesses, if one was indeed targeting her sister-in-law. Before she told Arya where Keelin was, she was at least going to give her friend a head's up. And she needed to talk to Drake first and get his opinion. She couldn't just completely betray Keelin like that. Knowing she'd likely anger Arya when she told her she'd have to wait, Victoria decided to tell her one more bit of information. Hopefully it would ease Arya's mind.

"Listen, I know you're worried about Keelin and I'm going to tell her everything you told me so she under-

228 | KATIE REUS

stands the dangers. She's not stupid and will likely come
home when she knows but just so you don't worry she's
with a very powerful Alpha right now. Well, technically
two since she's in another one's territory, but Bran
Devlin is watching out for her twenty-four-seven so
she's—"

Arya let out a growl so terrifying Victoria shouted
and ducked under the desk as the whole house seemed to
shake. Okay, the windows actually were shaking. Holy
crazy, what had she said?

A loud bang reverberated through the room, as if a
door had been thrown open. Arya's growling came to a
halt and a second later Drake was kneeling in front of
Victoria where she still crouched under the desk, his
expression worried. "Are you okay?"

"I think you should be more worried about your
mother," she whispered.

He pulled her into his arms as she crawled out from
under the desk. Victoria knew she was a strong shifter,
but she had no problem admitting that the other female
was older and a lot more powerful and yeah, Arya was
freaking scary. So she wasn't even embarrassed that
she'd hidden under the desk. Her wolf side had wanted
to jump out the freaking window and high-tail it for the
mountains.

Instead of doing that, she wrapped her arm around
Drake and soaked up his strong embrace as he shielded
her with his big body, holding her close as he faced Arya
and Dragos, who were both staring at them.

Dragos looked confused as he glanced between the two of them. "What's going on?" he asked.

Victoria looked up at her mate, not quite sure what she'd said to piss the other female off but she had a feeling it was Bran Devlin's name.

"Our daughter is with Bran Devlin," Arya said, practically breathing fire. Literally. The scent of it filled the air.

"He's a good male," Drake responded before anyone else could speak. "When Keelin and Victoria were taken he searched the mountains for them with all of us. All his clan members present did. And our former clan member Fia is mated to his brother—who is one of my oldest friends."

Victoria knew that his parents actually hadn't been aware of Drake's friendship with Gavin Devlin, but that was a conversation for another day.

Arya took a deep, steadying breath. "Yes, your brother told me of your friendship with Gavin. But Bran Devlin is strong. He is a *true* Alpha. And Keelin is…" She trailed off, looking at her mate for support.

The big male pulled her into his arms and for the first time since meeting her, Victoria could see a little bit of softness in the woman.

"My sister is smart," Drake said, breaking into the silence, an annoyed note in his voice. "And Bran would die for her."

That made both of his parents still before turning to them again. "He wishes to mate her then?" Dragos asked, his voice a growly rumble.

Drake nodded. "I believe so."

"It's worse than I thought," Arya muttered.

"What's worse?" Victoria asked, not understanding any of this. "Keelin is with a trained Alpha warrior who will kill and die for her. Not only that, but she's smart and capable all by herself. She was smart enough to call me for help in research and it's not like the two of them are going it alone. They're working with…" She paused, not wanting to give away too much. "Other shifters and supernatural beings who will be able to help them."

Arya's gaze narrowed on Victoria. "Other supernatural beings?"

Victoria snapped her lips together and glanced at Drake. She wasn't answering any more questions. Not when it was clear she'd said enough already.

Drake shrugged though. "A half-demon, probably a vampire or two and wolf shifters. She is completely protected right now."

And that was when both parents exploded into a litany of curses.

* * *

Bo half-smiled at Nyx as she entered his kitchen. He had to leave soon to meet Bran and Keelin, but wished he could stay with her instead. She was off work tonight and he had no problem leaving his employees in charge. Especially after the shitty night he'd had last night. Some asshole had thought he could get too rough with a female so he'd had to clean house.

He'd been more than happy to destroy that guy but it meant he now needed to inform Finn Stavros. Not that he minded the Alpha shifter, but it sometimes rubbed him the wrong way to check in with anyone. Even so, the Alpha needed to know Bo had killed someone in his territory. Technically he didn't always tell Finn about things like that, but enough people who worked for him last night knew what had gone down that it would be in his best interest to be honest.

"What are you up to this afternoon?" Nyx asked, heading for the refrigerator. Wearing jeans and a navy blue shirt with some kind of frilly lacy thing going on, she looked good enough to eat. As always.

He glanced down at his phone as a ding signaled an incoming text. Keelin and Bran were running late, not that he was surprised. An employee had already told him the gold fire was back at the club so he'd known they'd been busy this morning. Another text dinged as soon as he responded to Bran's. "Just meeting Bran and Keelin for lunch," he said while pulling up the next message.

"Can I join you or is it business stuff?"

He quickly responded to the unfortunately unhelpful text from an old contact before setting his phone on the countertop of the granite-topped island. "It's supernatural business, but I don't think they'll have an issue." And he wanted her with him so he didn't care.

"What's going on?" she asked, leaning against one of the counters, water bottle in hand.

"Nothing you need to worry about."

Her eyes narrowed. "Why, because I'm female?"

He blinked at the pop of annoyance in her voice, surprised she'd even ask that. "Uh, no. But unless you know what kind of being can pull an Akkadian demon out of Hell without the use of a Hell Gate then you don't need to worry."

Nyx's fingers tightened around the bottle, the crinkling sound of the plastic seeming overly loud in the kitchen.

"Look, everything is fine," he said soothingly. He wouldn't bother trying to comfort most people, but he didn't want Nyx to worry about anything. "Those things won't come near my club no matter who pulls them from Hell." Something he wouldn't necessarily bet money on, but he wanted to reassure her. And he didn't plan to let Nyx out of his sight anyway.

"It's not that. It's just... When are you meeting them?"

He glanced at the time on his phone. "Forty-five minutes."

"Okay, well, I think I know what pulled them from Hell. Were the demons in this area?"

Sliding off his chair, he nodded, more than curious about what she might know. "Yeah." He moved around the island, now realizing it wasn't fear on her face, but something else. "What do you know?"

Her expression became shuttered. "Maybe nothing but I'm pretty certain there's a demigod in the area. If anything could do it, it's him."

Shit, a *demigod*. Why the fuck didn't he think of that? Bo wanted to punch himself. It was so obvious but hell, there weren't many of them in existence. And how the hell did Nyx know about this? "Him?"

"Well, I don't *know* him or anything, but the demigod is a male. I'm certain." Her softly spoken words were filled with authority.

He took the bottle from her hands and set it on the counter next to her before placing his hands on either side of her, caging her in. "How the hell could you possibly know that?" He wanted to know what the hell she was. Over the last month or so he hadn't pushed her about what kind of supernatural being she was, but clearly it was time for her to come clean.

"Because I sensed him a couple weeks ago. More than once," she whispered, her blue eyes dilating as she stared at him.

Shock reverberated through him and he thought he knew the answer but decided to ask anyway. "How'd you do that?"

She bit her bottom lip and it took all his control not to follow suit and nibble on her. "Because I'm one too."

CHAPTER SEVENTEEN

As Keelin sat next to Bran in a booth at the quiet diner he'd chosen for an early lunch, she read over one of the files he'd printed out on the missing dragons. So far the main things they seemed to have in common was that they'd all been to Bo Broussard's club and liked sex. Well that and the obvious factor of them being dragons. Which she was certain was the reason they'd been taken. And none of the dragons taken were warriors. That was telling in itself. If you wanted to target a dragon, you'd go after a non-warrior.

Dragon blood was powerful and could be used in a myriad of sick ways for power hungry monsters. Her brother's kidnapping when he was a boy and subsequent sacrifice was a prime example. She couldn't think of that though, it made her want to cry.

"Bo just texted, said he and Nyx are almost here and have something big to tell us. Might have a lead." Bran didn't look at her as he spoke, instead scanning the quiet parking lot.

The diner was across the street from the beach. She'd been there before and it normally had a decent amount of foot traffic but today it was quiet with only a couple customers.

Their server returned again with a half-full pot of coffee in her hand. Her long, espresso-colored hair was pulled back into a ponytail and she looked dead on her feet. Faint dark smudges were under her eyes, pulling at Keelin's heartstrings. Especially since the human gave them a real smile that met her eyes. The girl looked to be maybe nineteen years old.

"Y'all need a refill?" she asked, looking between the two of them.

When her gaze focused on Keelin she got another flash of insight. Everything around her faded away as she saw the woman sitting in a nursery, feeding a baby maybe six months old a bottle. The room was small and she could hear what the woman was hearing, shouting from next door as if someone was having an argument. The woman looked at a digital clock on a dresser. It was two in the morning. And as loud as if they were her own thoughts she felt the woman's fears; that she wouldn't be able to pay the rent due in a few days, wouldn't be able to continue paying for childcare and wondering why her once loving boyfriend had abandoned her when she got pregnant with their child—after she'd moved from another state to be with him. The girl wanted to call her parents and tell them about their grandchild, but was too afraid. They'd hated her boyfriend and she was ashamed that they'd been right.

"I'm okay," Bran murmured to the server, breaking Keelin out of her spell and she murmured the same and glanced away as emotions overwhelmed her.

"What's wrong?" he asked as the woman moved on to the next occupied booth, which was thankfully on the other side of diner.

Keelin swallowed hard and shook her head. "Got another vision. Just sad, not dark like the other two." The woman's problems made Keelin feel like an ass. She might have an over-protective family but there were certainly worse things. And no matter what, she had financial stability, something she understood that so many didn't have. People like their server just trying to make ends meet. "How much money do you have on you?" she asked, digging into her purse and pulling out her wallet. She had about eight hundred dollars.

He raised an eyebrow. "I think about a grand but I can get more. What's up?"

"We're giving all our money to our waitress when we leave."

"Okay."

She frowned at him. "You're not going to ask me why?"

He shrugged. "No."

"Okay then." Her brother would have grilled her. Heck, any male from her clan would have. "Can I ask you something?"

Nodding, his gaze flicked to the parking lot again. He was always so watchful, something she appreciated.

Even though she knew the booth behind them was empty she looked over her shoulder out of instinct. Still empty. "That vision I had of you and that other male.

Will you tell me more about it?" It had been so dark and bloody, Bran's rage so intense. She wanted to know more about his past. It didn't matter that she told herself this thing between them was casual, she was falling harder and harder every second.

He scrubbed a hand over his face before setting it on her thigh. He rubbed up and down her leg almost absently. "Before I moved home to take over for my clan I worked in black ops for the government."

She blinked. Okay, maybe she should have expected it considering the file she'd seen earlier. But she'd wondered if he'd stolen the file. Twisting slightly in her seat, she stared at him. "Seriously?"

A short nod. "Yep. They have a supernatural division."

"I...can't even say that I'm surprised. It makes sense that they know about supernaturals with all this technology." After coming out of her Protective Hibernation she was still adjusting to everything. Smart phones made her feel stupid sometimes, but she still liked them.

A ghost of a smile played across his lips. "Pretty much. The male I killed was a traitor to not only this country, but his own kind. He was selling out supernaturals. I understand that political allegiances can change, but betraying shifters?" His jaw clenched tight. "That is unforgiveable." The deadly bite to his words sent a shiver down her spine. Reaching out, he surprised her by gently cupping her cheek and stroking his thumb over her skin.

She fought off a shiver, this time a very good one. She loved it when he touched her.

After a long moment, he dropped his hand and his expression grew pained. "He'd been a friend. Or I thought he was. We all did. He was a bear shifter and my boss took it harder than all of us."

"August?" She remembered what Nalani had said, though Keelin pushed thoughts of the other female away. It made her want to unleash her claws.

"Yeah. He's a bear too and they'd been close so... I killed that fucker so August wouldn't have to. It was a dark time in my life."

She took the hand he'd dropped back into his lap and linked her fingers through his, pulling it into her lap and squeezing. "I'm sorry you had to do that."

He lifted his shoulders in what he probably meant to be casual but he couldn't hide the pain in his gaze. "Just one of those things."

Killing a friend wasn't something anyone should have to do but she didn't say that aloud. She lifted his hand and kissed it. "Why did you tell me?" Because when she'd asked she'd thought he would deny answering her. It would have given her another reason to keep a wall between them. Now it appeared that Bran was determined to knock down any reason for her to keep resisting him.

"I trust you and... I think of you as an equal, no matter what you think. Am I going to be crazy fucking protective of you all the time?" The question came out as a sexy, possessive growl. "Yep," he answered, continuing. He clearly wasn't apologetic about it either. Which was annoyingly hot. "But that doesn't mean I don't respect you. I trust you to keep my secrets."

Keelin squeezed his hand again, unable to find her voice. Even if she could she wasn't sure what to say anyway. Damn this male. He was knocking down all of her defenses against him. The reasons she had for not wanting to mate were solid. She didn't want her independence limited ever again.

But those were reasons for not wanting a mate in general. Bran wasn't just anyone. The longer she was around him, the harder it was to put him in the category of Alpha asshole. Because he simply wasn't one. Was he dominating and possessive? Oh yeah. But he actually listened to her. And now he'd told her something so huge about his past.

"Was it hard to leave your job?" When his parents had died he'd probably had the Alpha role thrust onto him. Kind of like how her own brother Conall had when she and their parents had gone into Protective Hibernation.

"Yeah." His jaw tensed, his gaze so intense it was like he could see right through to her thoughts. "No one's ever asked me that before."

"Really?"

"Well, not many people know what I did before but even my brother didn't ask. Everyone just assumed I'd take over and since there was no one else I stepped up."

God, she just wanted to give him a big hug. But she didn't want him to think she felt pity for him. There was no way she could ever pity this male.

"How are they dealing with your absence?"

"They're fine. I've been in contact with Gavin and other warriors a couple times a day and unlike my father, I delegate. And honestly, I don't give a shit about them right now." Her eyes widened at his blunt remark, but he continued. "All I care about is you."

Her mouth parted slightly at his words and she earned a low growl from him when she absently licked her lips.

"I want to kiss you so bad, but if I do, we'll give the humans too much of a show," he rasped out.

She only nodded because that was about all she could manage. If their lips touched, she knew she'd start glowing. That would be bad enough, but if Bran's fire coated this place it would be complete pandemonium. After the way he'd shared part of his past she wanted to tell him more about herself. "When we all thought Drake died, my parents went into lockdown mode. Conall was only ten but they started training him hard to make sure he was able to always defend himself."

Bran's eyebrows pulled together. "But they didn't train you?"

Annoyance surged up as she shook her head. They should have, but she'd been a 'princess'. Looking back she couldn't believe the way her mother had treated her. Not when the woman was so fierce herself. "No. They coddled me to the point that I wasn't allowed to leave our land even in dragon form."

"That's…"

"Not good, I know." He was clearly too nice to say anything disparaging but dragons needed to roam free, especially when they were young. It was part of their biological makeup. Hers had been stunted. "For so long I felt like I had no choice in anything, but the truth is, I've always had choices. I'm just now exercising my right to live on my own terms." She hated that female she'd been and couldn't imagine going back to living like that. She might not know what she wanted in life, but it wasn't that. The last year out of her Hibernation had taught her a lot about herself.

With his free hand, he cupped her cheek again. His touch grounded her and made her senses go haywire at the same time. She had to consciously lock down her hunger for him so she wouldn't accidentally start glowing.

"I don't want to clip your wings," he murmured. "Pun intended."

A grin pulled at her lips even as his words struck her deep. That was her deepest fear, being stripped of who she was and given no freedom again. "I think I'm beginning to see that." It was true. Which meant she needed to start looking at this relationship as having a future, not just something casual. That alone was scary. She'd never thought she wanted to be mated and now to have this perfect male pursuing her…

He dropped his hand suddenly and turned toward the window. "They're here."

Keelin followed his gaze and saw Bo and Nyx getting out of a sleek two-door black sports car. They both looked grim. A healthy dose of worry slid through her veins. Nyx was usually smiling and the fact that she was here was odd enough. When Bo had texted to let them know the female was coming it had been a surprise since they'd just been expecting him.

The little bell above the door jingled as they came inside, with Bo scanning the place the same way Bran had. Bo nodded when he saw them. To Keelin's surprise, Bo had his hand on the small of Nyx's back as they approached and only dropped it when they slid into the booth opposite her and Bran.

After the waitress took their drink orders Bran said, "Talk."

Nyx's eyes widened at his tone but Bo didn't seem surprised at all. "Nyx has something to tell you. Something that's not going to leave this fucking table." He said it as a warning, clearly to both of them, but his focus was on Bran.

"Deal." Bran didn't hesitate in his response. When Bo looked at Keelin, Nyx nudged him.

"Keelin would never say anything," her friend muttered before half-smiling at Keelin.

The statement made her think that this was about Nyx specifically. Keelin returned her friend's smile.

"Look, whatever's going on, if there's a threat to Nyx we'll do anything we can to help."

"It's not that." Nyx stopped talking as the waitress returned with two more coffees. Once Nyx had ordered a surprising amount of food for just herself, because Bo apparently wasn't eating, the server left them in peace again. With no one sitting remotely close to them, they had privacy.

Keelin's purse was against her thigh and she felt her phone buzzing in it, signaling an incoming text, but she ignored it. "Are you in trouble?"

"No, but Bo told me about the Akkadian demon thing. There are almost no beings with that kind of power except a god or demigod."

Next to her Bran let out a low curse. "Fuck me."

"Yeah, I had the same reaction. Can't believe I didn't think of it," Bo muttered, clearly as disgusted with himself.

Keelin hadn't thought of it either though. Demigods were so rare and gods weren't even on this plane anymore. They didn't *like* anyone but themselves. She felt her phone buzzing again, but kept ignoring it as Nyx continued.

The female bit her bottom lip nervously, looking back and forth between Bran and Keelin.

"Just say it." Bo rubbed her back in another surprisingly intimate gesture.

Nyx sighed. "My mother is the goddess of chaos and my father is a fae prince."

Bran and Keelin both went still, but Keelin spoke first. "You're a demigod?" she whispered.

Looking miserable, Nyx nodded. "Yeah. Both my parents are horrible, horrible people. I have nothing to do with either of them, but... okay, let me back up a little. A couple weeks ago I sensed another demigod in the area for the first time. It was vague and brief and I'm not sure who the male is, but I know what I sensed. I sensed him again recently."

"Where'd you feel him?" Bran asked.

"Bo's place."

"You remember the times and dates?" he continued, his tone all business.

"Well, yeah, I think. I was working when it happened both times." Nyx looked unsure why he was asking and Keelin didn't know either.

Bo started nodding, however, clearly understanding. "I keep backups of all video surveillance. We'll head back there as soon as we eat."

"It's a good start," Bran said.

"There's more," Nyx continued, her nervousness seeming to grow. "I could contact my mother for help. She'd be able to track the male to where he was, but like I said she's a horrible being. She'll demand a payment in return for her help—and it won't be something you'll want to give. Plus she'll hate all of you. Bo on principal since he's a half-demon but you two..." Nyx shook her head. "She actually might not even meet with you, Bran. I can sense your power so it might keep her away."

Keelin nodded, understanding. Dragons were one of the few beings that could destroy a god. It wasn't easy and she didn't know of it ever happening in the last five or six thousand years, but it could theoretically happen. It would have to be an incredibly powerful dragon shifter though.

"Why can't I sense yours?" Bran asked, saying what Keelin was thinking.

Supernatural beings often put off a pulse of sorts. It was the only way she could think to describe it. And Bran's pulse of power was incredible, like a throb of energy rolling against her. Nyx's on the other hand felt like a breeze on her skin.

Nyx's cheeks flushed. "I keep it locked down. Easier that way if people think I'm just a random supernatural being." She inhaled deeply then pushed out a long breath, glancing around almost nervously.

As she did, Keelin could feel an incredible pulse of the female's power roll over her. And almost simultaneously a car alarm in the parking lot went off, the blare loud and obnoxious. At the same time one of the waitresses dropped a tray of drinks and the sound of glass shattering in the back of the kitchen filled the air as more dishes were destroyed.

Nyx grimaced and must have cloaked herself again because Keelin could no longer feel her power. "That's another reason I keep everything locked down. I don't have much control on my powers and things always seem to go haywire around me no matter what I do.

And my mother refuses to train me. She thinks causing havoc and well, chaos, is wonderful. She thinks I should embrace the insanity of my heritage, even going so far as to call it a 'gift'." Nyx rolled her eyes, her annoyance clear.

Their server chose that moment to arrive with a plate of pancakes, sausage, hash browns and a side of fruit for Nyx. She smiled as she placed the food in front of Nyx. "We had a bit of an accident in the back and your plate is the only one unscathed."

Nyx didn't look surprised by that as she smiled and thanked the woman.

"Hey, how much money do you two have on you?" Keelin asked abruptly.

Bo and Nyx both appeared surprised but Bo shrugged. "Maybe a couple grand."

"Five hundred, I think," Nyx said.

She shouldn't be surprised. Supernaturals tended to use cash in favor of credit cards. It was accepted everywhere and there was no chance of it being declined. And of course it was harder to be tracked if you paid for everything in cash. "Good. I would appreciate it if you'd give your money to our waitress when we leave. She needs the help. I'll pay you guys back."

Nyx shrugged. "It's no problem. You don't have to."

Bo lifted his shoulders in the same casual way. "Same here. I'll leave it."

When they didn't question her further, Keelin wanted to kiss both of them. Bo might try to pretend to be a badass demon—and he clearly was—but he also had a soft streak no matter how much he might want to hide it. "Thank you, guys."

Next to her Bran squeezed her leg gently before wrapping his arm around her shoulders and kissing the top of her head. She leaned into his hold, loving his protective embrace.

Once they were done, they all cleared out, with Keelin leaving the stash of cash under Nyx's empty plate along with a note urging the girl to call her parents. Keelin knew the girl would wonder about the note, but figured it didn't matter. She wanted to nudge the human into getting help from her family. She waited in the parking lot, watching to make sure the woman got the money. When the server saw it, her eyes widened and she started crying as she put the cash into one of her pockets.

Feeling satisfied, Keelin looked over at Bran. "We can head out now."

"That was really nice."

She shrugged, liking the feeling of what they'd done but wanting to do something more. And on a bigger scale. "Yeah."

"What's that hesitation in your voice?" he asked as he steered out of the parking lot. They'd be at Bo's club in less than ten minutes.

"Nothing really. Just thinking I'd like to do something... more organized and for more people, I guess." Something that gave her purpose.

"Are you talking for supernaturals or humans?"

"Both. Women specifically." She'd had a good life with a supportive clan and loving parents, even if they'd smothered her to the point where she'd basically run away. But she knew what it was to feel powerless, to not have a voice. And women of all species dealt with that on a much bigger scale. She wondered if there was something she could do about that. Her clan certainly had the money and she could dedicate her time.

"Good. You should if that's what you want to do. I'll help in any way I can." He gave her a half-smile as they pulled up to a stoplight and her heart about flipped over.

The male was too sweet for his own good. That was the moment she realized she wasn't just falling hard, that she'd absolutely, positively, fallen over a cliff and there was no going back for her.

He must have sensed her change in mood because he frowned and reached out to gently cup her cheek. "What's wrong?"

"Nothing, I…" She racked her brain trying to think of something halfway decent to say. "I just remembered that Victoria texted me a few times." The female's name had popped up on Keelin's phone as having texted and she still needed to check her messages.

He dropped his hand and pulled through the now green light as she grabbed her phone from her purse. When she saw the message on her phone she willed herself not to outwardly react as she read through the multiple texts.

Talked to your mom. Don't worry, she doesn't know where you are. Demigods and gods can release demons w/out using a Hell Gate. She told me a demigod wants to destroy your line. Your grandmother imprisoned one a long time ago. She's vague on deets but is scared for you. A demigod could have nothing to do with it, but when I told her about the Akkadian demons, she confirmed that a demigod could release them. I believe her, this isn't a ploy to get you home. I'm telling Finn about the demigod angle. He needs to know what's going on. Call me asap. You need to talk to your mom. She knows more than she's letting on, I feel it.

"What is it?" Bran asked.

Casually turning her screen off, Keelin slid her phone back into her purse. Closing her eyes, she leaned her head back against the headrest. "Victoria confirmed that demigods and gods are capable of releasing Akkadian demons." Keelin decided not to say anymore. She needed to call Victoria first and she wanted to do it while she was alone. She cared for Bran—okay, more than just cared for him—but she needed to get more details and she needed to see her parents.

And if she did that, she definitely wasn't taking him with her. Unfortunately she knew he'd argue the point and just follow her no matter what she did.

She wanted to face her parents on her own and show them she was living her life on her terms. If she was being honest, she also didn't want to subject Bran to her likely irate parents. It wasn't rational but her parents would flip out if she brought an Alpha with her to their clan's land. When they'd gone into Protective Hibernation the world had been so different and she didn't think they'd adjust well to seeing her with a male from a neighboring clan. And she didn't want to deal with that crap right now.

Not when she needed information about this apparent demigod who wanted to destroy her line. It would be much easier to get that info without Bran there.

The thought of leaving him, even for just a couple days, clawed at her insides, making her dragon edgy, but she knew what she had to do. She'd leave him a note of course, but she knew he wasn't going to be happy. She closed her eyes again and resisted the urge to massage her temple. She couldn't let him know that she was planning anything. If he had even an inkling of what she planned to do, he'd never let her out of his sight.

CHAPTER EIGHTEEN

"Should we wait for Keelin?" Bo asked as he activated the two largest television screens in his security room. He had twenty screens and even more video cameras, which were all on, but since no one was in the building other than employees right now he'd taken over the security room.

He, Bran and Nyx were all in his office ready to scan his video logs. He had a few other businesses and all those were strictly normal; meaning they were run by humans who had no idea the owner was a half-demon. For those businesses, his security feeds were all sent to an outside source and stored. But he kept all his security videos from his club stored in one place: his club. And everything was heavily encrypted. He couldn't risk prying eyes seeing supernatural happenings.

"No. She's got some phone calls to make," Bran said, the energy rolling off the male intense. He wasn't nervous, but the male was agitated.

Good. He didn't want to waste more time. Bo didn't respond as he entered the correct timeframe Nyx had given them for when she'd sensed the other demigod.

Freaking *demigod.*

He was still trying to wrap his mind around the fact that she was so powerful. Unfortunately without training she was a danger to herself and others. He knew he should care about the others part, but he was only concerned with Nyx's safety and well-being. She was all that mattered and whatever it took, he was going to find someone to help her understand and control her powers since her mother wouldn't.

"Okay," he said, motioning to the two large screens in the center of the wall. They were surrounded by eighteen other smaller screens. "The one on the left is from the first time frame and the one on the right is from the second time frame Nyx sensed the male. I'm going to run a facial recognition software program to see who shows up at the same time."

"Can you run the program for the missing dragons?" Bran asked. "I know they've all been here and I want to see how often and who they were with."

Bo nodded and keyed in the command to activate more screens. As his program started scanning the other screens, he pressed play for the two middle screens. Less than five minutes later the two middle screens paused and the face of the same man was highlighted with a green outline of dots and lines.

"According to my program, this male is the only person in a thirty foot radius to you in both time frames," Bo said, looking at Nyx. On the way to his club she'd told him that distance mattered.

"Can you run his face through your system and see if he shows up again?" Bran asked.

"I can do that and more." He turned away from Nyx and typed in more commands. "I'll run his face here and see if we can get a hit in other databases—human databases."

"I'll take care of the supernatural ones. Forward me his picture," Bran said. "Email me but text Keelin. I want to see if she recognizes him."

Bo did that first, guessing that the Alpha had a lot of resources. Then he started the scan for the male's face. As he did there were multiple soft dings, alerting them that his other program had gotten hits on the missing dragons. Glancing up, he started scanning the screens, looking at the paused images.

His blood iced over when he spotted one of them because he was in it. He was kissing one of the females and had his hand on the barely-covered breast of the other. The three of them were in an intimate embrace with him practically sandwiched between the females. Cringing, he remembered that night. His demon had been particularly edgy and out of control and he'd needed to calm down. The two females who he hadn't known were dragon shifters had propositioned him and he'd taken them up on their offer. Now he wanted to gut himself. He'd never felt an ounce of guilt about his sexual past— until now. He immediately clicked the screen off but when he looked over at Nyx he knew she'd seen.

For the briefest moment, hurt flared in her ocean-blue eyes before her expression went completely neutral. She looked away from him and back at the other screens.

"Those females meant nothing to me," he blurted, unable to stop himself. For all he knew she didn't even care but he hadn't imagined the hurt in her gaze.

She looked back at him and it was as if she was looking at a stranger. There was no warmth in her gaze now. She lifted one shoulder casually. "I don't care who you...are intimate with." There was pure ice in her voice.

Before he could respond, she looked at Bran, effectively dismissing Bo. "When we were outside the fights and I told you I felt as if we were being watched, I think it might have been the same male. The presence was almost muted, as if he had something blocking him. Or more likely he was on the fringe of where I could sense him, distance-wise, but now that I really think about it, I think it might have been him."

Bran frowned but didn't respond as he looked back at the screens. Then he started taking pictures of the screens with his phone, likely cataloguing the other individuals who'd been with the missing dragons.

Bo only had eyes for Nyx and couldn't stand her shutting him out. "Nyx, I—"

Her lips curved up into a fake smile, the sight scraping against all his senses as she took a step back from him. "If you two don't need me, I'm going to go visit with Keelin."

"We're good," Bran murmured as he swiped over the screen on his phone, likely forwarding the picture Bo had sent him along with the ones he'd taken to someone else.

But Bo wasn't *good*. He couldn't stand what was happening between him and Nyx. He also didn't know what to say to make it right. It wasn't like they were in a relationship. And he hadn't been with anyone since he'd met her. He wanted to tell her that but not in front of someone else. She shouldn't even be angry at him but if he saw some video or picture of her with two males he'd lose his shit, no doubt. It didn't matter that it wasn't rational. He hated that she thought he was some sort of male slut—even if he had been. Sort of. Sex had been the only way to keep his demon on lockdown. Until Nyx had strolled into his life. Just her presence calmed him and he still wasn't certain why.

She opened the office door and a solid glass paperweight exploded on his desk as she stepped out. It was messed up but in a dark way he liked her reaction. At least she felt something for him. He froze the pieces in midair before putting it back together then inwardly cursed.

"She do that?" Bran asked, not looking up from his phone as he typed out a message.

"Yep." When Bran didn't say anything else, Bo cleared his throat. He didn't have many friends, mainly because he found most people to be devious assholes, but right now... "Should I go after her?" He felt like an idiot that he even had to ask. But he didn't know anything about females and relationships. Fucking? Yeah, he knew a lot about that. But this emotional crap? No.

The Alpha slid his phone into his jeans pocket and looked up. "I'd give her space."

"I should talk to her though."

Bran gave him a pitying look that made him want to punch the male. "Do you have a clue what to say that will make her un-see what she just saw?"

Bo cringed. He didn't know what to say at all. "I haven't fucked anyone since I met her."

Bran shook his head, the pitying look even worse now. "Don't lead with that. At least not phrased like that."

When the screens started dinging again, he shifted thoughts of Nyx to the back of his brain—as much as he could, anyway—before focusing on the wall of frozen images. He had other stuff to worry about. He'd figure out how to make things right with Nyx later.

He hoped.

* * *

Keelin nearly jumped out of her skin at the sound of someone knocking on the door then chastised herself. Someone wanting to attack her wouldn't knock. She could barely smell anything over the scent of sex and

Bran in the room. It was as if Bran permeated everything. She went to the door and looked through the peephole. She'd noticed there was one installed in all of the rooms behind the red door. When she saw Nyx she opened it immediately. The smile on her face froze when she saw her friend's dark expression. "Hey, come in," she said, stepping back. "Is everything okay?"

Nyx nodded. "Yeah." Keelin couldn't scent a lie but that could be because of Nyx's powers.

"Seriously?"

Her friend wrapped her arms around herself and shook her head. "I'm just mad about something I have no right to be mad about. And, ugh, men are annoying."

Keelin snorted. "No kidding. You want to talk about it?"

Nyx dropped her arms. "Not right now."

"Okay. I won't push but seriously, anytime you want to talk let me know." Someone else's issues would be a welcome change from focusing on her own. "Are the guys still in Bo's office?"

A flicker of annoyance flashed across Nyx's face. "Yeah."

"Will they be there long?"

Now Nyx raised an eyebrow. "Maybe. *Why?*"

"I know someone who can help us with our problem. My problem." Because those demons and the demigod were after her, not anyone else. "It'll be a hassle but it's a lot better than you going to your mother. And it will probably save time on investigating." She didn't bother going into detail about the texts she'd received from Victoria because that wasn't the point. The point was that she could help. Keelin just needed to get over her own issues with her mother and go see the woman. And Keelin refused to let Nyx ask her own mother for any sort of favor. Not after Nyx's description of the female goddess.

"Who?"

"My mom. The only thing is, Bran can't come with me. It's complicated," she muttered when it looked as if Nyx would ask why.

"But if you tell him what you want to do, he'll insist on going, right?"

Feeling miserable, Keelin nodded, but was glad her friend understood. "Yeah. But I feel bad leaving without telling him."

Nyx glanced at the door then back at Keelin. "Leave a note for him and I can get you where you want to go in seconds. But we've got to land somewhere without any buildings or people."

"Land? I don't need you to fly with me." Keelin didn't plan on taking anyone with her. She'd get there fast in dragon form. And what did she mean in seconds?

"I can transport myself and anyone I'm touching to pretty much anyplace on the planet. It's a demigod thing." Nyx said it casually, as if this was totally normal. "My gift can be erratic though so I can't land near any structures. You said your family's land was in the mountains, right?"

"Yeah, it's near a ski lodge but our village has plenty of open space surrounding it. You can really just transport us there?" She supposed it shouldn't be surprising considering the female was a demigod but still, it was pretty amazing.

Nyx nodded. "Yes but I'll need to see a picture of where we're going. And I'm not kidding, no buildings or people in the vicinity. I… might have made a gas station implode once. It was at night and in the middle of nowhere—and no one got hurt—but it was horrible. The whole place was a ball of fire. I could have seriously hurt someone. Since then I only do it rarely and to remote places."

"What's the radius you'll need to be away from people or structures?"

Nyx shrugged. "To be safe, about a hundred yards all around."

Keelin pulled up a picture she'd taken a month ago when she'd been out flying and had landed and shifted. It was far from the village and once they arrived there she could shift and fly them both home. She held it out. "Can you get us here?"

Nyx studied it for a long moment before nodding. "I might knock over a few trees but I can do it."

"Okay, let me write a note for Bran." Guilt surged through her as she searched for a pad and paper. She hated just leaving him like this but a quick visit to see her mother without him would be so much easier and faster. He might be angry at first, but this would spare him the drama of her parents' reaction to their relationship. She could find out what she needed to know about this demigod who wanted to destroy her line, and figure out what the next step in protecting herself and Bran was. When she was done she looked up at Nyx. "Can you bring me back the same way?"

"Yes, but we'll have to land outside the building."

"And can I bring my cell phone?"

"Anything on your person will travel with you."

She took a deep breath and set the note in the middle of the bed where Bran couldn't miss it. "Let's do this."

Nyx reached out and held onto Keelin's forearm. Before she could blink it was as if she'd been sucked into a vortex of rushing wind.

When she opened her eyes a wall of snow exploded around her and Nyx, shooting high into the air before crashing back down around them. The rain of white iciness pelted them, the rush of cold a shock to her senses.

Silence reigned for long moments as Keelin looked around them. She and Nyx both sat in a crater of snow. All around them trees were uprooted completely or broken in half.

"You weren't kidding," she murmured, awed by her friend's power. "That was awesome."

"Really?" Nyx's eyes were huge, as if she was worried Keelin would be upset.

"We just traveled thousands of miles in the blink of an eye. Thank you so much for doing this." But still, it was a *little* scary to think what her friend was capable of. With a trembling hand, she pushed up and reached out for Nyx to pull her to her feet.

"The shaking is normal," Nyx said. "It only lasts for a minute."

Keelin consciously slowed her heart rate. "We're a few miles from the village so I'm going to shift and fly us but only if you're comfortable riding on me in my dragon form. Okay, saying that out loud is a little weird," she muttered. Shifting now would alleviate her jitters and give her body an outlet for the adrenaline coursing through her.

Nyx laughed. "I'm fine doing that but will your clan be okay with me? I thought dragons were pretty secretive about well, everything."

"They are but times are changing and besides, you're my friend. You're more than welcome here. And... I'm going to have to get naked. You can turn around or not but I don't want to make you uncomfortable."

"Oh, right. Uh, is it weird that I want to watch you shift? I've never seen a dragon shift before. Is that okay?"

Grinning, Keelin nodded. "I think this is a new stage in our friendship."

CHAPTER NINETEEN

Keelin glanced behind her as she knocked on Drake and Victoria's door. They were living in what had once been a guesthouse but was now theirs—unless they decided to build something else. Keelin had dropped Nyx off at her home but was going to get her friend as soon as she rounded her brothers up. Since neither of them had answered their cell phones she was coming to see Drake first. He was by far the more understanding of the two.

She'd been back in the village about ten minutes and knew it was only a matter of time before her parents found out she was here. She wanted to talk to her brothers before that happened.

Victoria answered the door, her long black hair rumpled and Drake's scent covering her.

A wide smile split her face and she practically lunged at Keelin. The taller female pulled her into a big hug. "I didn't know you were coming!"

Laughing, she returned Victoria's embrace. "It's a last minute sort of thing."

Stepping back, Victoria motioned for Keelin to follow. "Drake's upstairs but I'll get him. I'm assuming this is about the demigod?"

"Yeah. I'm—"

The front door that Victoria hadn't completely closed swung open behind them and Conall stepped through. "Keelin, I just saw you head up the walk. Why didn't you tell us you were coming?"

"I called you."

"Ten *minutes* ago. I couldn't get out of a meeting. Is everything okay?"

"Everything's good but I need to talk to Mother. And, just so you guys know, there's a demigod in my house. I'm going to get her once I've seen Mother." Translation: once she'd seen that her mom wasn't going to lose it that Keelin was friends with a demigod.

Both of them stared at her seemingly in shock as Drake reached the bottom stair, meeting them in the foyer.

"My favorite little sister," he said warmly, pulling her into a hug that rivaled his mate's.

She was his only sister but his words warmed her from the inside out. She hugged him back tightly, still amazed that he was living with them once again.

"You should have told us you were coming," he admonished.

Victoria snorted. "Lack of communication on travel plans must run in the family."

Keelin didn't know what she meant but Drake just smiled at his mate as he stepped back from Keelin.

"Where's Bran? Why are you alone?" he asked her suddenly, his gaze narrowing.

Keelin's eyebrows raised. "Why would Bran be with me?"

Drake and Conall exchanged a look she couldn't quite decipher before both focusing on her again. Their gray eyes, normally pale, were glowing silver as they watched her.

"He should be watching out for you," Drake said, condemnation for Bran clear in his voice.

"Especially since you two will be mating," Conall finished.

"Excuse me? Who the hell said I was mating him?" Keelin knew they had more important things to talk about but didn't understand her brothers' assumptions.

"We can scent him on you." Conall's expression was dark as he spoke.

"So what? Have you two mated every female you've slept with?" she demanded.

"I've only been with one female and yes, I'm mated to her." Drake looked smug as he pulled Victoria closer against him. Victoria seemed to be fighting a smile.

"That's not the point! I, gah, just forget about Bran. He doesn't even know I'm here." And she needed to talk to her mother about the demigod. When both her brothers stilled, a thread of panic slid up her spine. "What's wrong?"

"You didn't tell Bran you were coming?" Conall asked quietly.

"No. That's what I wanted to tell you. Nyx is a demigod and she transported us here. I knew if I told Bran he'd want to come and I didn't feel like dealing with the fallout from our parents. They still think I'm a child. If they have to come face-to-face with the male I'm sleeping with, I don't think they'll handle it well."

"Nyx is the one Bo has a thing for, right?" Victoria asked.

Victoria hadn't met Nyx but Keelin had told her about the female. And Victoria knew Bo since she'd lived in Biloxi for most of her life before mating with Drake. Keelin nodded. "Yes."

Conall frowned as he pulled out his cell phone. "We're going to go back to the demigod thing but give me a second." He started making calls and barking out orders that if Bran arrived on their land without warning not to attack. It was clear he was talking to their security team. He also ordered them to spread the word to everyone in the village.

"Okay, Bran has no idea I'm here and he's not going to follow me even if he did," she said as soon as he hung up.

Both Drake and Conall snorted.

"I left him a note. He knows I won't be gone long and that I'm safe." He was going to be angry at her for sure, but it wouldn't make any sense for him to fly here either via a plane or his dragon form. The trip would take too long. Besides, he didn't know where she was. She'd been a little vague on the specifics.

They both made that obnoxious 'I-know-better-than-you' sound before Victoria nudged Drake. "Your parents will be here for dinner in about half an hour but we can call them now if you'd like," she said to Keelin, changing the subject.

"That would be great, thanks. And I'll get Nyx over here. She might have some more insight about the demigod." At least Keelin hoped so. They needed all the help they could get.

* * *

Bran stared at the note in his hand before incinerating it. He hadn't meant to destroy it but his dragon clawed at the surface, rage like he'd never known pumping through him.

His dragon side knew only one thing mattered right now. His future mate had left him. Of her own volition. And left a pathetic note.

She said she was coming back. He didn't care. She could be in danger. Or hurt. And he wasn't there to protect her.

Unacceptable.

His dragon swiped at him again, its claws jagged, his beast demanding to be released so he could track his little mate down as fast as possible.

On the edge of losing it completely, he pulled his cell phone out and called a male he was certain would be truthful with him.

Drake answered on the first ring. "Yeah?"

"Is she coming to see you?" Keelin hadn't been gone long and her fucking note hadn't told him where she was going but he had a pretty good idea.

"She's here." Before he could say that was impossible Drake continued. "Her friend Nyx."

That was all the explanation Bran needed. If Nyx was truly a demigod then she'd be able to transport them to a different location quickly. "Don't let her leave," he growled, his voice more animal than man. He knew he shouldn't be giving orders to the male but couldn't stop himself.

"I don't control my sister." Drake's words were straightforward, with no malice.

But they pushed Bran over the edge. He didn't want to control Keelin either. But he hated that she'd left without him, had basically shut him out. She had to know that he'd have gone with her, would do anything for her. Without warning, Bran's dragon took over. He dropped his phone and though he tried to control himself, to stop the change, it was too intense.

The room in Bo's club was spacious but he was bigger. Ignoring the twinge of guilt, he burned a hole through the ceiling and burst into the darkening sky, destroying part of the roof as he flew through it. Ordering his invisibility cloak in place he surged through the air, savoring the feel of the wind rushing over him.

His beast was free and had one goal.

Find his mate—and convince her never to leave him again.

CHAPTER TWENTY

"**B**reathe," Nyx murmured to Keelin. "And drink more wine."

The light words from her friend made something in Keelin's chest loosen. She took another sip of the light white wine Victoria had poured for them. Victoria, Drake and Conall had disappeared from the kitchen a few minutes ago so it was just the two of them sitting at the center island.

"Who keeps calling you?" Keelin asked when Nyx glanced at her phone screen for the tenth time and silenced the call. Right about now she wanted to talk about anything that didn't involve her impending visit with her parents.

Nyx's blue eyes turned angry, the blue like storm clouds. It was the first time Keelin had ever seen that expression on the female. It was a little scary. "No one."

"Really? Come on, distract me," she practically begged.

Nyx sighed and shot a glare at her now silent phone. "Bo."

Keelin's eyebrows raised. "You two seemed pretty, uh, friendly in the diner earlier."

272 | KATIE REUS

Nyx lifted her shoulders, the action jerky. When she did some of the copper pots and pans on the rack above them shook. Wincing, the female cursed. "Sorry, I'm just feeling weird now and I'm having trouble controlling my emotions."

"If you don't want to talk about it, it's okay." Even if Keelin was dying of curiosity and it would definitely distract her from her own worries.

Nyx bit her bottom lip and for a moment looked incredibly young. "No, I do. I've never really had girlfriends before until you and Ophelia. And Cynara. I don't want to overshare."

Keelin snorted. "I'm from a huge clan of dragons who don't know how to keep secrets. Trust me, you can't overshare with me. Or pretty much any shifter. There is no such thing as TMI."

She half-smiled. "Okay but I feel stupid being mad at him. When we were looking at the videos for shots of the demigod, Bran also wanted to do a search for the missing dragons. There was an image of two of the females with Bo. They were all...being intimate."

Her eyes widened. "*Oh.* You saw them all..." Keelin fluttered her hands wildly for a second then stopped. "How bad was it?"

"He was kissing one and groping the other," Nyx said through gritted teeth and the pots started to tremble again. They stopped as Nyx took a steadying breath. "We're not dating or anything, we're just friends but, I don't know, it made me really angry. Is that stupid?"

Keelin shook her head. "You can't help the way you feel so it's not stupid. Do you like him then?"

To her surprise, Nyx's cheeks tinged pink as she nodded. "Yes, but after what I saw it's just a reminder that he's out of my league."

"You're a *demigod*."

"Not like that, I mean sexually. He's obviously had threesomes before. Probably done more than that considering his club." Now her cheeks were full-on crimson.

"I don't know Bo well enough to speak to that but I don't think your lack of experience will matter to him. I haven't had much experience but it didn't matter with Bran." And he'd clearly been pleased with everything they'd done in the bedroom. She had too.

"Try *no* experience," Nyx muttered. "And he's so obviously a player."

Keelin wasn't exactly surprised by the virgin revelation but still... "How old are you?"

Nyx paused but finally said, "Twenty-three."

"Bo hasn't been with anyone since you started working at the club." Keelin wasn't sure if that was common knowledge but even if it wasn't, she figured Nyx should know. It might ease some of her anger at the male.

The female blinked. "Truly?"

"Truly."

Nyx bit her bottom lip again, her expression growing thoughtful as Keelin scented her parents nearby. She hadn't heard the front door open but her family could be stealth personified when they wanted.

She slid off her chair and smoothed her hands down her dress. She'd worn a leopard print faux wraparound dress with three-quarter sleeves. Her shoes were strappy five inch heels that laced around her ankles. The added height put her at all of five feet six inches.

Before she found time to panic the swinging door to the huge kitchen opened and in a blur of movement and exclamations she found herself being hugged by both her parents at the same time.

Statements and questions blurred together as they pretty much sandwiched her between them, embracing her fiercely. "We're so glad you're okay." "You look wonderful." "Are you eating enough?" "Why didn't you tell us you were coming in?" "How long are you staying?" She'd barely digested the questions before her parents abruptly stopped and stepped back from her a fraction, both of them staring down at her in surprise.

It was subtle but she realized they were scenting the air. No doubt scenting Bran on her because the male was definitely in her skin. And she'd be lying if she said she didn't like him there.

"Where's the Devlin male?" her father finally asked, the question more of a demand. His eyes had gone su-pernova.

"Not here." This was exactly why she hadn't wanted to involve Bran. Her parents might have attacked first and asked questions later.

"Did he hurt you?" her mother asked quietly.

Keelin rolled her eyes. "I love you guys but we need to set things straight. My personal life is mine alone. Bran and I are seeing each other." Because that sounded a lot better than 'hooking up'. And who was she kidding? They were more than hooking up anyway. "I don't know where we're headed but I don't need any interference. I'm a grown woman and I'm a *dragon*, the same as you. I appreciate your concern but I can take care of myself, and Bran is a good male." Saying the words was such a relief, as if a huge boulder had been lifted off her chest in one swoop.

To her surprise, her dad's expression became less foreboding and he gave a half-smile, as if pleased by what she'd said but her mom just frowned in typical Arya Petronilla fashion. Her mom was definitely a force of nature. Right now she wore dark cargo pants and a long-sleeved fitted T-shirt under a puffy vest and boots. The female had two modes; elegant or warrior. Tonight she was clearly in warrior mode. Keelin was surprised she didn't have a sword or blades strapped to her body because her mother definitely favored carrying them.

"Where are Victoria and my brothers?" she asked when neither of them spoke.

"Conall is dealing with clan business, something to do with the ski lodge, and Drake and his mate are on their way. I believe they wanted to give us time to catch up."

Unfortunately they would have to do that later. Time was too crucial now. Keelin half-turned and started to motion with her hand to Nyx so she could introduce them, but when she lifted her arm her mother let out a strange yelp of surprise.

Her mom grasped her wrist and eyed the bracelet Keelin had been wearing on and off for the last month.

"Where did you find this?" she asked, her gaze troubled as she met Keelin's eyes.

"In one of our storage containers." Over the years her clan had collected many valuable things; art, ancient books, priceless jewelry and so much more. The bracelet wasn't particularly valuable compared to some of her other jewelry, but Keelin loved the intricate detail of the two dragons intertwined together. The eyes on both dragons were diamonds. Though it appeared platinum, it wasn't, and she wasn't sure what type of metal it was made of. "Is it yours?" Because she'd never seen her mother wear it.

"No, it was your grandmother's." A deeper frown tugged at her lips as she glanced at Keelin's father.

He just looked thoughtful before he glanced at Nyx, who was still sitting quietly behind them. As if suddenly remembering the other female, Keelin's mother straightened and dropped Keelin's wrist. "Why don't you introduce us to your friend?"

Keelin turned to find Nyx sliding off her chair. She looked like an elementary school teacher with her dark jeans, feminine top, pearl necklace and ballerina flats.

"Mom, dad, this is Nyx. Nyx, this is Arya and Dragos Petronilla."

After they exchanged polite greetings her father spoke first. "So you are the demigod?"

Nyx nodded, her expression almost apologetic. "Yes, but not a very good one I'm afraid."

"I trust her completely," Keelin said before either of her parents could respond. She might not have known the female very long but she felt as if she could truly trust Nyx. It was one of those bone-deep convictions and she wanted her friend to feel welcome and secure here. "While I would love to catch up, I believe it's prudent for us to start discussing the demigod who apparently wants to kill me. And you too I suppose, since Victoria said he wants to eliminate every female in our line?" She said the last part as a question.

Her mother nodded. "Correct."

"Have you ever seen the male?" she asked.

"I was a girl but yes, I remember who he was. He terrorized a village close to our clan's at the time. He thought he had a right to any female he chose. My mother made it clear he did *not*." That deadly edge she'd heard more than once in her long life was clear in her mom's voice.

"I have a picture of someone we believe is the male." She didn't think it was necessary to go into detail about how Nyx had sensed the male and how they'd discovered who he was. Plus she didn't want to explain that she'd gotten the picture from a half-demon. She grabbed her phone from the counter—and found herself incredibly depressed that Bran hadn't even texted or called her since she'd left—and pulled up the picture.

As soon as she saw it, Arya nodded, her expression darkening. "This is the male. His name is Naram. Unfortunately," she added, looking at Keelin's father for a long moment before turning her grim expression on Keelin, "because of the bracelet you're wearing, he is most definitely hunting you."

CHAPTER TWENTY-ONE

E nergy rippled through Bran.

    She was so close.

Wind rushed over him as he rocketed through the air, flying faster than he'd ever gone before. The need to be with her, near her, was making him crazy.

He knew her clan's land was protected but he was cloaked and didn't care that he was there regardless. As he flew over the entrance gates he immediately slowed his pace. His muscles burned at the abrupt shift from full throttle to gliding.

Minutes later he was hovering over her house. Without caring about propriety or the consequences of an Alpha infiltrating another clan's land without permission, he landed silently in her front yard. Keelin was his and his dragon couldn't settle down until he saw her, knew she was okay.

Immediately he let his invisibility cloak drop and shifted to his human form. His claws and tail left heavy imprints in the snow.

Unconcerned about his naked state he stalked to her front door. When he tried the handle and it was locked he knocked once. Loudly. Impatient, he broke off the handle and shoved the door open. He was aware that he'd ventured into crazy territory, but yeah, he didn't give a shit. He'd taken two steps when Keelin and Nyx appeared from down a hallway.

Nyx immediately turned back around and made herself scarce.

Good.

Wearing a pink and black pajama set and her blonde hair pulled up on top of her head in a messy bun, Keelin was the sexiest thing he'd ever seen. It was like years had passed since he'd seen her and not mere hours. Relief like he'd never experienced detonated inside him, all the fear from the past few hours settling now that he could see with his own eyes that she was safe, alive.

"Bran, what are you—"

"Are you fucking *kidding* me? What am I *doing* here?" He couldn't even let her finish the question. The fact that she seemed surprised to see him pissed him off almost as much as the fact that she'd left.

"I left you a note," she whispered, seeming unsure of herself as her gaze flicked down his naked body before moving back up to his face.

He stalked forward a few steps and his dragon side cheered when she actually stepped back. She should feel like prey because right now he was all out stalking his mate. He was tired of playing games. "A note," he rasped out, his animal in his voice. How could she have left him a damn note? As if their relationship meant so little to her that he didn't deserve a conversation. Or hell, to come with her. How could she not want him to be with her right now when she was in clear danger?

"I told you I wouldn't be gone long and that I'd be safe."

So that made it all right? He couldn't even find his voice. He took another step forward when he scented two males.

All his hackles rose until he realized who it was. Turning around, he took a few more steps backward to Keelin, blocking her from the approaching males with his body. He didn't care that they were her relatives. Right now all he cared about was claiming her, and making it clear to her brothers and anyone else that Keelin was his to protect.

Drake and Conall stood just inside the entryway staring at him with equally grim expressions. He knew what he must look like, naked and angry. He felt more than heard Keelin moving closer to him.

She was the first to speak. "You two need to leave right now." Her voice was soft and it was a good thing she was talking to her brothers because he wasn't going anywhere.

Drake watched him for a long moment before nodding at his sister and stepping back toward the door.

Conall didn't move. "You can't come onto our land without warning." The dark edge to his voice was unmistakable and Bran understood the other leader's anger.

He'd trespassed and if someone had done that to his clan's land he'd incinerate them. But this wasn't about moving into someone's territory and Conall knew it. "This isn't about our clans. You know why I'm here." To his surprise he felt Keelin's hand on his forearm, holding him tight, as if she was afraid he'd attack her brothers.

Both males watched the action and seemed to relax. He couldn't be sure though. Every muscle in his body was tense and he could barely think straight.

"Can you two leave please? And can Nyx stay with you, Drake?" Keelin asked.

As if on cue, the other female hurried past them, also in pajamas, but not before shooting Keelin a questioning look, clearly making sure she was alright. That just pissed him off. "I'd never hurt her," he snapped at Nyx who just rolled her eyes at him. "Now everyone get the fuck out!"

Bran didn't care how rude he was or that he was practically inviting war between their clans. He needed to be alone with Keelin. Now. He knew he was being irrational. There was no doubt his behavior was insane. His female had left him a note, which made him angry, sure, but something dark inside him had awakened with her leaving him. He figured it had something to do with the mating process but couldn't be sure. All his dragon was sure of was that he couldn't be separated from Keelin right now. He needed to touch her, hold her, take care of her.

Conall took a step forward but Drake grabbed his arm and murmured something too low for Bran to hear.

Conall finally nodded but continued glaring at him. "We're talking in the morning."

Whatever. He turned his back on them and looked down at Keelin. He was vaguely aware of them shutting the door behind them. There was no lock now but it still shut.

"I would have come with you," he gritted out, unable to hide the hurt in his voice. Because more than anything, more than the deep desire to protect her, it killed him that she hadn't thought enough of him to bring him with her.

She started to place her hands on his chest but he took a step back. He couldn't have her touching him now that they were alone. If she did he'd pounce and they'd never talk. Not that talking was particularly high on his priority list now but some things needed to be said.

Her gray eyes flickered with hurt.

That pissed him off. "No. You don't get to be hurt. You fucking *left* me." It hurt more than he wanted to admit.

That nervousness was back in her gaze as she wrapped her arms around herself. "I didn't leave you. I just didn't want you to have to deal with my parents."

"Are you ashamed of me?" After everything they'd shared she seemed to be more than just attracted to him. He'd thought she respected him.

"What? No! I just knew my mother would be able to help with the demigod situation, but I also wasn't sure what their reception of you would be. I figured it would be easier to get all the information we needed instead of dealing with any drama from them over my relationship with you."

One word made him pause. "Relationship?" Was she actually admitting they were in one?

"Well, *yeah*. And I didn't want to argue with you over it. I knew it would turn into this big thing." She bit her bottom lip and he resisted the urge to lean down and do the same.

His cock throbbed between his legs, heavy and insistent. And his fire had already started to coat the entryway around them, covering the floor and bottom half of the staircase. He was glad she could see his reaction to her, wanted her to know what she did to him. All the time.

Her eyes widened as she looked around them. Until now he'd only reacted like this when they were kissing but he knew what was happening. They were pushing closer and closer to mating and he was barely in control of his response to her.

While he was still holding onto the last shred of his sanity he spoke again. "I'd rather argue with you any day of the week than deal with this shit of you running away." When it looked as if she wanted to interrupt, he continued. "Do I want to protect you from the world? Fuck yeah. But that doesn't mean I want to wrap you in cotton and keep you from experiencing everything. I'm sorry for the way your parents sheltered you but I'm *not* them. I want a partner, a mate, an equal. That's you, Keelin. We're definitely going to argue and I'm *definitely* going to be an overprotective asshole. If you'd told me you wanted to come here without me we definitely would have fought. And I don't know if I'd have let you go alone. Now we'll never know because you didn't give me the choice. But I trust that you can put me in my place in any situation." Not to mention the makeup sex with her would be explosive whenever they argued. "Now get naked." Because he was done talking.

Her lips parted in clear surprise but he scented her desire and her soft glow lit up the high-ceilinged room. Still, she wasn't getting undressed so he tried something he hadn't had a chance to yet.

Ordering the mating fire to incinerate her clothes, it did just that, eating them up in seconds until ashes fell away and she stood in front of him with wide eyes and oh-so hard nipples. She glanced down at herself in surprise but didn't make a move to cover her body.

He hungrily drank in the sight of her soft curves. Letting out a groan, he covered the distance between them, grasping her hips as he reached her. He needed to cover her in his scent, to let her and everyone know she was his. Thankfully she wrapped her legs around him as he lifted her up. She leaned into him, just as hungry for his touch as he was for hers. That soothed some of his edginess.

286 | KATIE REUS

His mouth crushed over hers as their bodies met. The feel of her breasts rubbing against his chest set him on fire. When she moaned into his mouth he rolled his hips against hers and started moving toward the closest room. A sitting room or something.

"I need in you now," he murmured, nipping her bottom lip between his teeth.

"Yes. Being away from you..." She trailed off and let her head fall back as he started feathering kisses up her jaw.

He lightly bit her earlobe. "What?"

She let out a little sigh as he tugged on it. "It was harder than I thought. Really hard. I felt so bad I called and texted you like a stalker." The regret in her voice was real.

He'd left his phone and all his belongings behind before coming after her. He just grunted a non-response and raked his teeth down her neck as he stepped into the room. In his peripheral he scanned the layout of the room. All delicate, feminine furniture that suited her perfectly. The biggest thing in there was a chaise near one of the long windows. Luckily drapes covered it. Not that he cared. He'd give her whole clan a show right now.

Let everyone know she belonged to him.

A small lamp in the corner emitted a soft glow, not that either of them needed it to see. Not with both their light and extrasensory abilities. Without asking her what she wanted, mainly because he was beyond words, he headed straight for the chaise. The urge to dominate, to possess, was too strong so he did something he rarely did.

Still holding her tight against him as they kissed and nipped at each other, he stretched out on the chaise and let her be on top.

As her knees sank into the upholstery on either side of him, his cock brushed against her slick folds. God, she was already so wet for him. Even though he could scent it, feeling her reaction made him that much crazier.

The faint scent of surprise rolled off Keelin as she pulled her head back and looked down at him. She splayed her hands over his chest, running her fingers over him in the most deliciously possessive way. A pleased rumble started in his chest. He loved her touching him.

"You set the pace," he said, needing her to know that she was in charge right now. Mostly. He'd acted like a complete caveman barging into her home and burning off her clothes that he needed to slow down.

The answering grin she gave him was pure sex as she lifted up on her knees and slid down onto him. He loved that she didn't even pause, just took what she wanted.

On instinct his canines descended. The feel of her tight sex clenching around his cock was enough to push him over the edge.

Closing her eyes, she placed her hands on his shoulders and let her head fall back. Her breasts pushed up, teasing him. He barely resisted the urge to grab her hips and start thrusting upward, but he had to give her this.

Cupping both her breasts, he lifted them, pushing them together before burying his face against her softness. He wanted to feast on every inch of her. The female was a true addiction. One he would never tire of.

Moaning, she threaded her fingers through his hair as he began kissing the underside of her breasts. Her skin was soft, smooth and she was all his. Just touching her had calmed him immensely.

When she began slowly riding him, letting out breathy little gasps each time he filled her to the hilt, his fire engulfed the room. There was no heat, just gold fire everywhere, competing with her own bright light.

Tingles already gathered at the base of his spine, his balls pulling up tight as her snug sheath milked him with each stroke. He wanted her for his mate so badly, his canines aching to the point he almost let nature take over and marked her. But he could never do that to her, even in this state. Not without her being a hundred percent willing.

He teased a path over both her breasts, worshipping her the way she deserved before he settled on one nipple and pressed down with his teeth, not hard but not gentle either.

"Bran," she gasped out, arching her back and pushing deeper into his mouth.

He flicked his tongue over the hardened bud as he cupped the other full mound and teased that nipple with his thumb. Each time he stroked her nipples, she tightened around his cock.

When she reached between their bodies and started stroking her clit, he growled against her breast. She was so close he could feel it with each thrust.

"Come for me." He was practically begging, was so desperate to feel her pleasure and empty himself inside her.

She began moving faster on top of him, up and down, her movements jerky and uncontrolled, until finally she let go. She dug her fingers into his shoulders, her claws pricking him as she shouted his name.

He couldn't hold back any longer either. Grabbing her hips, he let go of his control and began thrusting hard, slamming into her as they both found their pleasure.

His orgasm overtook him. He kept thrusting into her as she chanted his name, the sound like a prayer, until she grabbed his face and slanted her mouth over his.

The intensity of her kiss overwhelmed him and another, unexpected orgasm surged through him. He hadn't thought it possible to climax so hard but as her tongue stroked against his, hungry and demanding, he flipped their positions so that she was under him. The animal inside him growled in a primal feeling of victory at having her beneath him. Something about dominating her, pleasing her, made every part of him come alive.

After what felt like an eternity, his and her orgasms finally abated and Keelin pulled back from the kiss, her eyes heavy-lidded and her expression completely sated. Her arms were wrapped around his back and she slowly trailed her fingers up and down his spine.

"I don't want casual," Keelin whispered, her eyes sparking bright silver even as her light and his fire had dimmed.

Her words were exactly what he'd been waiting to hear. Deep down he knew that if he pushed he could get her to mate with him tonight. But he wanted her fully invested in this relationship with no doubts first. Shifting their positions, he rolled them over so that she was stretched out on top of him, her body a perfect fit with his.

"Me neither." He gently kissed her forehead, her nose, then claimed her mouth again. "And I'll never hurt you. My animal side might have claimed you first, but *I* want to claim you now," he murmured against her lips. All of him wanted her. Admitting that to her made him feel even more vulnerable than he already did around her, but she was worth the risk.

"Would your clan accept me?" she asked quietly, the insecurity in her voice taking him off guard.

But he loved that she was actually asking. It meant she was seriously contemplating mating with him. Hell yeah. "Of course." And if someone didn't, he'd deal with them.

She bit her bottom lip and laid her head against his chest. He stroked up and down her back, loving the feel of just holding her. When she didn't respond he decided to push.

"Why would you think my clan wouldn't accept you? You're pretty much royalty for your clan. It would be a strong alliance, not that I care about that, something you already know." Or she should know. While his role as Alpha had been thrust on him, he wasn't changing who he was or making bullshit political alliances.

"I'm not a warrior," she said quietly, tracing a finger over one of his pecs as she remained stretched out on top of him.

"So?" He didn't want someone just like him. He simply wanted Keelin. Sweet, compassionate, smart, and oh-so-soft. She was so different from him and he loved it.

She glanced up at him and arched a perfect eyebrow at him. "Have you ever known an Alpha couple unmatched like that?"

He started to respond when he realized that all the known Alpha dragon couples were warriors. "I guess you're right. But who gives a fuck? If my clan doesn't like it I'll step down and someone else can take over. Physical strength isn't the only necessity for a good leader. I've seen you in action, especially the way you handle Fia when she gets crazy. You're very diplomatic, something our people need more of." And at the end of the day, none of that mattered to him. Just Keelin mattered.

She pressed her lips together, seeming unconvinced, but he could tell his comment had pleased her. She snuggled up against him, curling into him in a way that warmed his entire body. He couldn't believe he'd lived most of his life without this female. "I'm not letting you go," he murmured against the top of her head.

She didn't look up, but he felt her smile against his chest. "Good. I'm not letting you go either."

That simple statement slammed through him. She might not have said the actual words that she was going to mate with him, but she had in a roundabout way. Just like that he was hard again, ready to take her slow this time. After he'd buried his face between her legs and made her scream his name. He rolled his hips once, nudging his cock against her hip.

She chuckled lightly against his chest, but remained curled up on top of him. "You're insatiable."

With her? Always.

Tonight he wanted to cement the bond between them, to show her exactly what she meant to him. Because for her, there was nothing he wouldn't give or do.

CHAPTER TWENTY-TWO

Naram leaned against the stone balcony of his castle and stared out at the bleak countryside.

"He'll return soon," Shar said, coming to stand next to him.

Naram just nodded, though he felt anything but certain. He hated being in this state of limbo and the female had apparently left Biloxi if the male dragon's erratic departure was anything to go on. One of Naram's demon spies had been watching the half-demon's club when the male dragon had burst through the roof in a rage and disappeared. No one had seen either Keelin or Bran since.

He could track her again but that would take a lot of power. Before he wasted that kind of energy, or blood, he'd sent a scout demon to Montana first. If Keelin was on her clan's land, getting to her would be difficult. Not impossible, but very, very difficult. It was why he wasn't going himself to search for her—yet. He would go after her when the time was right. It was possible that someone in her clan might sense him even if he was cloaked. Sometimes the ancient dragons had different gifts. There was simply no way of knowing.

He wouldn't risk the chance. Not when he was close to getting what he wanted. And he hated having to wait for anything. He'd already waited for thousands of years. His patience was growing thin.

As if he'd been summoned by Shar's words, the scout demon appeared on the balcony, his expression grim. He hadn't bothered with a human form, but his body was humanoid. Two small horns protruded from his bald head, his eyes glowing a faint blue and his skin was a grayish-blue. He wore simple loose black harem-style pants and a black tunic. Naram didn't remember his name and didn't care.

"Well?" he demanded. This male was just a tool he was using. Something he'd called on from Hell to do his bidding. It was one of his favorite gifts as a demigod, even if it did piss off those who ruled Hell. He just took who he wanted, when he wanted, then flung them back into their home.

The male's eyes narrowed the slightest fraction but he spoke. "She is there. So is the male. They're not mated yet but they will be soon."

"How can you be sure?"

"They were fucking in her home and their mating manifestation could be seen from the outside."

"You didn't go inside?"

The male snorted softly. "I will not interfere with a male dragon while he is rutting."

Naram nodded and flicked his wrist at the male. He vanished as Naram sent him back to where he came from. When he was alone with Shar he frowned at him. "What did the scout mean by mating manifestation?"

Shar paused, his human face and form perfection. On this plane Naram had glamored Shar to look similar to himself. Tall with dark eyes and dark hair, though his was shorter than Naram's. He was well built at over six feet tall, muscular and had the same bronze coloring as Naram. He was pleasing to look at, but right now Naram didn't like that confused expression.

"I assumed you knew," Shar said.

"No."

"I do not either. Should we call the scout back?"

There was no *we*. He would be the one who had to call the male back and that would expend more of his power. In addition it would reveal that he didn't know as much as the scout demon did about dragons. That was weak and unacceptable. "Not yet. If they haven't joined then to strike now would be preferred," he said more to himself than Shar.

Shar simply nodded in agreement.

"But we need her alone." Naram had transported his captives to his current residence with his demigod gift. They were far from their home and unable to escape once he'd locked them in his dungeon. Getting to Keelin on her own land would be incredibly difficult. Despite his earlier reservation, at this point it was a risk he would have to take.

"Your timing will have to be perfect," Shar said, understanding what Naram meant to do without him having to say the words aloud.

"Yes." Which meant he'd have to be very careful when he made his next move. In the end it would all be worth it though. He'd have his talisman, another dead dragon—from the line that had cursed him to prison for so long—and all his power returned.

Then there would be no stopping him.

He nodded back toward the French doors open to his bedroom. "Let's go see the prisoners." He had a direct stairwell entrance from his room down to the dungeon.

"You mean to do it now?"

Naram nodded, his blood pumping wildly. "I will drain them all dry and when I'm at my peak I'll transport to see the female." Of course he'd have to figure out exactly where she was on her clan's land, which would take some scouting. Then he'd make his move.

"You will need to disable her."

"I know." He softly patted one of the blades strapped over his chest. He'd learned many things since returning to this human world, but some things hadn't changed, including battle tactics. He was going to engage in a rapid dominance move and snatch the female dragon before anyone could do a damn thing. He would just have to make sure she was alone. It meant entering the clan's land cloaked and being discovered, but he would just have to risk it.

* * *

Bran felt like he was ten feet tall as he knocked on Drake's front door. Keelin's words from last night, or this morning really, played through his head on auto-repeat. *I'm not letting you go either.*

She might not have officially admitted it yet, but she was his. And that made him feel like a fucking king, invincible.

A moment later Dragos Petronilla answered the door, his mate right behind him. They were dressed to kill. Literally. Both looked like the type of bloodthirsty assassins he'd worked with and sometimes killed over the years. It wasn't just their military-style fatigues or the blades strapped to their thighs—which he knew was a show all for him—it was the deadly gleam in their eyes as they watched him.

Well, he'd come here for a reason. Time to get this over with. He nodded politely at them, the small act of civility pretty much all he was willing to give them. If they didn't approve of him and Keelin he didn't care. She was his and he was hers.

Dragos stepped back, his eyes supernova silver as he watched Bran carefully. He motioned with his hand for Bran to enter. "You're late."

He was actually ten minutes early but he wasn't going to argue the point. "My apologies," he said, his voice wry as he stepped inside.

Arya shut the door behind him with way more force than necessary.

When the two of them just stared at him he cleared his throat. "I'd like to speak to you about Keelin. We can do it here in the foyer or somewhere more comfortable."

Jaw clenched tight, Dragos jerked his head to the sitting room then turned his back on Bran, his mate falling in line with him.

The way they turned their back on him was a sign that they didn't view him as a threat. The sign of disrespect rankled his dragon but Bran just rolled his eyes. He'd known he'd have to deal with this. And he wasn't going to make small talk either.

As soon as they were all sitting, Dragos and Arya across from him on an uncomfortable looking couch, and him on an equally uncomfortable high-backed chair, he spoke. "I'm mating your daughter." Unlike humans and their strange customs of asking for a bride's hand in marriage, dragon shifters didn't do that. They had to prove they were a worthy mate. Asking would make him look weak.

"Is that right?" Dragos rumbled, his dragon clear in his gaze.

"If she'll have me." Because the choice was hers.

At that, Arya sniffed haughtily. "We all saw your little light show last night. Don't think sex is enough to keep my daughter happy."

Next to her Dragos growled and shot daggers at Bran with his eyes.

Yeah, he didn't want to talk about sex with Keelin in front of them either. "What we have is more than physical. I love your daughter." Something he hadn't told her but she had to know. He planned to tell her today anyway in case she wasn't crystal clear on the matter. Saying the words were daunting though.

"Love can be fleeting. She's not like your brother's mate so if you think that's what you're getting you are sorely mistaken," Arya said with Dragos just watching and likely cataloging the hundred ways he wanted to kill Bran.

At her comment about his brother's mate, Fia, Bran wondered if that was part of their issue with him in general. "I adore my sister-in-law but I don't want a female like her. I didn't even think I wanted a mate until I met Keelin. She's everything an Alpha needs and whether you can see her strength or not, *I* can." He felt his temper rising with each word he spoke. It pissed him off that they dared compare her to Fia, as if... He actually wasn't sure what Arya's statement meant. It was so vague but if she was trying to insinuate that Keelin was weaker than the other female, she didn't know her daughter at all.

"She cares for others, seems to have no prejudice against any supernatural beings and is incredibly diplomatic. An attitude our kind definitely needs more of." Something he'd told her last night. "Unlike Fia, she doesn't throw fits when she doesn't get her way. She doesn't panic in the face of danger. My Keelin is strong and you should know that. And for the record, Conall would have been miserable with Fia." The female was a perfect fit for his brother, who loved catering to her and taking care of her, but Conall needed a warrior. Bran could see that much from the little time he'd gotten to know the male.

To his surprise, Arya and Dragos leaned back a fraction as if they'd choreographed it, the scent rolling off them no longer acidic but pleasing to the senses. Dragos didn't smile but he also wasn't glaring anymore. That had to be a good sign. Right?

Arya gave him a half-smile. "You are correct in what you say about my son and Fia. We were pleased when she ran off with Gavin. And you are also correct that Keelin is strong. Thankfully she's not like Fia and I was not insulting my daughter as you seem to think. Keelin is not physically as strong as the rest of our family so we do worry about her, that's true. But the fact that she left you shows her strength. We weren't sure of your true intentions until just now."

When they didn't say anything further, he figured he should speak. "I will do everything in my power to make her happy and I'll never hurt her. I would rather lose a body part than cause her grief."

"If you *do* hurt her, that can be arranged." Dragos said, his dragon back in his gaze.

"Fair enough."

After another long moment of silence, Arya continued. "Everything we've heard about you from both our sons and the difference we've seen in Keelin indicates that you are a worthy male. We won't stand in the way of your pursuing her."

He nodded once. "Respectfully, it wouldn't matter if you did. She's mine." If a human said something like that he knew it would be considered rude, but not among his kind. They had to know that no matter what, his mate came first. Not the needs or cares of others, not even her parents.

Dragos gave him a ghost of a smile and Arya glanced at her mate. They seemed to be having an unspoken conversation before she turned back to Bran. "Now that we are on the same page, let's go meet with Keelin. Dragos and I will retrieve our sons and meet you at Conall's house. We have some decisions to make."

Bran nodded and stood with them, relieved this part of it was over. Keelin had filled him in earlier that morning on who the demigod was so he'd passed the info on to both Finn and Bo in the hopes that the males might be able to reach out to any one of their supernatural contacts. He'd also informed his former boss about what was going on. August hadn't been pleased about the new development but was glad for the intel. Hunting a demigod wasn't easy and Bran wasn't above using every resource necessary to find the male.

And eliminate him for good.

CHAPTER TWENTY-THREE

Keelin glanced at her cell phone and frowned. No call or text from Bran. She wasn't exactly worried for him but he'd been going to visit with her parents so yeah, she was a little nervous. Not that she thought he couldn't take care of himself. The male was fierce and strong and could easily handle himself. She didn't like the thought of her parents threatening him though. What if he changed his mind, decided she wasn't worth the trouble of her family?

That was a fear she'd kept locked down tight but it was pushing to the surface now, no matter how hard she tried to ignore it.

"Do you think this set of books has enough information to help me control my powers?" Nyx asked Victoria, drawing Keelin back to the present.

The three of them were in Conall's library going over books, ancient texts, and some of the files Bran's former boss had sent him on all the supernatural beings who'd been captured in images around the missing dragons at one time or another in Bo's club. So far Keelin recognized some of the people but that was normal considering she worked there. Same with Nyx. And they didn't remember anyone being seen with the demigod,

Naram. So it was more or less a dead end for the time being. However, with the demigod's name and his history with her clan now known, Keelin had started scouring a couple diaries her grandmother had kept. Nothing important stuck out yet, but it was still early. Her parents would be here soon too, but they were meeting with Bran.

Something she needed to stop thinking about.

Nyx had taken up reviewing a set of old books on Greek gods and goddesses and was like a kid on Christmas morning. They weren't the type of thing you could get at a library or find on the Internet either.

Victoria shrugged. "It appears to have information you can use but putting things into practice are always different than theoretic ideas. Do you think any of your relatives could help you?"

Nyx snorted. "Unlikely. Gods are assholes."

"Well maybe we can try a couple things out in the mountains so you're away from everyone. Not that I think you could really hurt anyone here but Keelin told me about your landing when you arrived." Victoria looked over at Keelin and half-smiled. "Stop worrying about him. He's fine."

Keelin tried to smile back as she pushed up from where she sat at one of the desks. Telling herself she just wanted to stretch her legs, she headed to one of the windows and oh-so-casually looked out over Conall's front yard and walkway.

No one was there and she felt a little insane keeping watch for Bran. But she wasn't embarrassed enough to stop. Behind her, Victoria and Nyx were still busy talking, the two women having become fast friends.

Rubbing a hand down her face, Keelin's gaze snagged on the bracelet she hadn't taken off since her mother had told her it had belonged to her grandmother. And the male named Naram before that. It was apparently linked to his powers so her grandmother had used all her battle skills to steal it before locking the male in a prison of her making.

Somehow the male had escaped that prison and her mother was convinced he wanted his bracelet back. So Keelin was wearing it for safe keeping. If she knew where it was at all times it meant *he* didn't have it. It was also part of the reason she'd been having visions, something Keelin wasn't sure how she felt about, but at this point, she didn't want them to stop. Of course her mother had demanded that she give it to her but Keelin had stood her ground, needing to set up new boundaries between them.

So far her parents actually seemed to be respecting those boundaries. Sure, it hadn't been long since she'd been home, but considering they hadn't stormed over last night when Bran had not-so-quietly arrived, that felt like progress.

Rolling her shoulders once to ease the tension there, she started to move back from the window when she saw Bran step through the heavy gate. A big smile spread across her face at the sight of him.

Unable to stop herself she drank in the way his broad shoulders stretched out his long-sleeved shirt and the way his thick thigh muscles flexed and strained under his cargo pants. The male was walking, talking sex and he was all hers.

More than her clear physical attraction to him, she genuinely liked Bran. Okay, more than liked him. He'd gotten to her when she hadn't even thought it was possible a male could. She was starting to see that he didn't want to take away her freedom and after his comments last night it was pretty clear he meant to put her first, even ahead of his own clan if necessary.

That knowledge had stunned her. Still did. She lifted a hand and waved at him, but then realized he probably couldn't see her because of the reflective coating.

Turning from the window, she started for the door, wanting to meet him in the foyer, but ran right into someone.

A male.

What the heck?

It took less than a second for who she was seeing to compute. The demigod. Panic slammed into her as she tried to step back from Naram. He grabbed her upper arm and fire instantly built in the back of her throat as she prepared to attack, her dragon seconds from taking over. Before she could release the flames, pain erupted inside her, sharp and punishing, coming from her stomach.

He'd stabbed her. Flashbacks of her last attack exploded in her mind, the memory vivid, but she called on all her strength and shoved at the male's chest.

Shouts of alarm from Nyx and Victoria sounded as she was suddenly sucked into a vortex of rushing wind.

Full-on terror forked through her in jagged pulses of energy as they flashed into a dungeon of sorts. Fire burst from her throat, the flames bright and scorching.

Unfortunately, they flowed around the male as if he was surrounded by an invisible force-field.

Then he laughed, the maniacal sound bouncing off the cold, damp prison walls and turning her veins to ice. Her fire wasn't affecting him and she was pretty certain she was trapped.

Her wound wasn't bad and she was already healing; she figured that had been more to stun and transport her than to truly hurt her. She knew it was likely an impossible hope but she prayed that Bran figured out a way to find her. Because she wasn't sure she could hold off a demigod by herself.

Though she was damn sure going to try.

* * *

What the *hell?* The sound of a female screaming pushed Bran into action. The front door slammed against the wall as he shoved it open. Not bothering to shut it, he raced for the library.

He jerked to a halt at the sight of Nyx shouting at the top of her lungs. Victoria was next to her, her green eyes wide with raw panic.

Keelin wasn't in the room.

She was supposed to be here. "Victoria—"

His words were cut off when a tall, Amazonian-looking woman with fiery red hair appeared out of nowhere, her expression pleased as she watched Nyx. Despite the difference in hair color, the female was clearly related to Nyx. Her mother. The goddess of Chaos.

Nyx stopped screaming, but the desks and books around them were all trembling, with some falling off the shelves. "Mother, I need your help."

"I know, silly girl."

Bran started to step forward but the tall female looked at him, her eyes turning a winter blue. "Don't take another step, dragon, or I leave this instant and you never see your pretty female again."

Fuck. Keelin was gone. Somehow, she was missing. It didn't seem possible but whatever was happening, Bran could swallow his pride and stay put. Fighting back his terror, however, wasn't as easy.

"Enough, Mother! I know you can tell me where he's taken her. Do it now."

The demigod had Keelin? No! His dragon clawed at him, all his rage threatening to burst through. Bran shoved down his growing fear, waiting for the goddess to do *something*.

The female smiled, all white teeth, red lips and pure calculation in her expression as she watched her daughter. "I'll tell you where your friend is but you will owe me a favor."

Nyx didn't even pause. "Fine. As long as it doesn't involve murder, rape, torture or maiming someone, I will owe you *one* favor."

The female smiled, a deadly predator's gleam in her blue eyes. "Deal." Then she held out her hand and touched Nyx's head.

Bran wanted to race toward her, afraid the female would leave without him but he forced himself to remain where he was. He couldn't risk the goddess not helping them.

A moment later the goddess disappeared into thin air and Nyx looked up and directly at him. "She showed me an image of where they are." Nyx ran toward him, her arm outstretched.

Bran started for her, knowing she intended to transport them.

Victoria was close behind but Nyx turned and threw out an arm. When she did, Victoria went flying onto a couch as if thrown by an invisible force. "I'm sorry, you can't come." Then she grabbed Bran and the world exploded into a kaleidoscope of color and noise.

CHAPTER TWENTY-FOUR

Internally cursing the fact that she had pretty much no battle moves, Keelin went with the only one she'd learned so far. Simultaneously screaming and breathing fire, she rushed at the male.

His screaming stopped as she slammed into him. Pain rippled through her from her stab wound but she was already healing. Using what she'd learned from Bran, she turned into Naram and slammed her hip into his crotch. Without pause she twisted in his hold, ignoring his groan of pain and surprise. Fluidly she bent over, using her momentum to slam him to the ground.

As he flew through the air he grabbed her wrist and too late she realized his intent. Yanking hard, he grabbed her bracelet.

The metal scraped against her skin as he slammed into the ground. No, no, no. He couldn't be allowed to possess it.

She lunged for him, releasing her fire even though it didn't seem to affect him. Her dragon just took over. She might not be trained but she was still strong. Tackling him to the ground, she screamed when he punched her in the stomach, the slam enflaming her wound.

He kicked her off him, metal glinting in his hand. A knife. He raised it high and she started to roll away when an explosion rent the air.

Stone and plaster rained down on them as the roof and walls around them crumbled to nothing. Bars on prison cells ripped apart, the metal tearing as if it was paper.

Flat on her back from the explosion, her ears rang as she stared up at what looked like a high, winding stone staircase. She shook off her pain and shoved up from the ground.

Bran! Joy surged through her at the sight of him standing near a crumbling wall until she saw a motionless Nyx. Her friend was curled on her side with blood trickling out of her nose and she was barely breathing.

"You stupid fucking dragon," Naram snarled at Bran as he climbed over a pile of rubble. He slid the bracelet onto his wrist and it was as if the air around him charged with energy.

Bran didn't pause, just unleashed a fire so hot and intense it coated everything, even licking high into the busted stairwell above them.

Naram laughed again, the evil sound raking against her senses. "Stupid fool! You can't touch me now!" he shouted, all his attention on Bran.

As if he'd forgotten she existed.

Bran's fire flowed around the demigod, not touching him at all. Keelin had no idea how to kill a demigod, but she was going to use his inattention to her advantage.

Think, think, *think.*

Suddenly Bran's fire was cut off as he flew backward through the air. Naram raised his arms high above him, shouting in victory as Bran slammed against the nearest wall. Bits of rock broke off under the impact.

The sight of her mate being injured made something snap inside her. Unable to control herself, a screech tore from her throat as she underwent the change faster than she ever had before.

Her wings burst from her body as something dark inside her she'd never known existed broke free. Her fire burned intensely hot, a pale blue stream of flame releasing from her as she dove for Naram.

She was vaguely aware of Bran shifting too, but she ignored him, all her focus on the threat to her mate. She had to destroy Naram, to keep him from hurting Bran and Nyx at all costs.

Screaming as his clothes caught on fire, Naram disappeared, transporting away, but reappeared ten feet away, naked and covered in soot.

"No!" he screamed, the fear rolling off him so potent it fed her dragon like the sweetest nectar.

He was having trouble transporting! Feeling victorious, she let out another stream of the same raging fire at the same time Bran did. His was just as pale and beautiful as hers, the blue nearly blinding as the demigod tried to run for the stairs. She'd heard that her brother had released a similar fire when his mate had been in trouble.

314 | KATIE REUS

Naram's body was burning, his screams echoing around the cavernous room until Bran lunged, snapping his head off without warning.

The male's body turned to ash but before her predator side could relish the demigod's death, she felt a presence behind her.

She turned in time to see a male pushing up from behind one of the dead bodies—one of the dead dragon shifters—a blade in his hand. His eyes flamed red as he lunged at Keelin.

If she could have laughed at his pathetic attempt she would have. Instead she released her fire, this time the flames their normal bright orange. The male screamed before bursting into flames and eventually turning to dust.

Tense, she turned to see Bran already shifting to his human form. She didn't scent anyone else in the dungeon but the smell of fire and death was potent so she could be wrong. Though she was unsure that they were alone, since Bran had shifted, instinct told her the threat was over.

The change flowed over her with a quickness she hadn't expected. Wincing as she stood, she was thankful to realize that she was almost healed, a faint purple bruise on her stomach the only souvenir from her injury. She didn't care about that though.

"*Keelin.*" Bran's face was tortured as he jumped over a couple fallen stones.

She rushed for him, thankful he was alive. "I'm okay. What's wrong with Nyx?"

Wrapping his arm around her waist, he pulled her close as they hurried to Nyx's fallen body. Bran checked the pulse in her neck as Keelin took her friend's hand. She was breathing but blood covered her upper lip and cheek.

"Her pulse is strong," Bran murmured, pulling his hand back from Nyx's neck.

No sooner had he said the words than Nyx's eyes popped open in alarm. She jerked upright, fists up as if to fight off an attacker until she realized it was just Keelin and Bran.

"What happened?" she asked, looking around the scene of destruction in horror.

Keelin followed her gaze and her heart twisted at the sight of the dead Moana dragons in the cells. She hated that they'd been too late to save them. They were clearly in a dungeon and if she had to guess it was part of a castle. Some part of her hindbrain recognized other scents and while she couldn't put her finger on exactly what it was, it smelled like Scotland.

The first place she'd ever called home so many years ago. That scent was embedded deep inside her. "We're in Scotland," she murmured.

To her surprise, Bran nodded and Nyx did the same. Keelin didn't think Nyx had the same sensory gifts as them but she must know where they were if she'd transported herself and Bran here.

"Are you okay?" she asked her friend.

Nyx nodded and started to stand so they both helped steady her. "The transport was just rocky. I was so emotional and worried I couldn't get a grip on anything. It was like being in a hurricane."

"Thank you for finding me." Later she'd ask Nyx how she'd even known where she was but for now she grabbed both Bran and Nyx into a big hug, pulling them close.

Nyx embraced them both but pulled back quickly. "Sorry, I just can't hug your male when his junk is hanging out."

Despite everything that had just happened, a burst of laughter escaped both her and Bran and Keelin threw herself into Bran's arms.

He lifted her off the ground, burying his face against her neck as she did the same to him. "I love you." It was a risk telling him how she felt first but she didn't care. She loved him and he needed to know, whether he returned the feelings or not. It would probably kill her if he didn't, but—

"I love you too." His grip tightened to the point it was almost painful but she didn't mind. "Never fucking scare me like that again." The soft growl of his words was laced with the kind of fear she'd felt earlier when she thought he'd been in mortal danger. When she'd thought that demigod would take away the male who'd come to mean everything to her.

"I'll try not to." Her voice was watery as tears escaped but she couldn't stop them. Too many emotions bubbled up inside her at once.

The threat was gone and everyone she cared about was safe, including the male she loved. After this, she was never letting him go.

CHAPTER TWENTY-FIVE

"I think I could sleep for a week. Maybe longer," Keelin groaned as she and Bran stepped through the front door of her house. It was quiet thankfully.

After about thirty-six hours of working nonstop, she knew he had to be exhausted too. Once they'd figured out they were in a castle owned by Naram—though it wasn't in his real name, but a fake human identity—Nyx had transported the deceased dragons back to Petronilla land. Then she'd transported Bran and Keelin. Nyx had even offered to take the dead dragons back to their home in Mississippi but she'd been exhausted and they didn't want to reveal her powers to anyone else, especially not another dragon clan. They didn't know enough about the Moana clan to make a judgment .on whether they could be trusted yet.

So the Alpha Nalani had arrived in Montana with members of her clan and retrieved her fallen people. She'd stayed for a while though, wanting to talk about alliances with Keelin's parents, Bran and Conall. At least she'd been fully clothed this time. Meanwhile Bran had let his former boss know that the threat was over and August had sent a cleanup crew to the castle. Keelin didn't actually care about that, she was just glad the male was dead and gone.

They'd found the dragon bracelet in the rubble, the talisman having survived the attack from her and Bran. She wasn't sure how she felt about it or if she wanted to wear it again. The visions had been interesting and helpful, but for now she just wanted to officially mate with her male and not worry about someone trying to kill her or those she cared about. And she didn't want to see anyone's dark or depressing thoughts.

"I'm not surprised Victoria was right about the blue fire either," she continued, still in awe over the pale blue flames she and Bran had both released on the demigod. Her brother Drake was the only one she knew who had used it before and it had been when his mate was in true danger. For months Victoria had been trying to figure out exactly what it was through research—though she'd already hypothesized that it was linked to mates—but once Keelin and Bran had returned from Scotland and told her family everything, her parents hadn't been surprised by it. They'd confirmed that it was indeed a mating fire that only emerged in the direst of circumstances—like when battling a demigod.

"I didn't think your parents were ever going to let you leave," Bran murmured, pulling her into his arms, his embrace warm and comforting. "And sleep is the last thing on my mind." His breath was warm on top of her head.

She silently agreed with his first statement. Her parents had understandably been crazy with worry but after Bran had told the entire clan how they'd killed the demigod together, with Keelin saving his ass—his words—it was like a weight had been lifted from her parents' shoulders. Maybe she was wrong, but she hoped they could stop worrying about her quite so much. She knew they wouldn't completely stop worrying because she was their child, but it felt as if they'd seen her in a different light.

"You sure?" she asked, pulling back so she could look at him, but she still kept her arms wrapped tightly around him. "I'm pretty tired." She fake yawned and yelped when he pinched her butt.

He rolled his hips against her, his erection pushing at her abdomen. "You're too tired for this?" he murmured.

She yawned again, this time more exaggerated. "I'm *so* tired and I'm not really sure anything you say can convince me otherwise." Fighting a grin, she stepped out of his hold and moved toward the stairs. He had to know she was kidding but the scowl on his face was adorable. "If you catch me, you get to keep me." Before he could respond she tore up the stairs, racing for her bedroom with him close behind.

The most primal part of her loved having him chase her. She knew it was her animal side, but her human side liked it a whole lot too. By the time she cleared her bedroom door, his arms were around her, his heartbeat an erratic tattoo against her back as he held her close.

"You're very brave to tease an Alpha dragon," he murmured against her neck, his teeth raking along her skin in a way that had her nipples tightening and heat flooding between her legs.

Oh yeah, she was definitely *not* too tired for him. "You like it."

"I do." He slid a hand up under her sweater, his big palm spanning her belly. "Mate with me, Keelin." In addition to the raw need she heard in his voice there was also a very real thread of fear.

The fact that he actually worried she'd say no sliced at her. She turned in his arms and laced her fingers behind his neck. "Yes." There was more she wanted to tell him, but that one word unleashed all the passion and hunger inside him.

His mouth slanted over hers, his tongue demanding entrance as he teased the seam of her lips. Grabbing her hips he hoisted her up so that she had to wrap her legs around his waist. He walked them to her bed and stripped her clothes in seconds. She was surprised he didn't burn them off this time.

Naked, splayed out for him, her breath hitched in her throat as she watched him strip. It was as if he was putting on a show just for her.

Gold fire rippled around him and her room, the flames coating her big bed and ceiling as he slowly peeled his shirt over his head. His chest and abs were nicked with scars she'd kissed—and looked forward to kissing and touching more over the years—and it took all her effort not to reach for him.

But she wanted to enjoy this.

Next went his shoes and pants. No surprise the male was commando. When he was finally bared completely to her, huge and strong, her entire body heated with a primal awareness. After tonight there was no going back.

Mated dragon shifters couldn't break up or part ways. Well, they could in the technical sense, but dragons mated for life and when one died, so did the other.

He paused at the edge of the bed, watching her. "Having second thoughts?" His jaw clenched tight.

The fears she'd let grow inside her had been her own insecurities. She was done letting fear rule her. Nothing would stop her from mating with this amazing male. She'd been alive for a long damn time and knew without a doubt that she wanted this. Wanted *him*.

"Not even a little bit. I'm just thinking how incredible you look standing there and I want to see you touch yourself."

He blinked once before his gaze went molten, her words having clearly surprised him. But he fisted his cock at the base and stroked upward once, then twice.

She let out a moan as another rush of heat flooded between her thighs. He was way too sexy for his own good.

Without thinking, she slid a hand between her legs and touched her clit. Before she'd even stroked herself once, Bran was on top of her, his big body covering hers, his lips devouring hers.

The male was so demanding and she loved it.

"I'm going to taste you later," he murmured, trailing kisses down her jaw as he cupped her mound.

She arched into his hold and dug her fingers into his back. "Right back at you." Because she wanted to kiss and tease every inch of him tonight. The need to mate was too strong.

His fire and her light lit up the room in a fiery blaze that told her he was just as crazed for her as she was for him.

Sliding her fingers down his back she grabbed his ass. "I want you in me now."

"Foreplay," he growled before biting her earlobe between his teeth.

She rolled her hips against his hand and he slid a finger inside her. Clenching around him, she shuddered. "I don't need it." Not now anyway. She nipped at his neck, sinking her teeth into his skin.

The low growl that filled the room was different than the playful one he'd just given her. It was primal and had her sex clenching around his finger.

"You're so damn demanding." He shifted lower, his kisses blazing a heated path down to her breasts as he slid another finger inside her.

She arched off the bed, her claws unleashing just a fraction. Immediately she went to grab the sheets but he lifted his head, pinning her with his gaze. "Don't hold back with me. Not tonight, not ever."

She didn't want to hurt him, but in that moment she realized she wouldn't. Bran wanted all of her and she wanted all of him. Still... "I'll scratch you."

"Good." His head dipped back to her breast and he sucked a nipple into his mouth. Hard.

She stopped thinking or worrying in that moment. As she raked her fingers down his back, her claws dragging over his skin, the rumble that came from his chest was so damn sexy it made her sex clench.

He withdrew his fingers but before she had the chance to protest, he thrust his cock deep inside her.

No polite asking or warning. Rough and raw and exactly what she wanted. He caged her in with his big body, his forearms bracketing her head as he looked right into her eyes. Then he started thrusting.

Slowly at first, his rhythm making her crazy. Unable to stop touching him, she stroked over his chest, upper arms, then around to his back as he continued his perfect rhythm inside her. She wanted to brand every inch of him in the same way he'd done to her.

The faster he moved, the closer she raced toward that edge. She knew he was close too. The tendons in his neck pulled tight and his expression was fierce and loving as he watched her. It was so damn intimate it almost made her want to look away, yet she couldn't.

She wanted to see him as he came, to see him right before he sank his canines into her neck. Each time he slammed into her, her inner walls tightened harder and harder around his thick length. She was so close.

Reaching between her legs, she tweaked her clit, the teasing action setting off her climax. Pleasure poured through her as her orgasm set her nerves on fire.

Just like that Bran groaned and buried his face against her neck. He didn't question or second-guess her again and for that she was glad. She knew her mind and was thankful he trusted her enough to know that.

When his teeth struck the sensitive area of skin between her neck and shoulder she expected pain or discomfort. Instead, another heavy dose of potent pleasure filled her until she could hardly stand it. After he withdrew his teeth, he sucked and kissed where he'd bitten her, his tender action exactly what she needed.

Her nipples tingled as her breasts rubbed against his chest and it was as if every inch of her body was oversensitized. Everywhere he touched her, she felt desire.

She wrapped her legs tighter around him and dug the heels of her feet into him, urging him to go harder, faster.

He groaned against her neck as he pulled back. When he did, she struck out with her own canines, biting him on pure instinct. She'd never heard that females did this but she didn't care. The urge to mark him, to claim him, was too damn strong. She couldn't fight it.

The moment she broke his skin, he cried out in pleasure, emptying himself inside her in long, hot strokes, his warmth filling her insides. She sunk her teeth in deeper, the taste of his blood sweet on her tongue, and he groaned even louder, his grip around her tight, reminding her that she belonged to him. And vice versa. Though she didn't want to, she finally withdrew, nuzzling where she'd bitten.

After what felt like an eternity, he slowly pulled out of her, but he didn't go far. He rolled so that he was on his back and she was splayed on top of him. Though he'd never said, she got the feeling he liked having her curled up on him like this. She loved it too. Bran made her feel safe and cherished in a way she'd never imagined possible.

"No going back now," he murmured, stroking a possessive hand down her spine. They'd carry each other's scent forever so that everyone supernatural would know they were mated. And she was going to ask him about exchanging rings, because she wanted that outward symbol for everyone to see.

She met his gaze. "Good. I can't imagine my life without you and I don't want to. I love you so much, Bran. You are the strongest, sweetest, most honorable male I've ever met and I'm proud to call you my mate." At her words, she felt his cock harden once more against her hip and grinned. The male was truly insatiable.

"I love you too, Keelin." It looked like he wanted to say more, but his jaw tightened and he swallowed hard as too many emotions for her to define filled his gaze.

She didn't need words anyway. She just needed Bran.

CHAPTER TWENTY-SIX

Bo swept an arm out, clearing everything off his desk. His laptop and papers went flying everywhere. He froze his laptop in midair, not wanting to deal with putting the thing back together. But his heavy paperweight hit the wood floor, shattering. The sound of breaking glass gave him a small sensation of pleasure. And naturally it reminded him of the last time Nyx had been here. Right now the urge to destroy was too great inside him.

It had been almost four days since he'd seen her.

Four damn days.

He'd contemplated going to the fights just to get rid of the excess energy inside him, something he'd never done, but he didn't trust his demon half right now.

It didn't make sense that being without Nyx for such a short period made him so crazy, but it did.

He just wanted to see her, to talk to her.

She'd been texting him and Bran had thankfully kept him up to date on what was going on, but the female had just dropped out of his life. Now he couldn't concentrate on anything. Especially since he knew she'd been in danger and could have over-exhausted herself with all that transporting she'd done.

"Hey, brother, Nyx is here. Wanted to know if you were free," Cynara said in his earpiece, her voice wry.

Relief slammed through him at her words. He'd been such a monster to work with the past few days and Cynara was the only one who knew why. Okay, he was lying to himself. Everyone probably knew why. "Send her back."

Less than two minutes later, there was a soft knock on his door. Since he'd been waiting by it like a pathetic excuse for a male, he opened it immediately, not caring how desperate he appeared to see her.

He drank in the sight of her. Wearing another one of those damn turtlenecks, a short plaid skirt and thigh-high black boots, he was surprised he didn't start drooling. From her texts he'd known she was okay, but actually seeing her in the flesh went a long way to calming him. "You're back." *Fucking genius, way to state the obvious.*

She smiled almost nervously and nodded. "Yeah, I, uh, I'm sorry I haven't called."

He stepped back and motioned for her to come inside. "I got your texts."

"I didn't want you to worry. Not that I thought you would," she added hurriedly.

"I would have." His words were blunt, but he needed for her to understand what she meant to him. Which, okay, he wasn't exactly sure what that was, but he knew he needed her in his life like he needed his next breath.

"Oh." She smoothed her hands down her skirt nervously so he sat on the edge of his desk.

What he really wanted to do was touch her, but he refrained. He wasn't sure what her reaction would be, especially after the way they'd left things between them. She'd seemed so angry at him before. At least his demon half was under control again. Just being near her made him feel different.

Wrapping her arms around herself in that way she did when she was unsure, she sat on one of his chairs and crossed her legs. What he wouldn't give to pull her into his arms, to take away her uncertainty.

He held back a groan at the flash of smooth skin and forced his gaze to her face.

"I feel weird about the way I reacted the other day in the security room."

He let out a sigh of relief that she brought it up. Moving from the desk, he sat on the chair next to her, but still didn't touch her. "I would have been pissed if I'd seen an image of you kissing some male." Or males. His demon rippled under his skin, angry at the imaginary males Bo was envisioning touching and kissing what he thought of as his.

Her blue eyes widened a fraction. "Really?"

He nodded. "Yeah, really. Fuck it, Nyx. I have feelings for you. I'm no good at this shit, but I care for you and for the record, I haven't been with anyone since the moment I met you." And he was being literal. It was like the second he'd laid eyes on her, his entire world had shifted.

Her cheeks flushed pink and he wanted to lean in and devour her pretty mouth.

"I have feelings for you too, but my life just got complicated." Now her expression darkened.

Elation jumped inside of him that she cared about him but it was tempered by concern. "What's wrong?"

"Nothing, it's just... I made a deal with someone I shouldn't have."

"Who?" The word came out dark and angry. Bran hadn't mentioned any of this to him.

Her eyes widened again, but at least she answered. "My mother."

The goddess? That couldn't be good. "I don't care about complicated. I just want you in my life. And I know I have no right to ask, but don't leave again without telling me."

A ghost of a smile teased her lips. "That doesn't sound like an actual request, but...I won't."

Tension he hadn't realized he'd been holding eased from him in a scorching wave. "Swear it."

"I swear." He started to respond, but she continued. "I can't offer you anything right now. I've got too much going on with both sides of my family and I'm afraid anyone I get involved with will get caught in the crossfire. I just can't risk that with you."

He wasn't worried about himself, but he nodded, not wanting to push her when it was clear she wasn't ready. "We can be friends though." The words were a complete lie, but he'd give her the illusion of just-friendship.

Meanwhile, he was going to approach their relationship like a battle. One he didn't plan to lose. He was going to claim her for his.

Her beautiful, ocean-blue eyes lit up. "Yes. I... your friendship has come to mean so much to me."

He held back a wince. It sounded like she was friend-zoning him, even if that wasn't her intent. "I feel the same about your friendship." That was the truth, even though he wanted a lot more. "I'd still like for you to stay with me." He forced the words to sound like a request when he wanted to order her to stay under his roof. No way was he letting her deal with her family on her own. He'd be there for backup.

She hesitated, but nodded. "For now, I will."

His demon half practically cheered at her words. As long as she was under his roof, he could start his slow plan of seduction. She might be worried for him, but he'd been around a long time and had learned a lot of dirty tricks. Killing him wouldn't be easy and he'd do damn near anything to stay in Nyx's life. She was a female worth fighting for and for once in his life he was finally going to be a male worthy enough to claim her.

Two months later

K eelin nudged open the front door of her home with her hip, not surprised to hear multiple male voices coming from Bran's office. As the Alpha of their clan, he was always busy.

She'd lived all over the world, but never Oregon before. She found she liked it, but something told her she'd like anywhere her mate was. After slipping off her sandals, she hooked her purse on the giant coatrack by the door. Clan members were always stopping by so she'd invested in a custom-made oak rack that would stand the test of time.

She'd made a lot of little changes like that over the past couple months. At first she'd been worried Bran wouldn't like the changes, but he'd made it clear that this was their home and she could do whatever she wanted.

The Devlin—now her clan—had a huge spread of acreage in northern Oregon on the outskirts of a small coastal town. It was different, yet the same as where she'd come from. Clans all figured out how to live in harmony with each other and their human counterparts. The big difference was the homes. Instead of chalet-type houses, they all had huge log homes. She liked the change.

Needing to see her mate, she headed down the hall-way and stepped into the cluttered office. Bran was sit-ting on the front edge of the desk, his arms crossed over his chest as he scowled at his brother Gavin and another warrior.

When he saw her his expression softened just a frac-tion, but he still looked annoyed. She knew it wasn't directed at her though. "Hey, sweetheart," he murmured before turning his gaze back on the other two males. "Get the fuck out and lock the front door on your way out," he growled at Gavin.

"Bran!" she admonished as Gavin and the other male just started laughing.

"Who's pussy-whipped now?" Gavin muttered under his breath as the two headed for the door.

"Damn right I am, now get out." He shoved up from the desk and stalked toward her, all beautiful predator sleekness.

Rolling her eyes, she gave both males an apologetic half-smile as they left. The door shut behind them with a click and she knew they would do as Bran ordered and lock the front door. Normally it was left unlocked dur-ing the daytime so if it was locked the clan knew not to disturb them.

"You didn't need to be so rude," she murmured, crossing the distance between them.

He just grunted and pulled her into his arms, his lips skating over hers in a far too chaste kiss. She started to protest when he deepened it, his tongue teasing against hers in a familiar dance that made her entire body flare to life with hunger.

"I missed you today," he said against her lips as he collapsed onto one of the chairs in front of his desk, pulling her with him.

She curled up into his lap, setting her head on his shoulder. "I missed you too. Today was long, but good."

"You should have let me come with you." The tension in his voice was hard to miss.

She snorted. "No way." Since moving to Oregon she'd started working with half a dozen clan members to get an organization for supernatural women who needed help in one way or another. Whether they were in abusive situations or simply needed shelter, she had big plans for the place. But for now she was taking things one step at a time. Last time Bran had come with her to the construction site he'd shouted at pretty much the entire crew and she wasn't dealing with the fallout of bruised egos again.

"I don't like the way any of those males looked at you," he muttered, practically sulking like an adolescent.

"You don't like the way *any* males look at me. And most of that crew is mated so don't play that game with me. You're being a big baby for no reason."

He pulled her tighter against him and nuzzled her neck. His masculine scent that reminded her of dark winter nights wrapped around her. "I know, I just miss you when you're not here."

She wasn't sure if it was because of what had happened with that demigod or if it was just the way all mated males were, but he got edgy when they weren't together. She missed and loved him more than anything when they were apart, but she liked having a purpose in life and still cherished her independence. And Bran, true to his word, hadn't once tried to keep her sheltered or take away any of her freedoms. She could put up with a little overprotectiveness.

Twisting in his lap, she straddled him. Her spring dress pushed up to her thighs. His gaze roved over her body hungrily. Without pause she grabbed the hem and pulled it up and over her head. Cool air rushed over her body, but the way her nipples hardened had little to do with that and everything to do with her mate's heated stare.

He sucked in a sharp breath, his eyes zeroing in on her breasts. "You're not wearing a bra?" he asked accusingly.

She started to tell him that it had a built-in one so she didn't need it, but her words were lost forever as his mouth descended on one of her nipples, his hands encircling her tight as he began teasing her into oblivion.

"I love you, Bran Devlin," she murmured with a smile, letting her head fall back as she clutched onto his shoulders. Some days she was afraid she'd wake up and find out this was all a dream, but she knew it wasn't.

Now that she'd found this beautiful, wonderful male, she was never letting go.

Thank you for reading Beyond the Darkness. If you don't want to miss any future releases, please feel free to join my newsletter. I only send out a newsletter for new releases or sales news. Find the signup link on my website: http://www.katiereus.com

ACKNOWLEDGMENTS

Once again it's time to thank some of my favorite people for their help in whipping this story into shape. Kari Walker, thank you (again) for reading the early version of this book. I'm always so grateful for your insight. Joan Turner, thank you for the final read through and your attention to detail. As always, I'm thankful to Jaycee with Sweet 'N Spicy Designs for her beautiful design work. For my readers, thank you for reading my various series and all your wonderfully supportive messages. Lastly, thank you to God for so many opportunities.

COMPLETE BOOKLIST

Red Stone Security Series
No One to Trust
Danger Next Door
Fatal Deception
Miami, Mistletoe & Murder
His to Protect
Breaking Her Rules
Protecting His Witness
Sinful Seduction
Under His Protection
Deadly Fallout

The Serafina: Sin City Series
First Surrender
Sensual Surrender
Sweetest Surrender
Dangerous Surrender

Deadly Ops Series
Targeted
Bound to Danger
Chasing Danger (novella)

Shattered Duty

Non-series Romantic Suspense
Running From the Past
Everything to Lose
Dangerous Deception
Dangerous Secrets
Killer Secrets
Deadly Obsession
Danger in Paradise
His Secret Past

Paranormal Romance
Destined Mate
Protector's Mate
A Jaguar's Kiss
Tempting the Jaguar
Enemy Mine
Heart of the Jaguar

Moon Shifter Series
Alpha Instinct
Lover's Instinct (novella)
Primal Possession
Mating Instinct
His Untamed Desire (novella)
Avenger's Heat
Hunter Reborn

Darkness Series
Darkness Awakened
Taste of Darkness
Beyond the Darkness

ABOUT THE AUTHOR

Katie Reus is the *New York Times* and *USA Today* bestselling author of the Red Stone Security series, the Moon Shifter series and the Deadly Ops series. She fell in love with romance at a young age thanks to books she pilfered from her mom's stash. Years later she loves reading romance almost as much as she loves writing it.

However, she didn't always know she wanted to be a writer. After changing majors many times, she finally graduated summa cum laude with a degree in psychology. Not long after that she discovered a new love. Writing. She now spends her days writing dark paranormal romance and sexy romantic suspense.

For more information on Katie please visit her website: www.katiereus.com. Also find her on twitter @katiereus or visit her on facebook at: www.facebook.com/katiereusauthor.